When Embers Fall

Hailey Bryant

Cover design: Muhammad Kaleem

1st edition 2024

To all of my villains,
your side of the story will never be forgotten.
Not by me.

DEAD Z

Figh

Fighter Castle

DEAD ZONE: WEST

Fighter Campsite

Fighter Hunting Ground

Fighter Campsite

ORTH
DEAD ZONE: EAST
End Mountains
Fighter Campsite
Light Field
Defender Campsite
Fractured Slopes
Hope Creek
Defender Castle
EAD ZONE: SOUTH
N
W
E
S

Prologue

The world was always going to be destroyed. It was inevitable. Of course, it was due to nuclear war, ravaged by humans. In the year 3000, bombs wiped out almost everything. Billions of people and animals died, and destruction was all that remained. Radiation poisoned the land, leaving only one small part of the world untouched. The land was still affected by earthquakes that arose from the bombs, and rubble and ashes littered the floor, but rebuilding was possible. The thousands of humans left carved out a new life. They built magnificent castles. They created a society without technology, without violence. But quickly, the peace they had, turned to war once again.

The radiation that filled the Dead Zone created a circle around everyone, and people began to fight over livable land. Eventually, society split into two sides. Proliators and Noctifiers, who more recently became known as Defenders and Fighters. The war between them has lasted one hundred years, and now, Alcmene, the new heir to the Fighters throne, is beginning to seek power. She wants the war to finally end by any means necessary. She wants to slaughter the enemy's side, instead of making a peace treaty. The Defenders, however, are pacifists. They defend themselves against the Fighters' attacks but never forge their own. They want peace, but don't have what it takes to earn it. Ember, the top Defender trainee, is different. She is prepared to make a new strategy to finally win.

Now, the tensions between the two sides are as brutal as ever, and magic runs through the poisoned land, threatening to change the fates of everyone involved. Only this magic is dark, and more deadly than any bomb or any radiation. Once it finds its way into someone, the costs could be catastrophic.

The world is hanging by a thread, and this war may lead to the end of it.

Chapter one

ALCMENE

I sit on the bed in my room, listening to my father berate me outside my door. It's nothing new, but it still hurts to know I'll never have a father who loves me.

"She will never get there. No matter what I do, that brat won't grow up. She's pathetic in training. I can't have a weak daughter. She is the heir," he tells my mother.

"She's only eight years old, Anwir. She doesn't understand that she will be the ruler of our people one day. For now, this training probably just seems like a bit of fun. She doesn't understand her obligation to the throne yet, but she will. In time." My father grunts in response. I know I will be ruling our people one day, and I've been trying my best in training. I'm just not good enough. Maybe I never will be.

I look around my room. It's small, but to me it's comforting. Drawings of the castle and war are scattered across my walls. I've never liked them, but my father insisted I grow up with them. The only drawing I appreciate is the one on my desk. My brother drew a picture of a bright and sunny meadow filled with flowers, and although he's not a very good artist, I still cherish it. I've always found nature beautiful, but the storms never end here, and the clouds are filled with darkness. There are no beautiful sunsets or blue skies, only rain and thunder.

My old desk sits in the corner, covered in dust. I spend most of my time training, although that clearly hasn't amounted to much. I close my curtains, shutting out the storm and leaving the room even darker than it was before. The only light comes from a single lantern on my desk. I lay back on my bed, thinking of today's humiliating events. I had training today, and I failed miserably. Younger kids beat me easily, as they always do, and they don't have the responsibility to be the heir. I'm supposed to be the greatest, but I'm not even decent. I grab my pillow and cover my ears with it. I can't stand to hear more of my parents' complaints about me. Most of all, my father's. Even at my young age, he expects me to be as good as him. He expects me to be ready to take his place, but I'm not.

I listen to the rain pouring outside the window for a few minutes. I don't think I'll ever get used to the weather. As I'm about to go to sleep, my door opens. A shiver runs down my spine. My father walks inside and stands beside my bed. I immediately sit up straight and force myself to meet his eyes. I squeeze my hands together to keep them from shaking. He places his lantern on the floor before staring at me with that same disappointed look he always wears when scolding me.

"I am disappointed in you," he finally says.

I look down, unable to meet his eyes. I'm afraid if I do, I won't be able to stop the tears that follow.

"Tell me, Alcmene, do you want to rule over the Fighters?" I hate how he calls me that fake name even inside the safety of my room. My father never chose my real name. My mother did. But he chose my alias, Alcmene. Maybe that's why he always calls me that. It's another one of his power schemes. Another way to get to me.

To answer his nagging question, I don't know what I want. I've never had the chance to know what life is like besides the one of the royal family. I've read books about kids going to school. A huge building with desks and computers and teachers. Now we have a form of school for younger kids to learn to read and write, administered in the training room by a Fighter with a heavy stutter. But after you reach ten years old, you learn to fight instead. Before the war, there was no training for kids. There was no constant fear of death. I find myself constantly wondering how different life would be without war. How peaceful.

"Father, I don't know what I want," I tell him truthfully. His disappointment quickly turns into a terrifying anger. I know the look. It's the one he gives my mother, brother, or me right before he hits us. I bite the inside of my cheek, drawing blood.

He clenches his jaw, staring at me with fire in his eyes. He grabs the collar of my shirt in his fist and yanks me toward him.

"You should know what you want! I've made it very clear that you will take my place one day. You have no other option. You will train. You will prepare. You will sit on my throne when I'm gone, whether you want to or not!" I see sparks ignite in his glare, as his hand reaches for the knife at his waist. *Oh no.*

He touches the blade to my cheek, and I freeze in place, trembling under the cold metal.

"I'm so sick of your weakness in training." He presses on the knife so the blade pierces my skin. I'm unable to move. Unable to breathe. I feel the knife slice into my flesh, warm blood streaming out of the wound.

"I'm sick of you disregarding your responsibilities." He pushes his hand forward, digging the knife deeper into the side of my cheek. I let out a cry, and try to pull away. He grabs the back of my neck to stop me, pressing his thumb into my throat. "Move again, and I'll cut more than just your face." I try as hard as I can to stop showing weakness, to stop my tears from falling, but I can't. His knife starts to slide down my cheek slowly, and I feel the searing pain intensify. It's the worst pain I've ever felt. I feel my blood drip down my face to my neck. I so badly want to pull away. I silently pray for the pain to end soon. For my father to walk out of my room and never come back.

"From now on," he releases a small amount of pressure on the knife, "you will train with me whenever I want you to. Training will come first, above everything else. That includes sleeping, eating, everything."

I gulp. My father will be the death of me. I'll die before I even have the chance to become the ruler. Maybe it would be better that way.

"And if you don't comply," he presses the knife down harder, slicing my flesh in a trail all the way down to my jaw, sending another surge of pain through my body. I clench my teeth together to hold in my sobs. "You'll be wishing you had."

I can only imagine what he will do to me if I don't listen.

"Is that understood?"

"Yes," my voice shakes, and the word is barely audible.

He doesn't let go.

"Yes, sir," I correct myself through sobs. He twists the blade before he finally lets go. He leaves, slamming the door behind him. I instantly let out a strangled cry. I wipe the blood from my face, but it continues to roll down. I grab a shirt from the corner of my room and press it to the gash. I try applying pressure, but it burns every time I touch it. I push myself through the pain, trying to stop the bleeding. I walk over to my mirror in the corner of the room and gasp. Looking at the width of the gash, it will need stitches. But the infirmary is empty tonight, and I doubt my father will let me patch it up. I hold the shirt to my face, silently crying as I let the night go by, dreading training tomorrow.

It's been ten years since then. I haven't changed much. I am stronger now, more skilled, and the Fighters fear me, but I'm still vulnerable to my father's abuse.

I look in the same mirror I did when he first cut me. There is a prominent scar from below my eye to my jaw, slightly jagged in the spot where my father twisted the knife. As much as I want to forget that day, I can't. He still abuses me, and I still take it. But eventually, one day, when I build up the courage and strength to kill him, I will. I told myself when I was eight, suffering from hunger and exhaustion from my father's demanding training, that eventually, I would end his life. With my mother still alive, I have been unable to fulfill that promise to myself, as I couldn't live with her being in pain over his death. But soon, with my brother by my side, my father will fall. Then I will be ruling this place better than he ever could. I will lead the Fighters to a victory he could never attain.

Chapter two

EMBER

I wake up to the sound of screaming. At first, I think I'm dreaming, but when my father rushes into my room with blood on his hands and a horrified look on his face, I jump out of bed, suddenly wide awake.

"What the hell is going on? Are you okay?"

"The Fighters," he pants. He wipes the blood on his pants, but the stain on his hands lingers. Terror dawns on me. Every battle brings death, and I have a good chance of being one of the fallen by the end of it. I notice he is weaponless. I swallow the lump in my throat and take my sword out from under my bed, handing it to him. I put on my knife holsters before placing three throwing knives and a spool of rope at my waist. I take my dagger from my desk drawer, trying to keep my hands from shaking. My father grabs me as I am about to exit the room.

"No. I won't let you die. Stay in here, block the door, and don't make a sound."

I rip my hands away from him.

"I must protect my people. I must protect Mom and Meadow. You can't make me stay here," I whisper yell. I try to push past him, but he shoves me back. I realize how disheveled he is. His blood-stained hands tremble, his clothes are torn, and there's a look of horror I've never seen before in his eyes.

"Whose blood is that?" My voice shakes.

"You didn't know them. Neither did I. I need to find your mother and sister. Please stay here." He holds my sword at his side as he runs out of my room. The screams continue, and I can only imagine the number of people we're losing. I have to fight. I've trained for five years to prepare myself for this day. My sister hasn't. I need to save her, wherever she is. I'm a Defender, and right now I need to defend.

I rush out of my room, dagger in hand. I instantly see a dead body. The only time I've seen dead Defenders is at funerals, laid to rest in wooden boxes before being put in the ground. Usually, the deaths are from old age or illness. It's different now, seeing someone lie in a pool of their own blood, their life gone. I wasn't old enough to remember the last Fighter attack, but now the sight of blood and the sound of screaming brings back memories I didn't know I had.

I keep running, and a knife flies past me, just missing my face. I see the Fighter and throw a knife back in his direction. It sticks in his arm, and he quickly rips it out, wincing. Anger floods his face, and he charges at me. I block his attack and after a few minutes of fighting, I manage to capture him with my rope. I tie him up and leave him on the castle floor, risking a look backward as I continue rushing towards the main castle doors. My heart beats faster. I need to find Meadow. I need to find Mom.

Meadow always stays out right before nightfall at the side of the castle under the trees with her boyfriend. I run outside and see that it's getting dark. She may be out there. I incapacitate a few more Fighters on my way to the woods, barely dodging knives being thrown my way as I make it into the forest, heaving from smoke clogging my throat. The trees are burning. I find my sister's spot in the woods and see her lying in the grass. I call out to her, but she doesn't answer. Why isn't she looking at me? Why isn't she answering? Her eyes are open, but she doesn't respond. Then I see the blood rushing out of the slit in her neck. Her body twisted like a gruesome piece of artwork. If only I got here a little sooner, maybe I could have saved her. I'm crying so hard, I can barely see. I fall to my knees beside her. She's still so beautiful. I brush her hair from her face, begging her to forgive me for not being here. For not saving her.

Meadow. What am I going to do? I hold my sister's body in my arms, my tears falling onto her blood-soaked shirt. Meadow was everything to me. She was a year older, and I've spent my whole life by her side. She grew up as a council member trainee, shadowing my father. She didn't learn to fight like I did. She wouldn't have been able to properly defend herself. I feel rage bubble up inside me. I need to fight. I need to kill whoever took her from me. I look at my sister, wiping the tears that fall. Killing is not our way. She wouldn't want me to kill someone as vengeance for her. We're supposed to capture the Fighters unless we have no other option. But I don't care.

"I'll come back for you." I place a kiss on her forehead, and close her eyes with my fingertips. I give her boyfriend beside her a long, sad look before I race out of the woods, with my sister's blood staining my hands. I hold my dagger tightly, itching to use it.

When I see the nearest Fighter, I don't hesitate. I strike him with my dagger and clip his shoulder. He stumbles backwards before lunging at me with a sword. I dodge his attack, rolling sideways and cutting his leg. He falls to one knee and I stand back up. He looks me in the eyes before I slash his throat. The sword easily rips through his flesh, the blood at first an outward burst, then a rich red stream. When he falls, I relish the sound of his body hitting the ground and savor the feeling of power and strength. He bleeds out, adding to the pool of blood on the grass.

I look at the Fighters in battle. They're winning, but we still have a chance. I think of my sister. Even if we win, I'll have lost her. The person who was always by my side. Just as I'm about to run into the conflict, I see something that stops me in my tracks. My father kneels by the castle doors, like he was just about to make it to some ounce of safety before he was attacked. But he isn't injured. He's crumbled on the ground, and I hear him sobbing. I see who he holds in his arms and a gasp escapes my throat.

It's my mother.

I rush over to them, and barely feel a knife slice my forearm as I run. I sit beside my father as tears run down his face. His hands shake as he presses on the gash on my mother's stomach, made by a sword. I can tell it's too deep. Blood runs out of the wound, and my mother's eyes close slowly. Her nails are coated in blood and dirt, like she tried to fight against whoever killed her but failed. Her skin is pale and clammy. Blood drips onto my skin. Fighting continues around us, but the Defenders push back, keeping us shielded. I don't move. My father doesn't speak. Life seeps out of my mother and he hugs her, rocking her slowly, his heartbreaking sobs tearing at his throat.

Screams echo around me, but soon I can't hear them. A piercing noise fills my ears and my breath escapes my lungs. I can't breathe. The smell of blood fills my nostrils as every feeling other than pain falls away. A despair I've never seen before lives in my father's eyes. And from that look, I know neither of us will ever be the same.

That battle was a little over a year ago. The Fighters fell back, and my father and I lived. We buried Meadow, her boyfriend, and my mother the next morning. Since that day, I have trained as much as humanly possible. Their deaths shadow every waking moment of my life. Their memory haunts me, but pushes me to never make the same mistake again. Next time the Fighters attack, I refuse to lose anyone else. I will be ready.

Chapter three

ALCMENE

My brother, Leviathan, means everything to me. He always tried to stand up against our father and protect me from his abuse. He wasn't afraid. I couldn't say the same about me. I'd let our father hurt me, and I thought I couldn't do anything about it. Leviathan, however, didn't let our father throw him around. He fought back as best he could, which never ended well. I told myself Levi was stronger than me simply because he was older, but I knew it wasn't that. I could have fought back, even at my younger age. But I didn't. Couldn't.

Leviathan was ten when I was eight. That was when things started getting bad. My father pushed me past my limits. He had me train and train until I collapsed. He wouldn't let me sleep, or sometimes even eat, before I mastered whatever skill he was teaching me. It could be anything from a simple strike in a close combat battle to mastering how to manipulate one of the simple-minded Defenders. But Leviathan was there when I was exhausted and broken, holding me up. He saved my life more times than I could count. He fed me when I was on the verge of starvation. He saved me when I tried to take my own life. In those dark times, he promised me that one day he would kill our father and end the war.

Levi helped me train. He didn't push me till I broke, like our father. Training with him was something I cherished. Levi prepared me to face our father and fight in the war. He was the reason why I became so strong. His guidance turned me into a real Fighter. That was something our father could never do.

My best memories with Levi are from when we were younger, when things weren't as bad. I haven't had many good nights in my life, but this was one of them. From four years ago, when I was fourteen, lives a memory I will never forget.

The screaming match with my father only ends in tears and pain. After our fight, I run into my room, falling onto my bed, my head diving straight into my pillow. I lay like this for a while, although I'm unsure how long. Every night seems to end the same. With a new bruise to add to my collection and my father, careless about how he's treated me. How does my mother love him? How can she still care, even after all the horrible things he has done? I lift my head to look out of the window next to my bed. The sky in the daytime is always dark and gloomy, but at night at least there are stars. From the history books I've read, I've learned that people used to go into space. They could be among the moon and the stars, away from this world.

Now, traveling into space is impossible. After the great war, so many things were destroyed, never to return again. My father talks so much about guns. They were able to kill so many people so easily. He said we would be able to defeat the Defenders in an instant with that kind of weapon. But the war wiped guns away, leaving us with nothing but knives, daggers, swords, and bows. The war took away countless other things, like cars, technology, and so much beautiful land. Most of all, it killed billions of people. Now, this world is inhabited by only tens of thousands, if that. And they all live on this one stretch of survivable land.

"Come with me." Levi beckons from my door frame.

I didn't even hear him come in. Sometimes he moves with such precision and grace that I can't hear the slightest sound. It's a useful skill to have in combat. I turn away from my window, from the beautiful stars, and look up at him. I throw on my tight black books and get up to follow. I don't ask where he wants to go, because I know I can trust him, no matter where he is taking me.

"Why does our mother even love him?" I whisper as we pass our father's room.

"That is a mystery to us both," Levi replies, shaking his head.

We travel down the familiar halls of the castle until we reach the door that leads to the outside world.

"You want to go outside? In the middle of the night?" I question.

"Trust me, sis."

I sigh in return and follow him out the huge castle doors.

Levi lies down on the grass, and gestures for me to join him. I wonder what he has possibly led me out here for, but again, I don't ask. I lie beside my brother and listen to the soft sound of his breathing before he points to the sky.

"Look, Alcmene." He wouldn't dare say my real name outside of the castle walls, so he uses my alias. The heir to the throne and the holder of the throne have one. It's a way of keeping the Defenders from acquiring any real information about who the ruler or heir really is. Alcmene, in another language, supposedly means wrath. I only mind the name when my father says it.

I look at the stars with Levi. They are even more beautiful and bright out here than from the view in my room. Some are brighter than others, while some almost appear to be dying out. It's like my father is the biggest, brightest star in the sky, while I am the smallest, the one that is dim and slowly dying. Powerless and weak in comparison. I feel drops of rain on my face. It's always raining.

"What are you thinking about?" Levi asks, looking at me.

"Just our father."

He frowns. "I wish he wasn't your problem, only mine. You shouldn't have to grow up like I did. With terror looming over your head. The thought that at any minute, he could snap, with mother just standing by, letting it happen."

I don't know how to respond to him, so I say nothing. I find myself at a loss for words often lately. Maybe I've grown so used to keeping my mouth shut when our father is around that I can't find words even when he's gone.

Levi faces the stars again. "I wanted you to have a better night, for once. I know Father hurt you earlier today. I am so sorry I didn't get there in time to stop him. But maybe this will make up for it."

I don't blame Levi for being unable to protect me today. Our father hit me again, and Levi walked in right after the fact. It's not his fault he wasn't there. It's my fault I couldn't protect myself. Just like a child, I still freeze when my father reaches for me. After he cut my face when I was eight, I've been more terrified than ever, even though it's been years since that day. I think my father is the only thing I'm afraid of in this world. I just wish Levi didn't always have to protect me. I don't want that burden on him.

"Want to know why I brought you out here, besides getting you out of the castle?" he asks.

"Yes," is all I say.

"To tell you a legend about the stars."

I wasn't expecting that, but I'll take it. Levi's stories are the best. When he tells them, I get lost in his words, which helps me keep my mind off of our brutal reality.

He points to the stars again. "See how some stars kind of flicker? The light goes dim, then comes back full force." I nod. "Every star is one of the dead. Most are from the old war, before we split into the Fighters and Defenders. But some are Fighters, lost in battle. Every time a star twinkles, it's their way of communicating with us. Telling us that they're still up there, in the sky. When we die, our bodies are no longer on this Earth, but a part of us will always be in the sky, among the stars. A part of us will never truly leave."

I take in his words, and look at the stars like I never have before. If the legend is real, the stars are much more beautiful than I ever thought. Our people are out there. And that is all the more reason to win this never-ending war. For them.

Chapter four

EMBER

My father asks to train with me one night, after not having the time to train for at least a month. He is on The Council, a group of leaders for the Defenders, which takes up almost all of his attention. I'm glad he has something he loves doing, but I wish it didn't always take him away from me. It's like he never leaves the meeting room. I miss having my sister and mother to talk to.

"Finally," I grin. It's been forever. Although my father never has time to see me, being a councilman's daughter has its perks. My room is one of the biggest in the castle. When I'm not training, I'm in my room, basking in solitude. I head to my bed and grab my weapons bag beneath it. The black case laced with a velvet interior holds my most valuable knives and daggers. I take out my favorite one. The dagger is lightweight and has a sharp point and shiny golden handle, with red and blue flowers painted along the silver blade.

After losing my mother, I keep this dagger close. It's a family heirloom, and was passed down from one of my great grandparents, to her, and finally to me. My mother never got much use out of it, as she didn't train in close combat like I do. But she painted the roses along the blade. She loved those flowers because they showed the two sides our world has always been split into. The light, beautiful blue for the Defenders, and the dark, blood red for the Fighters. Her roses are painted in various places around the castle. I didn't look at them very often before she died, never thinking much of it, but now I stop to see at least one every day. Only a year ago she left me, and her flowers are the only piece of her left in this cruel world. I want to remember her as she was; kind, bright, carefree, and elegant. A painter at heart. But all my memories of her are fogged over by the day she died. The blood dripping from her stomach. My father's pleading cries.

"You know, I thought this war would be over by now," my father says. His dark brown hair is neatly trimmed, as required by The Council. He has bright blue eyes and a soft smile that accentuates the crows feet by his temples. His Council uniform is a deep blue color. A tunic with black slacks and a shiny belt. It's not exactly the best thing to spar in. I wear my training outfit, loose and comfortable, perfect for exercising.

We walk, heading outside of the castle as he speaks. I hold onto my mother's dagger tightly. The sun is just beginning to set. "The Council has thought of everything, but somehow, every time the Fighters attack, they are one step ahead. I don't want more of your life to be filled with the terror that comes with war, like mine was. I want you to be happy."

"I know, Dad. And maybe I could be." He looks at me with a tightened jaw, knowing what I'm about to say.

"I won't have this conversation again with you," he sighs.

"You know it's true. If we fought back and planned our own attacks, the war could end. Maybe we could win. But all we do is hide out in this castle and hope it'll be over one day. The war won't stop until the Fighters have conquered everything. It will never end if we don't try to stop it."

He looks away. "That's not who we are. We don't attack them unless they attack us. We cannot be the instigators in this war."

I think of the Fighter I killed after I found my sister dead in the woods. Although he saw me, my father and I never spoke of the act I committed. But I don't regret it. I needed revenge, and in a way, I wish I could have earned more of it.

We get to our training spot just outside the castle. Rocks make a circle around the training zone filled with dirt. The space is large enough for multiple sets of people to practice at once, but most Defenders choose to stay inside the safety of the castle. It doesn't surprise me. After the last attack, I never wanted to go outside again. But I felt so suffocated inside the stone walls, staying inside would have killed me.

I don't bother trying to argue with my father any further. I've always suggested planning an attack ourselves, with The Council leading it, but he disregards my ideas whenever I bring them up. We've all lost people. I can't help but think that if we actually fought back, less of us would have died. Maybe my mother and my sister wouldn't be gone. I get teary-eyed just thinking about them, and my thoughts immediately drift to them rotting underground, the names on their graves slowly fading to nothing. I force the thoughts out of my mind and prepare to fight. The key to winning a battle is to have a clear head. I've tried fighting with things on my mind before, and to say the least, it never ended well.

My father and I get in position for combat. He takes out his dagger from his waist holster. On the count of three, we start.

"Don't go easy on me," I tell him.

"You know I won't."

I charge towards him, knife in hand.

When I'm a few feet from him, he moves to the side of me and strikes. I effortlessly block his attack. I swing at his head, which he dodges and immediately counterattacks. He jabs his knife towards my stomach, and I quickly move out of the way. Attacks continue, with both of us easily deflecting them.

I strike toward his chest, and he jumps backwards, but the knife just catches his shoulder on the way back.

"You've gotten better," my father says.

"I've been practicing," I grunt, as I send another strike his way.

He laughs. "I can tell. It seems I'm a bit rusty."

I dodge and attack, over and over. It's like a game with my father. We always match each other's rhythm, and wait for the second the other makes the smallest mistake. This time, it's me who makes the wrong move. I jab toward his side, and he sweeps my legs out from under me, sending me crashing to the ground.

"Seems like you still have much to learn."

"You know that's my weakness," I retort.

"Fighters are trained to find weaknesses. If they know you are defenseless against a sweep to the leg, they will continue to use it." He helps me up.

"Sorry about your shoulder," I say. A small trickle of blood pours from the wound.

"Just a scratch. It's all part of training."

We train a little longer, with him teaching me how to better fend off takedowns.

As we walk back to our rooms in the castle, I ask him something I've been wondering.

"What if some of the people on the Fighter's side think they're the good guys?"

My father takes a minute to answer. "Everyone has a conscience, Ember. If they were in the attack on us last year, then they saw the destruction they've caused. They should know killing is not the answer. Not for land, or control, or anything. Nothing is a good enough reason for murder."

I nod. The Fighters attacked me at the last battle without thinking twice. Even if their ruler tells them they are doing the right thing, they must have some morality that tells them they're not.

"If the Fighters attack again, I need you to be ready. If I die in battle, you need to be able to protect yourself."

I cringe at the thought of him leaving me completely alone, but I tell him, "I am ready."

"It's been a year since they've attacked. They must be planning something big," he says. I've thought the same. They could attack any day.

Although I've had nightmares about the Fighters storming the castle again, killing more of us, something inside me wants them to attack again. I want revenge for what they did to my family. But wishing for a battle is foolish.

My father heads off to bed. I hear other people walking in the halls. They must be settling in, too. The castle is so huge that it fits almost all of our people inside. Some Defenders live in smaller camps in the woods, because they want to have their own areas and some think it'll be safer to spread out. It's smart, as one attack on our castle could kill nearly all of us.

I have never met the other people rumored to be this world's inhabitants. They are allegedly not from either group, not Fighters or Defenders. They are just a myth, as far as I know, but they are called the People in Between and don't belong to anyone. To me, that sounds nice. Everything I do revolves around protecting my people and preparing for war. It's always been that way. It would feel nice to live freely for once. However, the Fighters would probably go after smaller groups of people since it would be easier to conquer them. So living freely as the People in Between may be dangerous, but I really wouldn't know.

I roll my shirt sleeve up, as I do every night, looking at the mark on my arm. It's hard to make out the odd lines, but the mark vaguely resembles a jagged-looking circle, with ascending swirling lines in the middle that remind me of smoke. I've had it since I was born, and my parents told me it was some sort of strange birthmark, but it feels like there's more to it than that. Although it hasn't changed in seventeen years, so I'm beginning to believe my parents were right. I shrug and roll my sleeve back down before I pull the covers over my head. I try to fall asleep, but every night it's the same. Thoughts keep me up for hours on end. Tonight I am constantly wondering about the People in Between, and how different my life would be if I were one of them. I think about the Fighters and how some of them may not know they are in the wrong. As I always do, I try to push the endless thoughts away, and instead focus on the sounds of the crickets outside until I finally fall asleep.

Chapter five

ALCMENE

Levi and I haven't visited our mother in a while. She's been sick for a long time. Every time we see her she seems to get worse. As much as I hate her for standing by while our father abuses us, it's still sad to see her in such bad shape.

We knock on the dark wooden door, and it opens after a minute. Our mother shakily walks from the door to her bed, groaning as she sets herself down. Levi and I sit next to her.

"Your father will be back soon," she mumbles, her voice hoarse. After over a month of silence, that is the first thing she says to us. I shouldn't be surprised.

I glare into her eyes and ask, "Why do you love him? After everything he's done to us? Done to you?" It's not really fair, asking this in her condition. But she never treated me fairly either. She never cared about what happened to me. What still happens.

My mother looks out the window. She says nothing for what feels like an eternity. Levi and I await her response. I begin to wonder if she'll ever have one.

"Honestly, I don't know. It's a hate kind of love. One that I can't rip myself away from. Believe me, I've tried." The dark circles under her eyes are more pronounced than when I saw her last. Her bones are so visible they seem as though they may pop out with a quick movement. Her body more deathly skinny than before. She's gotten way worse.

I don't acknowledge my mother's ridiculous excuse for staying with our father. I know it's because he's the ruler. She wants that kind of royalty. That kind of power.

Levi seems to notice her quickly changing appearance as well.

"Mom. You're not getting better," he says. She just stares out the window, her eyes glossy and tired.

She doesn't look at us but says, "You should go now. Your father will be back any minute." Levi and I don't try to argue. We leave without a word. I knew there was no use seeing her. Nothing ever comes out of it.

Levi leads me outside of the castle, knowing the fresh air is exactly what I need. We walk over the bridge that separates the castle from the moat, and into the outskirts of the forest. "Mother's not well," he says.

"Not at all," I reply, looking at the sky.

Levi sits on the grass and gestures for me to join him.

"If she dies, our father will be even worse. No matter how much of a bastard he is, he loves her. Without her stopping him, he'll surely kill us." Our mother is the only reason Levi and I are alive. The minute she's gone, our father won't have anyone holding him back. He'll get rid of us for good. It doesn't matter that I'm his heir. He'll find someone he actually wants as his second. "We need to kill him soon before he kills us." The thought of murdering my own father has always been in the back of my mind, as dark as it is, but it's never been so prominent before.

I look at Levi. "We're not ready. We won't win."

"Actually," Levi takes a long breath, "I think we'll stand a chance."

"How?" I can't think of any plan that would end in us surviving. Even with both of us fighting against him, he has many years of experience and knows how we attack.

"There's something I've been keeping from you. I didn't tell you because I wasn't sure what was happening or how to control it, but I have no choice other than to figure it out now."

I never thought Levi would hide something from me. Especially not something that seems so important. I furrow my brows. "What are you talking about?"

"I've known for a while that there was something different about me. Whenever I get angry at our father, the rage consumes me. It's like I can't control it. The last few times I got angry at him, I felt some kind of pressure surrounding me. Like a weight. But not the kind that paralyzes you. A kind of weight that made me feel stronger, in a way. My eyes felt like they were on fire, they burned so bad. The only thing I could see was our father. Everything else went dark, like my vision was zoning in on him, and everything else was background. Every time this happened, I'd leave the room, afraid of what would occur if I acted upon what I was feeling. But recently, after I left, I went to the training room and punched a hole through the stone wall. Then I lifted both the heavy dirt bags in one hand like they weighed nothing." He hesitates before saying his next words. "My eyes, they were white. Like completely white. The blue was gone." He looks down at his hands. "I think I have some kind of power. Not always, but sometimes. Enhanced strength."

I almost laugh. The thought of Levi having a power is insane. But by the look in his eyes, he isn't kidding. Before I say anything, something registers in my brain. A memory.

About a year ago, our father had me torture a Defender. His only instructions were to make him suffer but keep him alive. Only, my rage against our father drove me to take it out on the Defender. I killed him. Brutally. Our father quickly got word of my act of defiance, and the minute I came upstairs from the dungeon, he hit me and I fell to the ground. I don't know where Levi came from, but he was immediately by my side. He saw my bleeding head and thought I had a concussion or worse. He may have thought that the blow to my skull was going to kill me. I thought I was delirious from the impact, but I remember seeing Levi's eyes. They weren't just cold and filled with anger. They were completely white. All of the pigment was gone, like a twisted version of an angel. But his eyes didn't remind me of light. Of anything good. They were dull and piercing. I saw him go after my father before I blacked out.

"Sister?" He snaps his fingers in front of my face. "You okay?"

I look up at him. Although more proof would help, I know my brother would never lie to me. And what I saw that day couldn't have been a coincidence. "I believe you."

"You do?" He looks astounded. He definitely didn't think I would believe him, at least not as quickly as I did. I could ask him how he figured all of this out, or what other times this power showed up, but there's no time. This could be the key to ending our father.

"We have to train. If we have any chance at taking our father down, it's with this."

Levi nods. "Let's start now."

Chapter six

EMBER

The bright, illuminating light shining through my window wakes me up. Every day is a constant, repetitive cycle of training and daydreaming. Wishing I could be somewhere else, without a war, with my sister back by my side. I can't help but wonder about the possibility of the People in Between. If they're real, are they being attacked? Are they training too? Or are they living freely in the woods, away from the Fighters, having the time of their lives? But I can't seem to wrap my head around a group of people being so carefree. So unaware of the shadow of death always looming above. Not when I can't get past it.

I get up, prepared to train. Honestly, I don't see the point of it anymore. No one can beat me but the training instructor and my father. Fighting with anyone else is useless. It's a win so easy I barely have to try. I would train with the instructor, but he's always busy. So I usually train in the solo area, practicing throwing knives and capturing techniques. Although I've trained so much that there are really no more techniques or weapons I need to work on. But even so, I still head to training after I get changed and ready. It's not like there's anything else to do. Not in war.

The walk to the training room isn't very long. It's down a hallway in the castle, to the right, downstairs, and the first huge door on the left. On the way, there are things to admire, like sculptures, paintings, and decorations. Even the walls are decorated with painted flowers and beautiful sights. I stop where I always do on the way to training. The small area of the wall with my mothers rose on it. She only painted one, because she said, "One flower means more than one thousand. Each individual flower loses meaning as the number of them increases." So there is only one every time she draws her beautiful blue rose. Except if she draws it with the red one, like the pair on my dagger. I look at the detail s. The fine brush strokes the petals are made of, the swirl of the rose, and the light blue color that signifies all of us. She was proud to be on the Defender's side.

After running my fingers along the delicate flower painting, wishing my mother was still here, I continue my walk to the training room. I run into a couple people who greet me as they walk by. I don't really have any friends; rather I just have acquaintances I know from training or mealtime. I've never been social enough to interact much. But I've always wanted one close friend, someone to whom I could spill all my thoughts, or even a romantic partner. But I haven't found that person yet, and maybe I never will. And that's okay. My main goal as the top combat trainee is to be the best I can, to someday defend my people without failing like last time. I don't need friends to do that.

I walk into the training room, where many of the same men as always are scattered about, engaging in combat. A couple of women, too. It seems as though fewer people have been coming to training, possibly because we haven't been attacked in over a year. I would love to put my guard down and take a long break, but I can't. Not after what happened last time.

The training room is a huge open space, the size of a gymnasium. Half of it is for sparring and partner exercises, while the other half is for solo training with targets for practice.

I find something unusual as I look around. A new trainee, sitting on the same wooden bench I sat on five years ago, when I was twelve. The bench has all of the trainees' names carved into it, so many that they are beginning to overlap. The bench is so worn that it's falling apart, but D'andre hasn't removed it for good reason. Trainees who have died in the war still have their names there, and getting rid of the bench would be like getting rid of a part of them.

The boy watches D'andre, the training instructor, as he gives him the introduction speech I know so well.

I walk over to the kid, excited to finally meet someone new. He's small, with curly hair and dark eyes. Light freckles dot his nose and cheeks from the sun. He isn't dressed in the training uniform yet. Instead, he wears clothes that look like he tried to come looking formal. He has a clean, pressed blue shirt and black slacks. I stand on the side, waiting for D'andre to finish his speech before I talk to him. It's been so long since a 12-year-old has come about, especially one who will learn to train instead of learning to do diplomatic things. I was lucky I got put in training. My father almost wanted to put me by his side, learning to lead as he does. He was a soldier when he was younger, but his compassion for our cause sent him to The Council. Although my father desperately wanted me to join The Council once I grew up, the training instructor insisted I learn to fight. He said it was because he saw something in me. I don't know how, because I was only twelve and had never picked up a weapon or fought in my life, but I'm glad he did. Otherwise, I would be stuck in meetings all the time, and would have never gotten to reach my full potential. I would never have learned the skills I need to avenge my mother and Meadow.

D'andre notices me and steps aside so I can meet the boy.

"Hi, I'm-"

He abruptly stands. "I know who you are." The boy stares at me with bright eyes and a huge grin, in what appears to be awe. "You're all my parents talk about. The girl who is an expert in training. The one I should be learning from. Your name is Ember."

I smile, surprised that he knows me already. "What's your name?"

"Austin," he says excitedly. "Can you teach me?" he asks, looking up at me with hope.

I've never thought about teaching anyone. I don't know if I'd even be allowed to. Teaching is something D'andre has always done alone. I don't know if I could ever live up to it.

"I'd love to, if it's okay with you, D'andre." He looks to Austin with his bright smile, then back to me.

"Yes," he says without hesitation. I almost fall over in shock. As long as I've been alive, I've never heard of anyone else training students besides D'andre. How is he willing to change that so quickly? It's incredibly surprising. A rush of excitement fills me. This will be something I've never done before. Something new is exactly what I've been needing. "I can't think of a trainee more suited for the job. You have my approval, Ember." He smiles and says, "I need a break anyway." I laugh and thank him multiple times before he walks away. Austin looks up at me with a lightness in his eyes I used to have in my own a year ago. Before my world came crashing down.

"Let's get started."

Austin changes and I bring him over to the solo training area so that no other people are around to cause distractions. He practically prances following me with excitement. The uniform is slightly big on his small build, and he rolls his sleeves off his hands. I look in the direction D'andre departed in, wondering if he will come running back, saying he's changed his mind. It's hard to believe I will actually train a new kid.

I think of what to teach first. When I was learning five years ago, D'andre had me practicing simple moves over and over again until my muscles ached and cramped. He had me sat in a horse stance, strengthening my legs while throwing punches forever. At least it felt like forever. I don't want to do exactly that, but Austin still needs to learn the basics. They are the foundation for everything else.

"So, I'm guessing the instructor went over the basics of strikes, blocks, and captures, is that right?"

He nods.

"Okay. What do you think is the most important of those three?" I was quizzed on questions like these countless times. I even had a written test, but I don't think D'andre gives out tests anymore.

"Blocking," he answers correctly.

"Why?" I ask, testing him.

"Because Defenders want to block attacks less than strike."

"Yes. We don't want to be the instigators."

He looks at me, puzzled. "What does that mean?"

"The person who starts the fight," I answer. Oh, how I miss being twelve.

"The next most important thing is capturing. If a Fighter gets away, they could hurt more people. That is what we want to prevent. We are the protectors of our people, and letting a Fighter run off is not protecting anyone." I think of my sister in the woods. If I got there earlier, if I realized what was happening sooner, I could have prevented her from being murdered. I'm supposed to be a protector of all Defenders, but I couldn't even protect my own family.

He nods again. I see his gaze shift to the array of knives on the wall.

I laugh slightly. "Don't worry. You'll get to use those eventually. For now, we just want to focus on those three major things." He nods. I remember picking up a knife for the first time. I obtained the honor of using weapons earlier than any trainee in history. I was always a quick learner. When I threw my first knife, I knew I was a natural. D'andre was proud.

"And finally, striking. You strike a Fighter to weaken them in preparation for a capture, not to kill them. We don't kill anyone unless we absolutely have to." I think of the man whose throat I slit. I didn't have to kill him. I was enraged. But I've learned to contain my anger since then, and I have to teach Austin the right way, even if I don't exactly think it's best.

After explaining more of the basics, I show Austin the different types of blocks, and soon I throw punches and strikes at him to defend. Usually a Fighter would have a knife or some sort of weapon, so I place emphasis on Austin protecting his heart, neck, and head.

Later, I teach him a few strikes and how to get out of a chokehold. In the coming days I will show him more defensive strategies and takedowns. But this is enough for today. The training room is slowly starting to clear out. Everyone is finishing up. I complete the lesson by explaining captures. He won't do them yet, since I want to teach him takedowns first, but I explain how vital capturing is, and show him the rope at my waist. When I'm satisfied with everything Austin has learned, we walk out of the training room. I bid Austin farewell, and he goes to his room on the bottom floor of the castle, after thanking me more than once. He's adorable. On my way back to my room I run into my father.

"Hey, why are you out?" I ask.

"Eh, I wanted to take a break from the strenuous meetings. Want to talk?"

"Sitting in a chair all day is hardly strenuous," I joke, but I know what he means. Anything gets tiring after doing it for long enough. Mother used to be exhausted after painting so precisely for hours on end.

He follows me over to a small seating area outside the meeting rooms.

"I'm guessing you have more pressing questions for me to answer."

He knows me too well. Almost every time I see him, I have some question I think he will know the answer to, or a story I want him to tell about his past.

"We have always had multiple people ruling us, right? A council that decides everything, not just one person?"

"As long as I've lived, yes. That's how it's been. But as far as the past goes, I'm sure we had a single ruler who gained too much power. We must have had some reason for switching to multiple people."

"But the Fighters only have one leader, right?"

"Yes, and their leader has a lot of power. Some of us wonder if that's why they are so evil. One ruler with too much power can turn their followers into something they're not out of fear. And the Fighters would have no way to stop that leader. They would have no choice but to obey."

I nod and look down. There have to be some good people on that side. People who have no choice but to obey the ruler, even if they don't want to.

"Do you know who it is?" I ask. Learning more about the ruler could be key if they attack.

He shakes his head. "None of our people have ever crossed paths with him before. He never steps foot outside of his territory. He sends his soldiers to do his work. I have, however, heard of the heir to the throne, the next in line."

My head pops up. Knowing about his second is valuable information. Knowing anything about the people in power of the Fighters could help us figure out more about them, and how and why they are so evil.

"The heir is his daughter, known as Alcmene, the ancient Greek word for 'wrath.' Her real name is unknown to any of us. You don't want to ever run into her. After the battle a year ago, a large number of Defenders split off from the castle, adding to the Defenders in separate camps. Some must have gotten captured on the way, because one was dropped back at our castle after a few weeks. He was burned alive and stabbed in the heart. Her name was carved into his head. Ever since that day, people have been sharing stories about her. Some, I have no doubt, are true." He looks into the distance. "She is crazy, and if she takes the throne, she will try to kill us all." Genuine terror fills my father's voice. It scares me. I never knew about this. I never knew one of our people was killed so ruthlessly and left for us to see. The Defenders who found him must have quickly disposed of the body before many of us saw.

"How could someone do that? Why?"

He shrugs. "Most rulers, or the heir in this case, from what I know, want power. But it must be more than that for her. I just haven't been able to figure out what."

Now I want to know. Why does anyone want power in general? What good comes out of it? If Alcmene tortured and killed a Defender so brutally, what else has she done? There must be some reason why Alcmene is as evil as she is made out to be. But why does anyone want to be evil? To torture and murder innocent people. How is power worth that?

My father disrupts my train of thought as he speaks.

"Anyway, I should be heading back. I'll see you soon. Maybe we can train again in a couple of days. You're so close to beating me." He smiles and gives me a wink, then enters the meeting room.

I walk back to my room, wondering about the Fighters, but mostly about Alcmene, as they call her. Wrath. I pass by my mother's flower painting on the way. I wonder if she's heard of her. I wonder what she would think. If only she were alive to ask. But Alcmene and the rest of the Fighters took her away from me. And for that, I want to capture the heir more than anything, and win this awful war.

Chapter seven

ALCMENE

Levi and I walk down to the training room. We pass by Fighters on the way, some even stopping to bow or curtsy. The ones who don't acknowledge me outright stare with fear in their eyes. My father is terrifying to them, and that makes them scared of me too. I hold power in this castle. It's one of the few nice things that comes from being the heir.

I look at Levi by my side, swiftly walking and avoiding eye contact with the trembling Fighters. Sometimes I wonder what he would be like if he was able to take the throne after our father's death. Although he's never expressed his thoughts about wanting that position, he can't have it. Every time a man holds the throne, it is passed down to his daughter, then the daughter passes it to her son, and so on. It is our tradition. The only time this can ever be broken is if you don't have children. Then you would pass it on to someone of your choosing, who can be either gender. I honestly think the whole dynamic is ridiculous, but it's not my place to change how we do things. The tradition has given me a chance at ruling this place better than my father, so I will gladly take it when the time comes.

One boy in particular makes his presence very known as Levi and I walk. He practically prances up to me, stopping about a pace away. He drops into a low bow, his head almost brushing the floor at my feet. "Good morning, my lady," he says as he lifts himself back up. I almost let out a laugh.

"Morning," I reply. He smiles before he continues passing by us. It's strange, how a select few Fighters are never afraid and have no shame, while the rest cower in fear.

Levi and I laugh when he's far enough away. Bowing is also traditional, but it usually isn't done unless my father or I are giving people orders.

We enter the training room to find it packed. We can't test out Levi's ability with others watching. No one can know about it, at least not yet. "Everyone out!" I yell. Everyone's eyes snap to me. All the Fighters drop whatever they're doing, and flee the room. The training room is filled with weapons: knives, daggers, swords, and a few bow and arrows. There is a space in the middle of the room to practice dueling, speckled with fresh blood from combative injuries. Targets line the walls to throw knives at, and a few dirt-filled bags lay against the wall for lifting. I look at the mirror on the wall, made from glass and a thin layer of silver. I look away when I see my scar reflected back at me. Considering the large number of Fighters we have in this main castle, our training room is pretty small.

Levi and I sit in the middle of the room.

"I have to get mad," he says, reading my mind.

"Think of our father. That should do the trick."

He scoots away from me slightly, probably worried about hurting me if his power actually works. He closes his eyes, and all is eerily silent for a few minutes. I sit there, wondering if I have any of my own magic, as it could be genetic for all I know. But I feel I would know by now if I did have any. I've gotten angry enough to know. I feel a twinge of jealousy, which quickly goes away when I realize how pointless the feeling is. Wanting a power won't get me one. Want won't get anyone anything.

I wait for Levi, absently wondering how much time our mother has left. Our lives depend on it. By the looks of her, I'm not expecting more than a week or two. I don't know if Levi will be ready by then. His power could have been a fluke. Maybe it will never work again. Or if it does work, he may never be able to control it, or keep it going long enough to kill our father.

Levi finally opens his eyes. The blue is gone, now completely white. It's haunting to see eyes so empty. I would be terrified if I saw this on anyone else. But my brother could never scare me.

Levi never would have been able to make his power rise to the surface so quickly without practice. He must have been training on his own for some time. The thought hurts. I always thought Levi told me everything. But I guess it makes sense, in a way. He didn't want me to get my hopes up, thinking that he would easily be able to kill our father. But now, we're out of time for secrets or waiting.

"What does it feel like?" I ask.

"Like weight surrounding my entire body," he winces. "And my eyes burn so bad it feels like someone is pouring lava into them." He tries to stand, but falls back down, wincing and rubbing his eyes furiously. “I don’t think I have control.” He lets out a cry of pain.

I grab his face in my hands. “What’s happening? Are you okay?” He darts away from me, breathing heavily with his face contorted in a painful expression. “Leave. I don’t want to hurt you.” He struggles against the pain, clawing at his eyes and throat like it’s killing him.

“I’m not leaving.” I move back towards my brother, who is now lying on the floor with tears rolling down his face. I've never seen him cry before. Not even after everything we’ve been through. I’ve never seen him in so much pain. It hurts just watching it. I wish I could take his place.

He gasps. “I can’t hold it in. Leave! I don’t want to hurt you!” he repeats, yelling this time. I want to help him, but there is nothing I can do. I don’t know the first thing about his power. I rush out of the room, the sounds of his sobs muffling as I close the training room door behind me. I wait outside the room for a few minutes, imagining Levi ripping his own eyes out to get rid of the agony. I hear a loud crashing noise, and I’m about to go back inside to check on him, when the door opens. I jump up, and luckily Levi’s eyes are still in his head. He hasn’t torn himself apart. In fact, he looks completely fine. The blue has returned, and there is no evidence that he is in any pain.

“How did you get your power to go away?” I ask, worried for the answer.

“I had to let it out.” He pushes the training room door open the rest of the way. The mirror is smashed, the dirt bags are open and spilling out on the opposite side of the room. The entire training area is a disaster. It looks like wild animals ripped the place to shreds. Anyone else would think that the person who did this has gone insane. But only I know it was my brother, and I could never think that.

"Wow," is all I'm able to say as I take in the damage.

Levi and I begin to pick up the mess as we talk. I watch his eyes to ensure he doesn't summon his power by accident while I'm so close to him. I'm not worried he'll hurt me, I've dealt with plenty of pain in my life. I'm scared that if he does, he'll never forgive himself.

"Do you think you'll ever have control of your power? To the point where you're not ready to tear your eyes out?" I pick up the glass from the mirror. I hold one of the shards up to my face, seeing my reflection. My long, black hair is a mess, the bags under my eyes are as dark as they were when my father was torturing me in training when I was eight, and the scar down my face is more prominent than ever.

"I don't kn-"

"I want him dead," I interrupt. I run my thumb across the scar. My father deserves to die for what he's done to both of us. I place the broken glass into a bucket in the corner.

"I'll train as much as I can before mother dies. When she does, I'll be ready, I know it."

What if she dies tomorrow? It's a possibility. She was able to walk the last time we saw her, but only for a few feet before her legs almost gave out. She was unbelievably frail. I don't see her lasting long. I give Levi a sad smile, hoping so desperately that he'll be able to save us. But hope is a fragile thing. It can't be depended on.

"What if you're never able to control it?" I ask.

Levi puts his hand on my shoulder. “I will be able to. And I will kill him.” He doesn’t promise me because he knows how much I hate it when he says it. Promises are just empty lies. Even worse than lies, because you expect a good outcome and never get one. “When I kill him and you take the throne, we will end this war for good, and no one will ever have power over us anymore. We will finally be happy,” he tells me. I don’t respond. Leviathan has enough hope for both of us.

Chapter eight

EMBER

I wake up in the morning a little earlier than usual. I decide to do something I haven't done in a while. Draw. I slowly get out of bed, reluctant to let my exhaustion pull me back under the covers. I open my curtains, letting the bright light of morning flood into my room. I sit at my desk and shuffle through the drawer until I find a piece of paper and a pencil.

One time, I tried drawing one of my mother's signature flowers. It didn't come out right and just made me sad. Another time I drew the training room, which came out okay, but it didn't really mean anything. The last drawing I ever made was of the dagger my mother gave me. I didn't draw the flowers on it because I knew they would never come out as good as hers, and it kind of felt wrong to draw something only she drew. I knew it would only make me sad like last time.

Finally, after staring at the blank paper for a good ten minutes, I think of something. I draw the Fighter Castle. I've seen drawings of it before, and my father has told me stories about the haunting place. Apparently it's always storming there, and the castle looks dark and horrifying amidst the rain and thunder. Looking through the window at the front of the castle on the top floor, you can see the huge throne room, lit by dim lanterns. I add the room I've heard about to my drawing, spending time drawing a glorious throne. I add an outline of a woman with a blank face sitting in the large chair, sharpening a knife. I imagine Alcmene would sit there after she becomes the ruler, plotting to kill us all. I wonder what she actually looks like. I wonder how seeing the castle in person would compare to drawings and stories. I finish the drawing by adding dead trees around the castle. My mother was an amazing painter and artist. I've definitely inherited some of her talent, but I'd rather train than spend all my time adding lead to paper.

I leave the drawing on my desk as I prepare to go downstairs for training. I take one last look at Alcmene's blank face before I depart. I wish I knew what my enemy looks like so I could imagine her face when I throw knives at targets. So I could know who I must capture once she finally shows herself.

I arrive at training early, even after routinely stopping at my mother's flower painting on the way. Every time I pass it by, I wonder how her death could have been prevented. How if we just stood up and attacked the Fighters castle, she could have stayed alive. If we fought back, maybe we could win. But I understand where The Council is coming from, because losing would bring devastating costs.

"You're here early," I say, as I notice Austin in the training room.

He smiles warmly. "I wanted to get a head start today. I'm glad you're here."

"Me too. With this attitude and practice, you'll be a master in no time. Able to defend against the Fighters by my side."

His smile drops slightly.

"What is it?"

"It-it's just..." he trails off.

"You can tell me, Austin." I grab his shoulder, trying to reassure him.

"What if I die in battle? What if you do? The Fighters haven't attacked in a long time. They could be building up for something big." I think of my dead sister, and imagine Austin lying beside her with his blood spilling out as the light leaves his innocent brown eyes. I swallow.

"Whatever the Fighters throw at us, we can handle it. We're ready. This is what training is for. We will defend our home." I won't let anyone else I love die, I add silently. Austin included.

He nods.

"Then let's start."

My training with Austin runs smoothly. He is better already. He must have been practicing on his own time. I briefly go over blocks, strikes, and chokeholds, before getting into takedowns. I show him how to take down a Fighter if they reach for him by bending their wrists backward, leg sweeps, and using their own body weight against them. Austin is small, so I tell him he is better off going for a Fighter's legs to knock them off balance.

"What about after I take them down? Won't they get back up?"

I chuckle and grab the rope by my side.

"You want to hold the Fighter down or knock them out so that you can tie them up with this. Capturing a Fighter is very important. We don't want a Fighter escaping, only to hurt more of us."

He nods again.

"What happens to Fighters after we capture them?" Austin asks.

I realize I have never really thought about it before. All I know is that The Council takes them. I know a few Fighters who have joined us in our cause, once they've established they could be trusted. I assume the rest are held somewhere for questioning, and only killed if they desperately have to be.

I tell Austin what I think.

"Oh." Austin looks up, probably wondering the same things I am. I asked my father where The Council takes captured Fighters years ago, but he wouldn't give me a direct answer. Although it thought it was odd, I haven't brought it up since. Maybe some things are meant to be left a mystery.

We continue with training. Austin is exceptionally good at leg sweeps, which is a skill I took a while to master. I promise him that soon he will learn how to use a knife or dagger to defend, but I need to be confident in his other abilities first.

D'andre walks over to us as Austin and I are sparring.

"I'm glad you took Austin under your guidance. He is doing very well."

I smile. "Thank you."

"And Austin, I look forward to the day we will spar." He gives the boy a warm grin and walks away. That day will definitely be an interesting one. I can't imagine Austin sparring with someone as big as D'andre. The first time I fought him, I lost in record time.

Later, Austin and I have lunch together right outside the castle. We sit on one of the beautiful benches that have blue and white floral designs. "Everything is so pretty here," he says.

That I can agree with.

"Yeah. I've always admired the castle for its beauty. Have you seen the light blue flower on the wall on the way to the training room?"

"I have, I've just never really stopped to look at it."

"I'll have to show it to you on our way back. My mother painted it before she died."

"Oh. I'm sorry, Ember."

"It's alright." I look at him. "I think my mother would have liked you a lot. You'd fit in with my family well." Austin's eyes shine, and he takes a bite of his sandwich. I worry for the day he will have to go into battle when the Fighters attack again, but I will protect him like a brother.

We sit in silence for a minute. I admire the sky. The sun shines over us, and the clouds appear in light pink and blue shades. It makes me wonder how the sky looks on the Fighter's side. Is it gloomy and dark, with barely any sun peeking through the clouds, like I've read? Or is it light, just like ours?

Austin starts to speak.

"If you don't mind me asking, how did your mom die?"

"In the battle a little over a year ago." By the look on Austin's face, he must remember that terrifying day as clearly as I do. I so badly wish I could forget, but nightmares and flashbacks will never go away. "A Fighter killed her. I found my father holding her in his arms just outside the castle. I know her death still haunts him." My father has never been the same since that day. He doesn't train with me as often, his eyes are tired and his beard is unkempt. He lost the spark he used to have. I'm still haunted by my mother and sister's deaths too, and I don't think the scene of her dying will ever leave my mind, but I don't tell Austin this. "The Fighters have been preparing for a year. I'm sure they will attack soon, this time to win." I try not to picture the screaming and deaths that will come with another attack. I still haven't recovered from last year's battle; another would rip me apart.

"I'm really sorry about your mom. That must be horrible."

"It was. I still think about her a lot, especially when I see her flowers painted on the castle walls. But if anything, remembering her is what's pushing me to want things to change."

Austin casts a curious glance my way. "What do you mean?"

I hardly know myself. Planning our own attacks against the Fighters is unheard of, unethical, and entirely against what we stand for. I probably shouldn't be telling Austin any of this, but it's too late now. And I trust him, even though we practically just met.

"I mean, what if we fought back? What if we didn't just defend our land? What if we planned our own attacks against the Fighters?" I look towards the woods, where Meadow died. "Wouldn't we have a better shot at winning this thing?"

Austin's eyes widen. "Wow. That is not what I was expecting." He gazes in the direction of the Fighter castle. "I get what you're saying, but we're not supposed to attack first."

"I know. But at the rate things are going, they may attack us any minute now. They wouldn't be expecting an attack from us. We would catch them off guard and-" I stop mid-sentence. "Sorry, I shouldn't be saying this. It's too risky, and The Council would never go for it."

What would my mother do? What would Meadow do? Now that they're both gone, they can't guide me anymore. I'm alone in this decision.

"Maybe if you made a plan, you could convince The Council."

I contemplate the idea. It's a good thought. Planning an attack on my own, and presenting it to The Council with all the details in front of them, would give me a better shot at convincing them versus showing up empty-handed. But Defending has always been our way. I doubt they would take advice from a teenager without authority in council matters.

"Trying can't hurt," I say.

Austin smiles. He finishes up his sandwich and crumples up the paper it was wrapped in, throwing it into a nearby bin.

"Have you ever been to other lands outside the castle?" he asks.

"No. There would be no reason to wander off to Defender camps in the middle of the war. Besides, most of the land is Fighters territory." I think for a minute. "Unless the People in Between are real, then there would be a reason to leave. But they're just a myth."

"What if they are real?"

I've been wondering that as well lately. We could live freely with them if they existed and I knew where they were. I wouldn't have to train every day or worry about an attack. But on the other hand, even if I could run off, I wouldn't have my revenge. I need to stay and win this war for Meadow and my mother. I don't have a choice anymore.

"Even if they did exist, they could be getting attacked too. The Fighters want land. And I don't think they'll stop until they get all that's left."

Austin looks down. The light in the sky starts to dim. A horn sounds, signaling nightfall. We have to return to the safety of the castle. Curfew is one of the many rules my father had a part in convincing The Council to make. Although it's somewhat annoying, I understand the need for precaution. Anyone outside the castle could be killed by a wandering Fighter. It's known that they do their hunting at night, and they don't mind crossing into our territory.

"Though I can promise you this." He looks back up at me, hopeful for what I am about to say next. "If the People In Between do exist, somehow, someway, we will find them. And once the war is over, we can all be together, in peace."

He smiles brighter than I've ever seen before. "That would be a dream."

Austin follows me back inside the castle. I remember to show him my mother's flower before I drop him off at his room. "It's beautiful. She was a great painter."

"She was." The words sting.

After a minute, I ask him about his parents. They weren't there on his first day of training, which is somewhat unusual.

"Oh, my dad isn't around much, and my mom is always kind of by herself. She doesn't talk a lot. I think she's sad about my dad being gone all the time."

"Where does he go?"

"Hunting outside the castle."

As far as I know, there is a big group of people set aside for hunting. Out of those people, a small amount goes out every week past the perimeter to find food. Then they switch with another small group inside the larger one the next week, and so on. No one person should always be out. Unless things changed. I decide not to question it. Austin's father's business is not mine.

He admires my mother's flower painting for a little while longer as we continue talking. Soon, we go our separate ways.

"Goodnight, Ember."

"Goodnight, Austin. I'm sure my mother would have loved to meet you. And I'm sure the People In Between, if we ever come across them, will too."

He hugs me before he enters his room. I head back to mine, to find my father standing by my desk.

"You're back early," I say.

"Yes, the discussion at the council meeting ended sooner than expected." He points to the small piece of paper on my desk. "What's this?" He holds up the drawing I made earlier.

"It's the Fighter castle. I drew it based on the stories I've heard and drawings I've seen. Then you told me about Alcmene, and I drew an outline of her on the throne. I was fascinated by her."

He nods slowly as he puts the paper back down. "Okay. Why are you so fascinated with the Fighters and her?" he questions, almost skeptically.

"I'm not." My voice comes out slightly higher pitched than normal, indicating my evident lie. My father glares at me.

"I-I don't really know," I tell him. I don't say what I'm really thinking. I want to know everything about the Fighters and Alcmene. Not just because I want information that would be useful in combat, but simply because I find them interesting. I want to know why the Fighters, and Alcmene specifically, are the way they are. What was the point where she decided to cross the line into evil? She burned a man to death and carved her name into his head. How did she get so monstrous?

My father stays silent for a minute. He looks back at the paper.

"Next time, maybe draw something more Defender-friendly, in case anyone comes here and sees it. People could get the wrong idea. As a council member, it won't look good if my daughter is labeled as obsessed with the opposite side of the war." I tense my jaw at the disgusted sound in his voice, but nod in agreement. He walks out of the room.

I go to my desk and pick up my drawing. My fingers trace along the outline of Alcmene. Out of all the questions I have about the Fighters, I think the one I want to know the answer to the most is what her real name is. Although the knowledge wouldn't be very useful, I desperately want to know.

Other questions plague my mind as well. What are the Fighters planning? Who is the current ruler, and why has he never been seen? Is Alcmene really as evil as my father believes her to be? If she is, and she takes the throne, she won't wait any longer to attack us. We will all crumble, and there will be nothing left to defend.

Chapter nine

ALCMENE

Levi has been practicing using his power everyday for a week. The pain is his biggest problem. It consumes him. Controls him. But if he can unleash his power right before he is about to attack our father, hopefully he can bear it for the time it takes to kill him. In any downtime, we've been gathering materials for another plan that will take down the Defenders for good. If Levi and I successfully kill our father, I want to attack the Defenders right away. We've been waiting too long, and I want this war to end. If this plan works, I have no doubt it will turn the tide our way.

For as long as I can remember, Levi has been fascinated with the books in the library. He read about materials we will need to make a weapon against the Defenders. When he wasn't arguing with our father or training, he was in the library with a stack of books beside him. They were usually science-related. He still tells me about technological inventions created before the war and the use of firearms for combat.

My father would benefit greatly from learning about old war methods, but he isn't the type to sit and read. It's definitely fascinating to know how different the world used to be and what technology did for people, but it's not the thing I usually read about when I have the time. I like fantasy stories, although they're limited in supply. By now, I've read almost every fiction and fantasy book in the library, even the children's ones.

While studying science books, Levi came across directions to make a pipe bomb. Knowing it would make a huge impact against the Defenders, we decided to try to make our own.

"We have the pipe and the lead, which is a good start, but we need to make gunpowder to put inside." For now, we're making one pipe bomb to test. But we will need many more to take down the castle.

We were lucky with the pipe. We found it in the unused tunnels under the castle. The tunnels were used in the early stages of the war, but since the Defenders never attack us, they have no use. Besides a small opening for the gunpowder and lead, the pipe is airtight. Levi explains that for the pipe to explode, we need charcoal, sulfur, and potassium nitrate. The three combined will make a sort of homemade gunpowder. Charcoal will be the easiest to obtain, but sulfur will require us to go to The Dead Zone. It's a dangerous place to be, one that is seldom traveled. But we don't have a choice if we want to win. Levi has been working on gathering the final necessity, potassium nitrate, from the manure and urine from the horse stables, but it will take a little while to start forming.

Levi and I work on chopping trees. We stay a good distance away from the castle, to keep the borders well surrounded. We will need plenty of wood in order to make charcoal.

"How long have you been planning this?" I ask. It seems like Levi already has everything figured out.

"A while. I knew that figuring out how to make bombs would give us a huge advantage against the Defenders. But I didn't want it to be our father who scored the winning attack. I wanted it to be us."

I understand that. I've always wanted this war to end. I thought that if it did, our father would have no reason to abuse us anymore. He wouldn't need us to be perfectly trained for the war, so he wouldn't be disappointed in me. But I never wanted him to get the power and glory that would come with ending the war himself. When he attacked the Defenders last year, I secretly hoped he would fail. When he did, he came home furious and took it out on me and Levi, but it left us a window of opportunity. I know our father won't attack again until he knows we'll be guaranteed to win, so we have time to take him down and win ourselves.

I slam my axe into the nearest tree multiple times, watching as it falls to the ground, sending the birds nearby flying away. Even one tree is a lot of effort, and if we want to make many bombs, we'll need a lot of wood for charcoal.

Levi and I work through the night, dreading our father's sudden appearance. Luckily, he doesn't show. He's probably happy that we're not "pestering" him. Even when we're not saying or doing anything, somehow, our presence angers our father. I don't understand how our mother could love someone like that.

We stack the wood on our arms and bring it in bundles to the place where we burn the dead. The fires have been left untouched for a while, as no one has died since the battle a year ago. I dread having to use them again. The last time I knew someone burned was about three years ago. I had a best friend, Amara. We were very close. Her brother died, and things were never the same. She stopped talking to me right after his body was burned. I think the despair and anger of losing her brother ruined her. No matter what I did, I couldn't get through to her. Eventually, I gave up. I could only imagine losing Levi. I doubt I would ever be the same. But I still miss Amara to this day. When I'm not thinking about my father or Levi, I'm thinking about her. Since she left, my life has been a lot worse.

We place tinder onto the fire pit first.

"You can do the honors." Levi hands me a match.

I light the tinder, and we place the chopped wood onto the fire after a minute. We barricade it, trying to keep out as much oxygen as possible.

"This needs to burn for about a day. Then we should have enough charcoal to make multiple bombs."

I stare at the fire. I hope our hard work isn't in vain. If the bombs don't work at the Defender's castle, it will be just as hard to defeat them as last time. We won't win.

I walk back to Levi's room with him and sit at his desk. Suddenly, I feel uneasy. I don't want to leave my brother's side. Maybe it's because our possible deaths are so close. I want every minute I may have left to be with him.

"You want to sleep on the floor?" he asks as if he can read my mind.

"Like old times." I smile. I used to stay with Levi after our father would hurt me when I was younger. I'd always feel safer with him beside me. When I got older, I kept to my own room, and once, I realized how big of a mistake that was. Our father came into my room to attack me again, and it was a long time before I got out of bed after that. Levi thought one of my ribs was broken and my ankle shattered. I could hardly walk. I didn't go to the infirmary for a week, scared that the minute I stepped out of my room, my father would be there to finish the job.

I'm not as scared of our father anymore. Although I never retaliate against him, it's not purely out of fear. Maybe somewhat, but it's mostly because I know it'll be no use. Just like when he cut my face and told me not to move. It would only make it worse. I know there's nothing I can do to make him stop other than kill him. And killing him is something Levi and I can't do until after our mother's death and until Levi's power is sure to work.

"Do you think the Defenders' lives are more normal than ours?" I watch Levi as he stares outside his window.

The random question catches me off guard. "What do you mean, normal?" I think that after the world was destroyed, nothing was ever normal again.

"Less painful."

I look at the ceiling. I've wondered that before. If being on the other side of the war would mean I'd have parents that love me. If it would mean I'd have a life without terror looming above my head. But the Defenders are probably worse off. We're the ones attacking them. I know I should care that we're the ones in the wrong, but I don't. I understand why we need to take them down. There isn't much land left in the world; they have half of it. They have another castle and more farmland. Sharing resources with them isn't possible. Not only that, but we want power. Our father does. I do. When I rule one day, I'll want everyone to fear me way more than they do now. I won't care if that involves killing innocent people. Not after what I've been through.

"No. I think this whole world is filled with pain. It's just how it is." With that, I roll over to face the wall, and drift off to sleep, listening to Levi's slow breathing.

When we wake up, we gather charcoal from the fire and ground it up. The charcoal, sulfur, and potassium nitrate all need to be mixed up separately before they're placed in the pipe. Mixing them together could lead to an early explosion. Levi leaves the pipe and charcoal in his room, and we gather supplies. I throw food, water, and knives into my backpack, leaving my sword behind. The journey to The Dead Zone isn't too far from here, only a few hours. Sulfur is found underground, and there are plenty of holes and deposits on the Earth where the bombs were dropped.

The land is unlivable in The Dead Zone. There are no animals for food, and the water is poisoned. With the amount of craters, there would be nowhere to set up camp. No one has gone far into it, afraid that the radiation is still evident in the air or that they won't find anything worth the travel. That is why the Fighters are so determined to kill the Defenders and take their land. There isn't much left.

Levi and I travel through the woods. He's soundless, like I am. I'm glad he's not my enemy because if he snuck up on me I would be doomed. We move like shadows, never snapping fallen branches, never announcing our presence in any way. The rain only stops when we reach The Dead Zone. I haven't been to the boundary in years. Destruction is everywhere. Crumbled buildings and craters from explosions. Skeletons litter the ground. I can imagine the smoke that was here a hundred years ago, followed by the smell of fire and burning bodies. The part of the world where I live was impacted too, but nowhere near as bad. There was chaos and almost no hope, but rebuilding was possible, and we did just that. But here, there is nothing. The trees will never grow back, and the collapse of structures is far too many to be built again.

It's been so many years I doubt the radiation would still be in the air, as much as people believe it. Levi and I should be fine for a short amount of time. We just need to find a crater that has dug deep into the Earth. That way, we will find sulfur.

I take a deep breath before I cross the tree line that makes the boundary between The Dead Zone and Fighters territory. Every few feet there is another skeleton to walk around. These people should have been burned. It was wrong for them to lie out here, like this, for so many years, getting eaten by maggots and rotting into the dirt. The Defenders bury their people, which I think is just as horrible.

Levi continues walking restlessly beside me. I almost have to jog to keep up with him.

"These craters are large, but not large enough. We need to find one of the main impact points." That could be a lot deeper into the wasteland, and he knows it. But we don't really have a choice. We've come this far, and this is the last thing we need to build bombs. We can't win the war without them, at least we won't anytime soon.

I see a flash of color to my left that quickly disappears when I turn to look at it. I hear a sound like a scuffle of feet, and I move away to catch up to Levi.

"This place gives me the creeps," I tell him.

He laughs. "Then let's make this quick." We keep walking, and I scan my surroundings for whatever I thought I saw. There's nothing here. Only ruins of a place that used to be full of life.

The sky begins to darken. We have to hurry this up. It will be harder to navigate through the wreckage in the dark. I've never had a hard time making my way through the woods when it's pitch-black outside, but I'm familiar with that environment. I can run without tripping in the dark and scale a tree without seeing the branches. I'm comfortable in the forest, but not here.

We finally find the center of the destruction, and a pit the size of our castle lies in front of us. This must have been where one of the huge bombs hit.

"How do you expect to get down there without breaking something? And how will you possibly get back up?" I ask. It's not like his power of strength will help him in a fall.

Levi rummages through his bag, pulling out a very long rope. "This will hold me. I've already tested it."

"How? Did you fling yourself off the top of the castle?" I laugh at the ludicrous thought.

"Something like that." He ties the rope around himself, securing it tightly. He walks a short distance to a sturdy piece of debris stuck in the dirt and wraps the other end around it. "See you on the other side, sister." With that, he jumps into the hole and swings around, placing his feet on the dirt like he's scaling a building. He slowly makes his way down. I watch the rope for the off chance it breaks and he falls to his death. But the rope doesn't fail him. It's the debris he tied it to. It rises out from the dirt and moves towards the hole. Levi falls faster. I run towards the crater and catch the rope just in time. He looks up at me as the rope hitches. "Everything good?" He asks. I nod and hold the rope tightly, steadying my breathing. Levi makes it to the bottom. He looks around for a minute before yelling up to me. "Can you pass the shovel?" I hold the unweighted rope in one hand and get the shovel out of his bag. I toss it to him, and the blade barely misses his head. He jerks out of the way.

"Sorry!" I yell. He laughs and rips the shovel out of the dirt. I watch as he digs into the side of the wall.

"Drop the bag too! Empty it first!" I dump out the contents of his bag and toss it to him. I quickly pull a knife into my hand when I hear the sound from earlier. I spin around to see a deer. How could a deer be all the way out here? I lower my knife. It looks completely normal at first, until it turns to face me. I almost fall over when I see It has two heads. Its eyes are melded together and pink flesh encases the connection. I raise my knife, but before I have the chance to do anything, it locks eyes with me and runs in the opposite direction. Did the radiation cause a mutation even after all these years? I shiver and place my knife into my holster. I've never seen such a thing.

"Are you almost done?" I shout. "I hate it here!"

"Pull me up!" he replies. He's heavier now that his bag is almost full, but I have enough strength to carry more weight.

When he places both feet firmly on the ground, I tell him what I saw.

I expect him to act shocked, but instead he laughs. "I'm not surprised. Like you said, this place is creepy." That means that the radiation could still be in effect. We need to get out of here fast.

We head back to the castle, navigating The Dead Zone through the light of the moon. The minute we step into Fighter's territory, I feel better. We make it into Levi's room and he empties his bag.

"We have enough sulfur to make plenty of bombs." I smile.

Chapter ten

EMBER

I'm walking back to my room from training when I hear a noise coming from the council room. I think nothing of it, until I hear it again. It's quiet, but I can just make out the sound of yelling. I immediately think of the screaming echoing around me when I knelt beside my mother in a pool of blood last year. I'm not allowed inside the council room, but my curiosity gets the better of me. I turn the handle on The Council's huge door. It opens with a slight creak, and the council room appears before me. I've only been in here once, with the council members watching me. It feels wrong to be here alone.

The room is alarmingly quiet, making me wonder if I imagined what I heard before. Pictures line the walls, some pretty with flowers and scenery, some horrifying, with pictures of war and death. My eyes immediately spot one of my mother's light blue flowers painted in the corner of the room, amongst the war pictures. I add this to my mental list of all the flowers she painted around the castle. This makes 52.

A gigantic table fills the center of the room, lined with chairs, all placed perfectly straight and neat. A map lies in the center of the table. There is no writing on it except for yesterday's date. Maybe The Council is considering a new strategy to defend against the Fighters. Hopefully, it's better than whatever strategy we used last year.

After taking a minute to look around, I hear the yelling again, and that's when I figure out where it's coming from. Below me.

"Hello? Can anyone hear me?" I whisper yell. As my face is inches away from the ground, I see a small split in the carpet under the table. "Weird," I say aloud.

I move the table as much as possible without messing up the perfect symmetry. Luckily, the carpet blocks the sound of the table being pushed. I will have to move it back after I investigate. Even an inch off, and my father will know something is amiss. He's a perfectionist like my mother used to be.

I debate not looking under the rug at all. I have no right to be in The Council room in the first place and definitely no right to snoop inside. I lost that privilege the minute I decided to train under D'andre. But even with that in mind, I lift the gray rug. To my surprise, I see what looks like a trapdoor. I step back, dropping the carpet, trying to decide if I really want to investigate my father's business. Since I heard yelling, I convince myself that what I'm doing is okay. Someone could be in danger.

With that, I lift the rug once more. Why is there a trapdoor under The Council room? What could possibly be under here? I think logically first that it's extra supplies or weapons. But what is the yelling I was hearing? My mind wanders. I hear footsteps outside but proceed anyway, swallowing my growing fear. I need to find out what's under here now, or else I may never know.

I slowly open the trap door, trying to prevent it from creaking as much as possible. When I open it completely, I see a ladder along a wall that goes down into a cellar. I take one more minute to ensure no one is coming in, before I go through the trap door.

I travel down the rungs of the ladder, and suppress the shivers going down my spine. What is this place? I hear the yelling again right as my feet hit the floor. Now it's piercingly loud. My heart starts to beat fast. Is someone stuck down here?

"Hello?" I ask. In front of me is a wall, and I hear shuffling from around the corner to my right. This is it. Once I turn this corner there's no going back. I take a deep breath before I go.

I see something I never imagined I'd see. Metal bars that make up at least ten prison-looking cells. What is this? I see men behind the bars, each one looking frailer and filthier than the next. Most men have collapsed on the floor or are sitting in a corner weeping.

As I step closer to each cell, they push themselves farther away from the bars separating us. I stop at one cell where a man with dark brown hair and piercing brown eyes stands and stares at me. He is the most beaten up out of all of them. His shirt is so ripped and torn he might as well not have one. He is so skinny you can see his ribs. His face is drawn and there are purple bags under his eyes. The smell hits me like a gust of wind. The stench is almost unbearable. My eyes water. They haven't bathed in what seems like months. And from the looks of them, fed a real meal. I gawk in horror at them.

The man looks at me, without cowering in fear like the rest.

"What is this place? What happened to all of you?" I ask. He looks at me, eyebrows raised, like he doesn't understand me. My mind drifts to the council room above us. Is The Council torturing these people? Does my father know about this? Is he the one authorizing it? I feel like I'm about to be sick.

"Who are you? Why are you acting like you don't know about this?" the man behind the bars asks, his voice breaking with almost every word.

"Is The Council doing this to you?" I whisper. The thought makes me woozy again. The man steps closer to me, his hands grasping the bars. I recognize the crimson red stitching on his torn gray shirt. I remember the clothing from the battle a year ago. He is a Fighter. Is this what happens to the Fighters after we capture them? I never imagined that The Council would keep them so close. Right under our feet. I assumed Fighters were kept somewhere outside the castle. Somewhere far away.

I look at the Fighters in their cages. From the looks of them, they've been here a while. Tortured this entire time. I thought The Council interrogated Fighters, and eventually let them join us if they were trustworthy. If not, they killed them. Of course I'm disgusted by how these people are being treated, but part of me is enraged because they're still alive. There is no point in torturing them. They should be in the ground along with my mother and sister.

The man doesn't answer my question, but I see his dark gaze linger on the birthmark on my arm. His eyes widen in what appears to be a form of recognition.

"Your mark," he gapes. "How-"

"Ember." My father's voice rings behind me, cutting the man off. I whip around to see him standing there with a neutral expression. Like he's not seeing the horror around us. "What the hell are you doing down here?" His voice raises instantly, as he sees me inches away from the cell bars.

"Did you know about this? Are you and The Council torturing Fighters?" I yell back at him. I see the men in the cells raise their heads to look at us. Their eyes are bloodshot. As much as I hate the Fighters, this is horribly wrong. We are pacifists. The last thing we should be doing is torturing people.

"Come upstairs with me. We can talk about this there," he says, holding his hand out.

"No! I want answers now!" I step back.

"You were never meant to see this. You have no right to demand answers from me. You're not on The Council." My father has never spoken to me this way before. He's not yelling, but somehow that's even worse. Would I have been a part of this If I joined The Council instead of becoming a trainee?

"Tell me what is going on. I'm not leaving until you do."

He tries to step closer to me, but I move away.

"He did this to me! Your people are not the good ones!" the man I was questioning earlier interrupts, showing me his back. Angry red whip lashes cover his pale skin. Bile rises in my throat. How could The Council do this?

"Are you a part of this?" I look to my father. "Have you been whipping them, starving them, and beating them? What kind of a monster are you?" I can't stop the words that spill out of my mouth. He says nothing in response. A part of me doesn't blame my father for hurting these people. I want my revenge as well, but this is not the way to get it. "Did you ever stop to think that not all the Fighters are terrible people? That they were born into it or that the ruler or Alcmene has been manipulating all of them?" He says nothing again. Not all of the Fighters deserve this, and he knows it too. Some of them must be good. "Tell me!"

"They're Fighters, Ember. They're the ones responsible for killing your mother and sister. They're the ones who are still trying to kill us. We needed information, and this was the only way to get it," he finally says. He tries to step closer to me again, and at this point I'm almost against the wall.

"This was not the only way." I push past my father and quickly get up the ladder before he has time to follow. Tears stream down my face. How could he keep this from me? How could he act like we're on the good side of this war when The Council is secretly torturing Fighters behind everyone's backs? We're supposed to defend peace. To fight for our home only because we have to. This is never what I grew up believing.

I rush back to my room, locking the door behind me. I don't want my father coming in, trying to deceive me with his never-ending stream of lies. So many questions run through my mind, but one sticks out. What am I going to do?

Chapter eleven

ALCMENE

About a year ago, the Fighters captured a Defender and put him in our holding cells. My father allowed me to torture the Defender as part of my training. He believed it would make me less weak. I couldn't refuse, but I told myself going into the whole thing that I wouldn't turn out like my father. Now, I'm not so sure I didn't. I've been thinking a lot about that day since it was the day I discovered Levi's power without realizing it. The day I saw his eyes turn white. But that isn't what's been sticking with me lately. That day marked my first kill and a continuous desire to do it again.

I walk down the steps to the holding cells on the lowest level of the castle. Noticing it's colder, I adjust my black coat, which Levi let me have once he grew out of it. The stone walls down to the cellar are lined with torches, which seem to dim more as I continue down the steps. My father suggested bringing something of my own to torture the Defender with, but I decided to use whatever was already in the cellar, not wanting to obey him further. I finally reach the last step, and I see the cells. There are five of them, all with reinforced iron bars and a keyhole for each one. Only my father holds the keys to the cells, but recently he entrusted me with one of my own. I see the Defender crouched in the corner, facing away from me. The other cells look bare without Defenders in them. Spiderwebs hang down in intricate patterns from the ceilings, and thread between the bars of the cells. It's been a long time since we've had Defenders down here. Too long. After the battle a year ago, my father insisted on only attacking small, outlying Defender camps for a while, because of how badly we lost at the main Defender castle. But at the same time, he is angry that we don't have more than one prisoner. Whose fault is that? I know that when I rule, I won't be so naive.

There's almost no light in this part of the cellar. My eyes strain to see in the dark. "Look at me," I tell the Defender. I light an unlit torch on the wall. He shifts around to face my direction. The man is younger than I expected. Hardly in his twenties. His clothes are ripped, hair in a mangled knot falling just above his shoulders. His hands are tied in front of him, and his eyes are wild, like he's just been to hell and back. His face is bloody, scratches and scars along his pale skin. The Fighters who captured him must have beat him before throwing him into the cell. I wish I could have been at the battle to capture my own Defenders, but of course my father wouldn't let me go, and now we're stuck with one measly prisoner. The Defender looks at me with fear in his tired eyes. The same look is reflected in my own eyes whenever my father is around. I don't want to be afraid of him anymore. Maybe this will help. Finally having someone under my own command. Someone who can feel the fear and pain I've felt too many times before.

"Please, don't hurt me," he says hoarsely.

I smile. "I think my Fighters have done a pretty good job of that already. But don't worry, boy. I'll only hurt you if I have to." The lie comes out easily. I will hurt him, no matter what information he gives up. My father ordered me to. I have no choice. But the voice in the back of my head tells me otherwise.

I always have a choice.

"Why did the Defenders start building separate camps away from the castle? I'm sure there's enough room to hold all of you." I make the venom in my voice as evident as possible. To rule one day, I have to speak the part. I don't care why the Defenders separated, I just like hearing the boy's ragged voice as he squirms beneath me.

He seems hesitant to talk at first. But one hard glare in his direction changes his mind, fast. I picked it up from my father, seeing him shoot daggers in my direction too many times to count. So much for not becoming like him.

He coughs before speaking. "The camps were made a long time ago for safety. They wanted to be more spread out. After the battle, even more of us left for the same reason."

The pathetic, incompetent Defenders only took ages to figure that one out. Of course you should spread out your people so that one attack isn't against everyone. The Fighters spread out in multiple castles and small camps forever ago. The Fighters in the small camps are especially vigilant. They move between different hunting spots and Fighter territory, gathering supplies and foraging, never staying in one place for too long.

"You must have known the trip to a smaller camp would have been dangerous. Why did you leave?" I question.

He wipes some of the blood from his face. "I wanted to look for something."

I grab onto the bars, and he falls backwards, away from me. "Something?" I raise my voice. "Now is not the time to leave out details, Defender."

He takes a breath, fixing his torn clothing. "The People In Between. Everyone thinks they're just a legend. But I know that's not true. They're out there, they must be, and I thought I would be safer with them, so I left."

I laugh. "That stupid Defender myth? Utter nonsense." He looks away from me.

I've heard of the legend. The Defenders believe there are outliers, neither Fighters nor Defenders, out in the wild somewhere. But If there was, my father would have found them already, and would have forced them to join us or killed them. He would love for our army to expand further. And so would I.

I don't bother asking the shaking Defender any more questions. I have to torture him. My father will punish me otherwise. But besides that, something deep within me wants this man to suffer.

The walls are lined with a few daggers, knives, and a sword. I contemplate stabbing him, but that would be too easy. Too quick. I smile as my eye catches the light gleaming from the torch I lit a few minutes ago. I hear the Defender gasp as I grab it, and unlock his cell. He scurries to the far corner, but that doesn't help him.

"The more you struggle, the more this will hurt." I smile brighter at the thought. It feels like I've taken the place of my father, holding someone at my own mercy. There's no way out for this boy.

"Please!" he cries out, "don't do this! I'll give you whatever you want. Anything!" he screams, as I near him with the torch.

"This is the only thing I want." I lower the torch to the Defender's leg. He tries to move away, but he doesn't escape the flames. I was explicitly ordered not to kill this boy, but I don't care. I hold him down as the torch burns through his flesh. His screams pierce my ears, and I press the torch down harder, watching as the fire tears away at him, turning his skin from a pale white to a welting red. His torn clothes light on fire, and the smell of burning flesh fills my nostrils. Bit by bit, the fire consumes him. As I grow tired of watching him thrash around like a fish out of water, I finish him off with my dagger to his heart. I watch as his eyes go dark, his burnt body slumping against the wall.

An idea sparks in my mind. I take my dagger out of the Defender's heart and carve my name into the boy's forehead, one of the only places the fire didn't turn his skin to welts or ashes.

Before walking into the cellar, I told myself I wouldn't be like my father. But as I walk back up with the boy's burned body behind me, I don't care. I don't regret torturing him, killing him. It was my first life taken, and even though I shouldn't admit it, I enjoyed it. Maybe I'm like my father, feeling no remorse after doing something horrible. But does that matter? I feel powerful, and it's a feeling I want to have again and again, no matter the cost.

I order a few Fighters to travel to the Defenders main castle and deposit the boy at the front entrance in the dead of night. When the Defenders wake, they will all know who killed the boy, and they will all fear me, not my father. When I kill him one day and take the throne, the Defenders will know who I am. And they will all wither before me.

Chapter twelve

ALCMENE

A few days later, Levi and I go into our mother's room when we know our father won't be around. We find her lying in bed, the life draining out of her.

We sit down beside her, expecting the worst.

"She's not getting better, Levi."

Her eyes open, and she tries to speak, but no words come out. Levi glances at me, eyes worried.

Our mother has almost always ignored what our father did to us and even what he did to her, but she's still our mother. As she looks up at us, her eyes foggy and barely remaining open, I know her time has come. I instantly think of ending her life myself. Maybe it would be better that way, quicker. Quicker than whatever sickness is slowly draining the life from her. Quicker than watching her face become shallower and darker. But it's not like killing a random Defender like I did a year ago. I don't want to kill my mother. I won't feel powerful after taking her life. The only way I can think of killing her in the most painless way possible would be to stab her in the heart. She would only feel it for a second before she'd be gone. But the thought makes my stomach churn. I imagine the knife piercing her skin, her blood starting to drip onto my shaking hands. I ball my hands into fists and look away from her.

I wonder if Levi is thinking the same thing. He stares at our mother with a soft sadness, and she shifts her head to look out the window. I don't know what intrigues her out there. Every day there is nothing but storms and darkness. It's always been that way. But every time I see our mother, she stares outside, with her gaze fixated on the dark. I hear the door to the bedroom squeak. I jump off the bed and practically crash into Levi when I see my father opening the door. He doesn't look as angry as he usually does. His expression is unreadable. He sits down next to our mother on the bed, without looking in our direction. He doesn't give us a chance to say goodbye to her. He doesn't even say a word, before he slices her neck open, catching the flowing blood in a cloth in his hands. Levi and I stand there, unable to speak. A single tear drops from my eye, rolling down my face and onto my shirt. I think I see a tear fall from my father's eye, too, but I must be imagining it. He would never cry in front of us.

I can't seem to rip my eyes away from my bleeding mother. The blood drowns out everything else I see. I stand frozen, replaying her throat getting slashed a thousand times. The blood pouring out. The last of the light leaving her eyes. Her final breath. My father sits on the bed, practically as motionless as our dead mother. The cloth he holds soaks with blood, and starts to drip onto him and the bed, leaving everything colored a crimson red. The room smells like metal now, which threatens to suffocate me. But I still can't move, can't escape this reality. I don't know how long I've been standing here, to me it feels like an eternity. Then Levi finally grabs my hand and drags me out of the room, leaving my mother's lifeless body behind.

The image doesn't leave my mind as he pulls me into his room. I feel his arms wrap around me, but I'm still not able to function. Love wouldn't be the right word to describe what I felt for our mother. I just feel hollow.

"I'm sorry," he mutters into my shoulder, "I'm so sorry." He doesn't cry, although I know he wants to. He's acting strong for me. He shouldn't. I shouldn't need him to take care of me anymore. Nevertheless, I let him hold onto me as my tears pour endlessly. A salty taste fills my mouth. In a way, our mother deserved to die for staying with our father, and watching as he hurt us. But dying by his hand isn't a death I'd wish on anyone.

Levi doesn't pull away for a while, but when he finally does, he looks into my eyes. "It's time."

I immediately know what he means and my expression turns dark. I wipe away my tears. I've cried enough. Now that our mother isn't here to persuade our father from killing us, we don't have a choice. We have to kill him first.

"You've trained enough?" I ask.

"Yes. I have. But it doesn't matter. We don't have time to wait anymore. I have no doubt Anwir will be coming for us soon."

I grab his hand. "I can't lose you too."

He smiles but it's sad. "You won't."

Levi practices his power in his room while I go to mine. He doesn't want to risk hurting me. I gather my knives before laying on my bedroom floor, thinking of our mother bleeding out, even though I don't want to. We didn't even get to say goodbye. Of course I was thinking of killing her myself right before our father walked in, but I would have talked to her first. I would have made sure I said everything I had to say. I would have made sure it was what she wanted.

Questions soar through my mind like birds on an endless flight. All the questions I could have asked her. One in particular makes me angrier than anything. Why did she pick her abusive husband over her own children? Not once did she apologize for the way she stood back while he tortured us. She said she loved and hated our father. That being with him threw her into a turmoil of emotions she couldn't pull herself away from. But how does that justify any of her actions? By staying with him and remaining a bystander, she ruined her children's lives. And she never cared. She never loved us. Not once did she mutter the words.

Time ticks by, and I still lay motionless on my floor, not even bothering to move to my bed. I lift my head to look out the window to my left. This is the view my mother saw right before she died. She never got a better one.

What did my father do with the body? Did he leave her there, in her bed, in a pool of her own blood? Did he mourn her? He didn't care enough to say one last word to her or warn us about his plan. He probably didn't care enough to mourn her after he slit her throat.

I wonder when Levi will come into my room, telling me he's ready for the final showdown with my father. Telling me how I can help him. But it seems as though hours have passed, and the castle remains silent. No word from Levi or my father, just the sounds of the raging storm outside.

Chapter thirteen

EMBER

Fortunately, my father doesn't come into my room. I lie in my bed, looking out my window. I don't want to get up tomorrow. I don't want to face my father. But so many questions will be left unanswered if I don't.

I'm unable to sleep. My mind can't drift away into a calm enough state sleep requires while the memories of the dungeon below The Council room plague my thoughts. The Fighters were malnourished, covered in whip marks and other scars, and they were terrified. Most were at the backs of their cells, cowering away from me. How could The Council do that to people who aren't strong enough to fight back? How could my father do that? The thought of him whipping them makes the nausea in my stomach rise. Even though I desperately want my revenge, I wouldn't take it from helpless people. Every fight should be fair. I rip the blankets off my bed and onto the floor, suddenly overwhelmed by the heat. I get out of my bed and sit down at my desk, opening the drawer that holds my drawing of the Fighter's castle. My father said that the ruler of the Fighters and Alcmene are pure evil. But how can I trust his words anymore? How can I trust anything from him after he's been hiding this from me all this time?

But if my twisted father is right, I can only imagine what Alcmene would do if she found out what The Council is doing to the Fighters. Her people. She would kill all of us.

I sit at my desk for what feels like a long time. Even though it's the middle of the night, I catch myself glancing at my bedroom door, dreading a knock from my father. I don't know what I would say to him. I look out the window, contemplating staying in my room forever. I sigh, knowing that's not possible. Maybe I can run to training tomorrow before my father tries to talk to me. I let out a breath, holding my face in my hands. What am I going to do?

The morning comes, and when the light shines through my window, I find myself still sitting at my desk. I must have drifted off at some point in the night. I rub my eyes and put the drawing of the Fighter castle back in my desk drawer. There's still no sign of my father. I quickly get dressed, having no option but to go to training. It seems like it's all I do. I often imagine what my life would be like, without a war or constant training. I would be able to wander outside the castle boundary, into the woods, into the world.

Austin meets up with me at the sparring end of the training room. We practice skills I believe he should work on. He wants to learn weapons training, but I only show him a small amount of knife techniques, knowing he's not completely ready for more. He notices my drifting mind as we train.

"What are you thinking about?" Austin asks.

I let out a light sigh and try to play my growing anxiety off as nothing. "Just the usual."

He furrows his brows, but nods.

"Okay," he adds.

After a minute he asks, "Are you thinking about planning your own attack on the Fighters?"

That wasn't what I was currently preoccupied with, but it's always in the back of my mind. If we don't plan our own attack, Alcmene will come after us once she takes the throne, and I could lose Austin. I can't lose anyone else.

"I always am," I answer honestly.

He gives me a knowing look, but remains silent. He knows it's too risky, and so do I. But the risk factor won't keep me from thinking about it.

Austin and I train for a while longer, have lunch, talk with D'andre, and walk around inside the castle, before we part ways.

I knew it would happen eventually, but running into my father makes me feel queasy all over again. I'm walking above the prison he had a part in making.

"Can I talk to you?" he asks, reaching for my arm. I pull away from his attempt at touching me, but I follow him into his room.

He pulls his door closed behind us, sitting at his small table in the corner of the room. I sit across from him, already wanting to be in my own room, alone, without this uneasy feeling in my chest.

He clears his throat and looks into my eyes before speaking. I immediately move my gaze off him and stare down at the table between us. I occupy myself with counting the ridges in the light-colored wood as he speaks.

"I'm sorry you came across the cellar that way," he says, running a hand through his light brown hair.

I tense. "Were you ever going to tell me? Were you ever going to admit what you've been doing to those people?"

He takes a small breath. "Yes, I was going to tell you eventually," he rubs his beard, "when the time was right." By the tone of his voice, it sounds like he was never going to.

"How could the time ever be right?" I take my eyes off the table and glare at him. "How could you torture them as they begged you to stop? What were you getting out of it?" My voice breaks.

He purses his lips. "This has been going on for ages, Ember. I am not the only one involved. Don't you see? This is how we get our revenge." His voice has a desperation in it now, like he's begging me to see the truth. I hate him for it.

I scoff and stand up from the table, wanting to get farther away from him.

"Violence is not who we are," I tell my father, anger rising in my voice.

"*Killing* is not who we are," he corrects me. I take a shallow breath, my mind spinning. I think of the blood spraying out of the throat of the Fighter I killed. His body falling limply onto the red grass. I want to leave the room, run out of the castle, and never come back. But I can't, as much as I want to. Not when I still need answers. Not when what is beyond the castle walls is far more dangerous than the man in front of me.

"Don't you want revenge for your mother and sister?" My father suddenly stands up, stalking towards me. I give him a look, silently telling him to back off. He clenches his jaw but doesn't move closer.

"Not like that," I say. I want to kill them, not torture them. I want to kill Alcmene. I want a real fight, the one my mother and sister were denied. But I don't tell him this. I don't want him to know my thoughts of murder and revenge. The ones that keep me up at night.

"You're saying that for years and years, the Defenders have been brought up with the knowledge that violence and bloodshed is not our way, but at the same time, The Council has been torturing the Fighters all along?"

He nods. "I know it's a lot to take in." He starts to come towards me again.

"Don't." He stays back, an ashamed look on his face. "What came out of torturing them? What did it give us?" He doesn't say anything, and that gives me my answer. Torturing the Fighters didn't give us any knowledge or anything useful for this war. It only gave The Council the satisfaction of hurting them. And for what? For all we know, those beaten Fighters downstairs have been brought up with the same lies I have. That they're the good guys.

"Who else knows about this?"

"About a quarter of our people. And they're on The Council's side in this situation. I hope you'll come to realize I'm not trying to hurt you. I'm doing what our people have done for generations. We deserve to hurt them, as they have hurt us. We haven't killed them. That's against who we are. But nowhere does it state that we can't do this." I think of the beaten Fighter who spoke to me. The terrified but resilient look in his eyes. The recognition in them when he saw my birthmark. He didn't deserve what my father did to him. None of them did. And the fact that my father thinks he had every right to torture people, simply because it didn't explicitly state anywhere that he couldn't, makes the matter worse. It's the wrong thing to do, whether it's a part of our values or not.

I feel the urge to be sick. "What you're doing to them is worse than killing them. I don't even know who you are anymore." I let the tears run down my face as I sprint out of the room and into the night. The breeze hits me, and although it's cold, I feel comfort in it. Outside, with the stars above, I feel free.

Chapter fourteen

ALCMENE

Levi never comes into my room to tell me he's ready. I wait for hours, drifting in and out of a nightmare-filled sleep, until I decide to get up and see what is happening for myself. Maybe he realized he wasn't ready and decided to hold off killing our father.

I open the door to Levi's room and walk inside. His bed is a mess, his curtains partly open, revealing the storm outside. Books and papers fill the floor from when he tried to find out more about his power, but my brother is gone. Where else could he be? I hear a crashing noise coming from my father's room. I run to my father's door and throw it open without a second thought. I quickly scan the room. I don't see my father. Broken glass and knocked-over paintings scatter the floor. Mother's body is gone, but I smell fresh blood. What the hell happened? I look down to see a line of thick blood trailing to the other side of my father's bed. Where is he? I follow the path of blood. When I get to the other side of the bed, my knees give out and I fall to the floor. My eyes fill with tears faster than they ever have.

Levi.

He's still breathing, but his breaths are shallow, just like our mother's before she gave way to the stars above. I crawl over to him, my legs refusing to hold my weight. I would be an easy target for my father if he walked in. He wouldn't even have to try. But right now, I don't care. Tears stream down my face, dripping onto the blood-stained floor. I've never seen Levi so broken. So not in control. I see the amount of blood that pools underneath him, no longer pulsing through his body but instead in a puddled mess. He has a gigantic gash covering most of his stomach, but I can't tell how deep it goes because of all the blood. From the amount he's lost, I can't comprehend how he's still alive. Did our father do this to him? Why did Levi attack him alone? Did his power stop working? The questions fill my mind, only to be pushed away by the pain that takes their place. The thought that he won't make it.

I grab his hand, letting his blood drench my clothes. I try to stop the blood flowing out of his open wound, but it keeps coming. It's too deep.

I've never told anyone I love them before. Not even Levi. The words just never seemed to come out. But now, without hesitation, I say them.

"Levi, please. Please don't go." I barely get the words out through my sobs. "I love you," I tell him, my voice cracking. I squeeze his hand tighter. My tears fall onto his ripped shirt. They cloud my vision. They taste of salt. I see his lips struggle to move, but they slant up the smallest amount, like he's trying to smile. He doesn't need to say it. He never needed to. I know he loves me too.

A choking noise comes from my throat, and I struggle to breathe. Levi has been the only person in my whole life who has been there for me. Trusted me. *Loved me.* And still, I never told him I loved him until now, when he's leaving me. When it's too late. I wish I told him sooner. I wish I was strong enough to kill our father earlier, so Levi wouldn't suffer the consequences. I wish it was my life slipping away, not his.

Levi's eyes close, and he's gone. I hear him take his last breath, and my heart shatters. Suddenly, the world goes quiet. The sounds of the storm outside and my heart pounding all stop at once. I'm trapped in this soundless, horrible moment. I let his hand go, allowing it to fall into the blood surrounding us. I remain kneeling beside him, not daring to move. I'm afraid if I do, his body will be gone. Just like our mother's. His body is all I have left of him now. Once it's gone, there will be nothing left.

The pain that courses through me is a pain unlike anything I've ever felt before. It's nothing like how I felt when I lost my mother. It's so much worse. The loss, the betrayal, the anger. I feel like collapsing next to him, lying here until I die, too. But I know I can't. I have to kill my father like Levi would want me to do. I have to avenge my brother's death and become the ruler of the Fighters. Only then can I win this war. My heart breaks at the thought of being alone at the end of everything. Levi always told me that we would have a normal, happy life together after the war. But now, even after I win, it will just be me. Alone forever, waiting for the day when I will join him among the stars.

I look back down at Levi. His blonde hair covers part of his face. His eyes are so delicately closed that it looks as if he's sleeping. He almost looks at peace. But I know he's not. I don't care if I die in the process. I will kill my father. *For him*.

Chapter fifteen

ALCMENE

I wake up the day after Levi's death. The storm brews outside my window, the noise drowning everything out. But even so, the pain in my heart doesn't waver. Not for a second. I so desperately wish I hadn't woken up at all. That I died yesterday with my brother by my side.

Yesterday I searched everywhere for my father, finding nothing. I searched the entire castle, the woods, and the hunting grounds, but there was no trace of him. Why did he leave after what he did to Levi? Is he dead somewhere too? I have no idea what happened, but if he returns, he won't be alive for long. I will get my revenge.

I ponder simply going back to sleep, letting this dreadful day pass by. But I know, no matter how much I want to, I can't. I have to train. But even with days of nonstop training, my father will still kill me if we fight. Somehow I have to outsmart him, not just outfight him. If only I wasn't fighting alone.

I slowly roll out of my bed with my brother firmly on my mind. It's like a part of me is gone. I feel empty and miserable. Levi was the only light in my life. He was the only reason I kept breathing. Now, my only reason is revenge. And once I get it, I can join him.

I prepare for training without my brother, which feels like a stab wound in my chest. Every time I'd train, it would be with him. He'd mentor me while he worked on his power. I still don't understand why his power didn't work when he fought my father. Surely if it did, my father would be among the stars instead of Levi. I would still have my light.

Before I train, there's one thing I have to do. Levi's corpse is still there. In that *room*. Everything in my body screams at me to just leave him there. Because I know facing that scene again will just kill me twice over. Realistically, I can have any servant take him to the burning site. They would do it without question. But that would feel wrong. I have to be the one to take him there, and I have to be the one to burn his body. It's my responsibility to do so, as much as I don't want to see his stab wound covered in dried blood or his closed eyes, never to reopen. I want to erase those memories altogether, not face them again. But I must.

I grab my dagger from my room before I head out, just in case my father turns up. It's my favorite dagger, with a silver handle and pure obsidian for the sharp blade. I remember the day Levi gave it to me. It was a few years ago, right after our father hurt me so badly that I couldn't get out of bed for days. Levi gave it to me as an apology for not being there to fend my father off and as a way to cheer me up. I hated that he needed to be responsible for me. That he always needed to be the older brother. And now, that's led to his death. My father killed him, but his blood is on my hands, too. This dagger and Levi's jacket will be the only things I have left of him after I burn his body. I will protect them with my life.

I holster the dagger, along with a few throwing knives. I'll need to practice with them when I go down to training today. Throwing knives is a skill most Fighters haven't been able to master. I want to be the one to change that. When I'm running this place, the Fighters will be masters at every skill possible. I know Levi would have been a better teacher than I ever will be, but I have to try. There's no chance of winning this war if the Fighters go into battle with what they've learned from my father, who hardly ever takes the time to teach them.

As I walk towards my father's room, a few Fighters pass by me. They look like they're about to say something, but once they see the look on my face, they know better than to speak to me. Maybe they've all gotten word of my brother's death. Maybe they all think I did it. I know they all think I'm cruel like my father. Maybe they're right, because when I kill him, I won't feel anything but pride. I will feel no remorse or regret when I take his life, just like he took my brother's from me. When my father returns, I'll be ready to kill him the minute he walks into the castle. I will have a complete plan. Once he falls, everyone will be terrified of me, not him. And I'll feel the power I've always wanted. The power I felt the day I killed my first Defender.

I walk into my father's room, and the thought of power immediately leaves my mind. Instead I feel overwhelming pain. The farther I walk into the room, the more the pain in my chest increases. I'll never talk to my brother again. I'll never train with him again. I'll never hear his hopeful voice or light laugh. He's just gone. And now every second that goes by feels like an eternity. I'm on my own.

When I see Levi, my heart shatters just as it did before. It still feels like I'll wake up tomorrow, and he'll be hovering over me, trying to get me up and out to train. And then we'll go stargazing at night, just like we used to. Leviathan was the one holding me together. With the constant terror of my father, he was the only one keeping me sane. I don't know how I would've survived my childhood without him.

I try not to look at my dead brother as I maneuver him onto a stretcher I took from the infirmary. I take a long look back at my father's room, still a mess from their fight. Dried blood lines the floor and scatters the spot where Levi took his last breath. I don't think I can ever come in here again. And there's no way I can ever clean the blood stains. Cleaning up the spot where he drifted away from me will be too painful. I turn around, leaving the memories in the room, dragging my brother's corpse behind me.

When I make it to the burning site, my arms are aching. Besides dragging Levi in the stretcher all the way here, I had to deal with petrified looks from countless Fighters. Thankfully, as I gather wood for the fire, the remaining Fighters disperse, leaving me alone with him. I stare at his pale skin. His closed eyes. The dried blood. I stare at him until I hear footsteps approach me. What kind of Fighter has the nerve to talk to me while I'm with my brother's body? I look up, and my scowl drops. I instantly recognize who the Fighter is and I freeze for a second.

She was my best friend when I was younger, or more than that. At least I felt like we were more than just friends. She was the only person besides Levi who I felt close to. But after her own brother died, she became distant. She never really talked to me again, and I had my own problems to deal with, so I didn't bother trying to become friends again. It hurt for a while, though. She was the only real friend I ever had. I understood why she became so distant, but that didn't mean it hurt any less. Lately I've seen her around the castle, usually in the training room or heading there, but she never acknowledged me. I thought she never would again. But now, she walks right up to me, like no time has passed. I haven't had a chance to see how much her appearance has changed, since I haven't seen her up close in years. She stands at my height, with emerald green eyes and auburn red hair that falls a few inches below the top of her spine in fiery waves. She has freckles that used to only speckle her nose and cheeks, but now cover her entire face. Her toned muscles show through her gray shirt. She must be training pretty hard. In a few ways, she reminds me of myself. She holds herself with a fake confidence I am familiar with, masking the pain behind her eyes that only I can recognize. Her slight smile reminds me of the days when we were seven years old, training and laughing together. Her presence, on top of Leviathan's, helped me deal with the horror of my father.

"Amara, what are you doing here?" The words come out sharper than I intend them to. I have never really forgiven her for leaving me, and that's evident in my tone.

She drops a few pieces of wood onto the unlit fire before she speaks. Her voice is low, but soft. She doesn't address me as royalty or someone to fear. She talks to me the same way she did years ago, like a friend. Only this time, everything is different.

"The Fighters have been talking." Her voice is the same as I remember it. Soft, but always has an edge to it.

"I figured they would be," I reply, adding an armful of wood onto the fire. I keep my answer short, already wanting to be out of this conversation. Why is she talking to me all of a sudden? It has been years since she's interacted with me. Years since I've heard her voice.

She reaches into her pocket, pulling out a match-box. "May I?" she asks. I look at her outstretched hand and imagine holding it in my own.

"Let me." I take a match from her, trying not to let an old, familiar blush rise to my cheeks as our hands touch. I light the fire and watch as it slowly devours the wood. The smoke and embers rise, slipping away into the morning sky. The blazing fire grows stronger, one bit at a time. I focus on the heat of the flames instead of the woman beside me.

"Most of the Fighters believe *you* killed Leviathan."

"I figured that too."

She says nothing but looks a little surprised. "Why didn't you tell them the truth?"

"And how would you know what the truth is?" I ask as I make my way towards Levi on his stretcher. I stop before picking him up, knowing I have to do this alone. I can tell Amara senses this as she keeps her space from Levi and me.

"I know you didn't kill your own brother. Anyone who saw you two together would know that. You were a different person around him. You were happy." My eyes shift away from hers as pain fills my chest again. I'll never be happy again with him dead.

I don't care what the other Fighters think, right now I just want to be alone. Amara shouldn't be here. She should be inside, telling stupid stories about my brother's death like the rest of them. Avoiding me like she always does. Burning his body is something I need to do alone.

"What would you know, Amara? Go inside with the other clueless Fighters, where you belong!" I can't help myself. Snapping at her is the only way she'll leave.

"I know you want me gone, so I'll go. But just know that I'm here if you need me."

She heads inside, leaving me alone with the burning fire. She's here if I need her? What the hell is that supposed to mean? She hasn't been here for years, and out of nowhere she shows up again and expects me to believe that? What a joke. I guarantee she only said that because she knows I'll be taking the throne in no time and wants to get on my good side before it's too late. She wants power, just like everyone else. She's not here for me and she never will be.

I sit down beside Levi, trying to calm down. I touch his pale, cold hand.

"What am I supposed to do without you? I'm already starting to feel crazy, and it's only been a day. I can't do this forever." I look down at him, almost expecting an answer. My tears threaten to fall, but I don't let them. I've cried enough. Now is the time to be strong. The only one that can take down our father is me. Crying won't help.

When I finally manage to get Levi's body into the fire, keeping my eyes on the flames is torture. I so badly want to run back into the castle, but one of the traditions of the burning ceremony is to stay the whole time. Usually, these ceremonies will have many people standing up, talking about the dead, and mourning together. But for Levi, it's just me. Levi was an outsider, as am I. He didn't talk to any other Fighters because he knew they would use him to get closer to our father. Becoming connected to the ruler is what everyone wants because they think they won't end up on the front lines of the war. But it's not true. Almost everyone has to go into battle at some point.

It feels as though I've spent the whole day getting Levi here and burning him, but in reality, it's only been an hour. I've used up almost all my energy, and I still have to train later. I'm already dreading it.

Levi has no one else here to talk about him, so I decide to say something myself, even if it is short. I look at the sky and clear my dry throat.

"I've never really thanked anyone in my life. There's never been anything to be thankful for. But now that you're gone, I realize I should have been thankful for you while you were still alive. You were always there for me. You always kept me safe, even if it meant getting yourself hurt. You showed me how to fight back. I promise you, I will fight back against our father, and I will kill him. For you."

I take a breath, holding back sobs I know are inevitable.

"You always loved me. I should have said it before it was too late. I would give anything to go back to when you showed me the stars for the first time when we were kids. I think that was my happiest moment. I feel like that was the first time in my life I felt free. It was the first time my mind didn't drift off to other horrible thoughts. I was just there, in that moment, with you. I should have said the words then." It takes everything in me to keep my tears from falling. I know Levi wouldn't want me to cry over him anymore.

"I know you're up there, looking after me. I will join you someday, and even though I want to join you now, my job here isn't done. I will kill our father for you. And then I will win the war for you. I love you, brother." I stand in one place until Leviathan's body is completely burned away. I break down the fire, crushing the last of the embers, before I head to the training room, throwing knives in hand.

Chapter sixteen

ALCMENE

I train nonstop for two days straight, only getting a few hours of sleep. There is no sign of my father in those two days, but I have a feeling he will be back at any moment. I will have to be prepared to face him. The anger of losing my brother keeps me going, and I continue training with various weapons and far-range vs. close-range combat.

I throw my knives angrily into the targets, hitting the bullseye over and over. How can I beat my father if he is always better than me? He is the one who trained me. He will know my every move. I throw another knife into the smallest target, ripping the red circle in half.

"Nice shot." I turn around and see Amara hovering in the training room doorway.

I tense my jaw, but I don't speak. She walks up to me.

"I know your father killed Leviathan. And I know you plan to kill him when he returns."

Is it really that obvious? I wipe the sweat from my forehead and pull my knives from the targets.

Thanks to my father, I'm usually pretty good at predicting people's next moves or words, even their intentions. But what Amara says next, I don't expect at all.

"I want in." I let out a small laugh, looking up at her in amusement. By the look in her green eyes, she isn't joking.

"Are you serious?"

"Very," she replies.

I scoff, walking over to the dirt-filled bags in the room's far corner. Amara follows.

"This is something I have to do alone," I tell her.

Amara looks into my eyes. "I understand that. But I only want to help. I've seen your father fight, and I don't know if you can beat him alone."

Suddenly I feel anger rush through me. I walk closer to her. "You don't know what I'm capable of. You haven't been around for years. You don't know anything about me," I growl.

Her expression remains neutral, her voice calm. "Maybe I don't know you anymore. But I do know what it's like to lose a brother." I clench my jaw. I want to scream at her for leaving me. I want to tell her how much it hurt, being without her for all those years, but I don't. The words refuse to leave my throat.

"And what do you propose? The kill will be mine, not yours."

Amara thinks for a second.

"Maybe I can help you weaken him before you deliver the final strike that ends his life."

I remember seeing Amara's eyes after she found out her brother died. They haunted me for a while, as that was the last time I saw her. They were filled with sadness and grief. She broke down crying. It was horrible to watch. She kissed me, the first and last one we ever shared before she walked away and never came back. Her eyes are lighter now, and I find myself staring at them. The pain of losing her brother will never leave her, that I know, but I can tell the pain doesn't consume her as much as it did back when he died.

Amara and I discuss possible options as we train. We don't speak of our past together, as much as I want to.

"We can't have you face him head-on," I tell her. I hardly want to myself. If she does, it would be a death wish. "With how much accuracy can you shoot an arrow?" I drop my dirt bag down, immediately feeling relief in my tense muscles. If she shoots him from a distance, she has a chance.

"Well enough." I follow her to the area with the targets I was using earlier. She takes her bow off her shoulder and an arrow from her side. She lines her bow up with the target, and slowly pulls a pointed arrow back, and releases, hitting a perfect bullseye.

"We may not have an hour for you to line up your shot before my father realizes what's happening." She rolls her eyes, before retrieving her arrow.

"Then I'll practice."

"My father could be back any minute! There's no time to practice! When he gets here, I need him gone before he has the chance to kill me." Amara tenses as I yell.

"Fine. He won't notice me. And I won't miss." Her voice holds confidence, but I'm unsure if I trust her abilities.

"Where do you want me to hit him?" she asks. I need to be the one to kill my father. Maybe a shot to the leg will put him off balance, giving me an opening. He will be shocked by the sudden pain, and he won't expect me to run over to him. Once I'm up close, I'll slit his throat. I tell Amara all of this, and she agrees. I barely use my bow, I've always been more proficient with throwing knives. So I give her mine from my room, as the training room one is old and unreliable. She takes it gingerly.

"If you miss..."

"I won't," she declares.

We continue training for a few more hours. Amara stays in my room that night, just in case my father comes back. She sleeps in my bed, and I try to drift off, but I can't. Thoughts of my father returning and Amara's warm body against mine make it impossible to sleep. Even in the darkness, I can make out Amara's freckled face and red hair. Her breathing is steady and her breath tingles my neck. Her lips are slightly parted, and I remember our first and only kiss. It was three years ago, long enough to forget what it felt like. But I didn't forget. I don't think I ever will. Having Amara back after our time apart is strange, but it almost feels like no time has passed. I want to kiss her. I want her to stay by my side. But she must be using me for the power I will have if I successfully kill my father and take the throne. As much as I want things back to the way they were, I can't fall for her trap. I won't give her my trust again, not after she left me when I needed her most. All I can do is listen to her long breaths and dread the day when I won't hear them anymore. When she'll abandon me once more.

Amara and I wait anxiously in the hopes my father will arrive today. The rain has stopped; it is the perfect time for my father to return. We stay in the throne room, knowing that is where he will go first. When we hear his footsteps, Amara runs into my father's room, which is connected to this one. She leaves the door ajar.

When my father walks in, he is covered in sweat and dirt. He looks exhausted. I have no idea why he went missing for multiple days, but whatever the reason, it couldn't have been good.

"Alcmene," he says through gritted teeth. He shrugs his coat off his shoulders, throwing it down to the floor. There's blood on his hands, and I think of my mother with her throat slit and the gash on Levi's stomach. I won't be next. I stare him down. His exhaustion will make it easier for me to win. I've never been one to care for a fair fight.

"You killed my brother." For some reason, I expect him to deny it. He doesn't.

He laughs. "Leviathan had it coming. As do you. Since you were a child, I knew you would never live up to your title. Once you're gone, I will be able to select my own heir rather than be forced to have you in power." Anger flashes behind my eyes. The only one that has it coming is him. He's abused my family our entire lives. He's held his spot on the throne, but hasn't had the courage to attack the Defenders Castle in a year. He killed the only person I ever loved. He deserves to die more than anyone.

"You will pay for Leviathan's death." As my father approaches me, I realize what I have walked into. I should have killed my father stealthily rather than attack him directly. But there's no turning back now. I have one shot at this. I have to make it count.

He draws his sword from his holster, and I do the same. I hope and pray that Amara doesn't miss. But hope is a fragile thing. As my father charges at me, sword in hand, I hear the door Amara is hidden behind squeak as it opens wider. My father hears it, too, as he swerves sideways, missing her arrow by less than an inch. My eyes widen. What now? Amara will never be able to hit him while he's attacking me. He will be moving too fast, and she'll probably hit me if she tries. Before I have another second to think, my father's sword hits mine, and my sword dips under the weight. He slashes his sword toward my stomach, and I barely dodge it. This is how Leviathan died. A swipe to the stomach. An endless stream of dark blood.

I see Amara spring out of the doorway in the corner of my eye. She pulls out her own sword and yells to my father.

"Two against one." My father's attacks don't waiver. Amara charges at him. I feel panic rush through me. I don't want her to die too. She can't. My father spins his body sideways, deflecting her sword with his. He throws her back, and I step up to him. Our swords clash. He swings the metal toward my head, and I duck, just missing the blade. He quickly takes out a throwing knife, sticking it into Amara's leg and disabling her. She falls to the floor, digging the knife out of her leg, trying to stop the bleeding. My father already has me on the ground when she stands back up. He hovers over me, his sword to my neck. I don't move. Maybe I was destined to die like this. At least I'll be with my brother. But as soon as the thought of death comes, I will it away. I told Levi when I burned his body that I would win this battle. Giving up would be breaking that promise. I look at my father as he nicks my neck. Fire is in his eyes now, the same look he wore when he cut my face when I was eight. It terrified me back then, but not anymore. Showing my father that I am afraid is practically giving him the win, and I won't let him have the satisfaction. Amara rushes over to us, but I yell at her to stop when she raises her sword to my father.

"This is my kill," I tell her. My father slams the point of his sword down, and I roll sideways just in time. It barely misses my head. Amara holds her leg as it bleeds onto the floor. I stand up, crashing my sword against my father's. He uses his weight to push my sword down toward me. The blade nears my throat, and I know he almost has me. I push my sword up with everything I have, but it doesn't budge. Just as his sword cuts into my neck, I put my left hand onto the blade. The sword rips through the flesh of my hand, and I hold back a scream as I push the blade away from me. Just as the swords become even again, I stab him in the leg with my brother's dagger. He falls to the floor, and blood spurts out of his wound as he rips it free.

He rolls, dodging my strike to his head. He hits the sword out of my hand, and as I reach for it on the floor, my father slashes at my leg. He cuts deep, and my blood spills. I move away before he has time to strike again. He's livid now, his movements less precise. Amara points her bow at my father.

"Don't move," she demands, scowling. This is *not* her kill. I take out one of the throwing knives at my waist, and without hesitation, I stab my father in the neck. I can feel the skin split and the tendons break. I've hit his carotid artery. By the look in his eyes, he knows he's a goner. I stand up, moving away from him. I almost fall to the floor from the wound in my leg, but I don't let myself. Amara also takes a step back, watching as the ruler of the Fighters bleeds out. He claws at the knife in his throat as his life drains away.

I stand watching with fire in my own eyes instead of his. Amara is so still I almost think she's stopped breathing. I pull the knife out of his throat, and more of his blood pours out. He holds his hand to the wound but it's no use. In a matter of a minute, his hands fall to the floor, and he stops struggling. Now he knows what it feels like to bleed to death. That is what he did to Levi, only worse, because Levi suffered for longer.

Suddenly, I wish my father was still alive so I could stab the knife into his neck repeatedly, having the satisfaction of finally watching him die, knowing I've won.

"You can leave now," I whisper to Amara, never tearing my eyes away from the man who ruined me. "Load up the bombs." She limps out without a word, but I feel her eyes on me before I hear the door shut behind her.

I stand over my father with a genuine grin on my face, clutching my bleeding leg. "I won." Anger and disbelief run through my words. If only Levi were here to see it.

Blood pools around my father, coloring the floor a crimson red.

"I am never going to wash this blood away." I look at the oozing wound on his neck. "I will always remember this day." Limping, I retrieve my brother's dagger and holster it at my waist. I take my father's sword from his side and hang it on the wall, where I will always be reminded of this monumental day. I'd mount his head on the wall if I could, but the sword will have to suffice. I wrap my bleeding hand and leg in bandages while I watch the last of my father's blood join the rest on the floor.

I think back to the day the Fighters captured a Defender from one of the smaller Defender camps. That was the day I got real experience. I was ordered to torture the man, and instead I killed him. I got backlash from my father for doing so, but I didn't care. I liked having the power of someone else's life in my hands. I liked taking that life away. I didn't feel remorse or regret, although I knew I probably should. I felt powerful, and that was a feeling I wanted to keep having. Once other Fighters heard of how cruel and evil I could be, I knew they would spread the word. I know the Defender's did too, after I left the burned man at their castle, with my name carved into his skin. There's no doubt in my mind that there are stories about my father and I all around the world. How monstrous we both are. How insane. I wouldn't deny them. As I stand over my father's dead body, I can't help but think of how far I've come. I would have never admitted this earlier, but I like being the cruel, evil villain my father always wanted me to be. When I tortured that Defender for the first time and took his life, I didn't think a villain was who I really was. But now, that's all I *want* to be. I want to end this war, the way my father never could. He was too *weak*. I killed him for my brother, but I won't stop until I end this war for Levi too. That is when I will finally have peace. I don't care what it costs to earn it. I don't care who I have to become. I've spent too many years of my life under someone else's control. It's time I started ruling in my own, ruthless way.

I take one last look at my father. I scream at the top of my lungs to the outside world, beckoning the Fighters to come to me. Seconds pass before they scramble into the throne room, practically falling over one another as they make their way inside. I cross to my father's throne and hold my head high as I take my place there. My fingernails dig into the hardwood, leaving small scratch marks in their wake. This throne seems as though it was made for me all along. I smile, knowing Levi would be proud. I finally took our father's life. I finally took the throne. All for him.

The Fighters gasp and cry out when they see my father's body and the huge pool of blood surrounding him. I laugh at the looks on their faces when they realize I did it. I look down at them, the throne lifting me above their insignificance. My father never trained them adequately enough. They look pathetic, but they're all I have. There is no time to train them further. The time to attack is now. The Defenders will fall this time because, unlike my father, I will go into this battle with my people. And I will *win*.

Chapter seventeen

EMBER

I open the training room doors, only to see the place empty. I slowly walk in, expecting to suddenly see a flood of people on one side training. But as I look around, I realize no one is inside. I hear footsteps behind me. I turn around fast, ready to attack.

"Woah, easy, easy," D'andre says, letting out a small smile.

I put my hands down. "Where is everyone? Did something happen?"

D'andre puts a hand on my shoulder, steadying me. "Nothing happened. I just canceled training today, that's all."

This must be the first time training has been canceled, ever.

"What? Why would you do that?"

"I think we all deserve a break. One day won't make a difference, Ember." His voice is calm. Reassuring. Like it always is. I don't think I've ever heard D'andre raise his voice, in all the years I've known him.

I let my breathing slow to a normal pace. "Why today?"

He shrugs. “Today just felt like a good day for it. There’s no particular reason if that’s what you’re asking.”

“Okay. I guess I should just go back to my room then.” I silently hope I don't run into my father on the way back. I don't want to speak to him again.

As I start to walk away, D'andre stops me.

“Walk with me instead.”

He turns to head in another direction, and I obediently follow. I wonder what he has in mind.

We walk in silence until we get outside. He sits on one of the rocks in front of the castle, and I sit beside him.

“Do you think the Fighters will attack soon?” I ask.

D'andre looks in the direction of the Fighter's castle, like he can see it from here. It would be a long walk to get there. Four or five days minimum at a fast pace.

“I don’t know. But we’ve all trained enough. You especially. One day off won’t change the fact that you’re ready.”

“But what about Austin? He’s not rea-”

“Nonsense. With him under your wing, he is ready for anything. If you feel the need to train with him today, you can always train outside of class.”

I let out a breath. I've trained everyday since the battle a year ago. I thought I had to after I lost everything that day. But D'andre is right. One day off won't hurt.

“Did you always want to be a trainer?” I ask. I’ve known D’andre for many years, and he feels like a second father to me after all his mentoring. But I've never had a real conversation with him outside of training talk. I've never asked him about his life. Now seems like a good time.

"Not always. When I was a boy, I just wanted peace, so I wanted to join The Council. But I decided against it after I saw that the Defenders lacked an adequate trainer. I devoted my young years to training to become the mentor the Defenders needed." He looks at me. "Now, training Defenders is all I know. Although the Fighters haven't attacked in a year, they may soon, and all I want is for the Defenders to be ready for it."

I nod in agreement. We have to be more prepared than we were last time.

"Do you think that the ruler of the Fighters just doesn't want to attack, and that's why we've had a year with nothing?"

"I have thought about that, and it is a possibility. However, I'm sure you've heard about Alcmene."

I nod again.

"Once she rules, I'm sure there will be an attack upon us. Let's just hope it isn't soon."

"Could she kill the current ruler?"

He looks me in the eyes. "It is forbidden to do so, but I'm certain she will. She wouldn't wait for his death to take the throne. It would be too long."

I haven't thought about it much, but it seems like something she would do from the little I know about her. I think of the Defender my father told me about. The one who was tortured by Alcmene's hands and dropped off here with her name carved into his head. I imagine his family finding him, grief shadowing their lives, just as it does mine.

"I have an idea," D'andre says, as he stands up on his feet, snapping me out of my thoughts.

He pulls out two knives from his holsters.

"Want to see if you can finally beat me?" He smiles.

I haven't challenged D'andre in a long time. I've been too preoccupied after the last attack, and now having Austin to train keeps me busy. Maybe I can actually win. I have improved greatly since the last time we sparred. I grin at him.

"You're on," I say as I grab a knife from his outstretched hand.

We step away from the rocks, into a clearer area before D'andre starts a countdown. The minute he gets to one, I charge.

My knife reaches for D'andre's stomach, and he easily deflects it. I block a high strike and counter with a jab towards his abdomen. He moves out of the way. He swipes his knife toward my shoulder, and I just miss it. D'andre and I used to spar together often, and I've seen him spar with other trainees, but his moves are still completely unpredictable. His strikes are hard to dodge, and recover from by the quick way he moves. But in order to best an opponent, you have to know them well. D'andre may be unpredictable, but I know him.

He gains on me, and soon he is close to taking me down. I focus more on dodging his attacks than striking back, playing on the defensive side. His knife swings toward my face, and I duck, the blade sweeping over my head, and I move forward. He steps back before my knife is able to make contact with his chest. I decide not to run away from his attacks anymore. I face him directly, and although I take a cut to my shoulder, I begin to gain some ground. I try not to focus on the blood slowly dripping down my shoulder to my arm as I attack.

"You've definitely improved since our last match," he tells me.

I lose my breath as our strikes and blocks get faster. We circle each other, jumping side to side and moving up and down to deflect and attack. Little by little, I gain more confidence. I dodge his strikes easier, and soon he is the one who almost gets cut.

After another minute, I know I almost have him. D'andre is in his forties, and although he is in great shape, he will never be as agile as I am now. He slowly begins to lose energy. At first glance, it would be hard for anyone to tell his moves are becoming less fluid. But I know him. This is a perfect opportunity for me to perform a takedown.

I use his waning momentum against him, and as he sends a strike toward my head, I duck and move closer to him. In one quick motion, I throw him to the ground. He falls, still holding onto his knife tightly. He lands lightly and looks up at me.

"Well done, Ember." He stands up, smiling gently. Then he sees the cut on my shoulder. "Let's get that patched up."

We head back to the empty training room, my head still spinning from my victory.

The solo training area has a cabinet full of first aid supplies. I apply ointment and cut a small piece of bandage to place on my shoulder wound.

We sit in silence for a minute, and my thoughts drift back to yesterday's events of the tortured Fighters and my father's part in it. I wasn't planning on telling anyone about what I saw, or what my father said, but D'andre can keep a secret.

"I found something yesterday. Underneath the council room." He can tell I'm hesitant about sharing the information with him.

"Whatever it is, you can trust me, Ember."

I tell him everything I saw and did that day. How I went into the council room and heard the yelling. How I discovered the secret underground room and the Fighters locked in cells, beaten and starved. How my father was a part of it all. How so many Defenders know, and still act like they're good people.

He listens intently without interrupting me once. He seems just as shocked as I was. He seems angry about it, too, but he keeps his thoughts mostly to himself. I let silence wash over us for a minute until a thought comes to my mind.

"How would The Council have Fighters to torture? I never see The Council or anyone go outside the perimeter for anything other than to hunt for food."

"They must be from the battle over a year ago." He says. Could the Fighters in the cells really have been tortured for a year? That seems insane. It's such a long time for someone to be locked away from the real world, only knowing darkness and pain.

"What should I do?" I ask, hoping his wisdom can help me in this crazy reality.

"Do what you think is right. I'm your mentor, Ember. I can't give you the answer. I don't know it. But I think you should talk to your father again. It's never smart to hold a grudge in a time of war."

He's right. He always is. But I don't want to face my father. I can't look him in the eyes after what he's done. I've been avoiding him completely for the last week.

"Can I ask you something? It's off-topic, but about you."

"Of course." I answer.

"It's really more of an observation," he says.

I let him continue before my curiosity sends me spiraling.

"I have known you long enough to know how you fight. You don't fight like a Defender." He pauses. It seems like he's waiting for a response.

But what is that supposed to mean? What do I fight like, if not a Defender?

"What do you mean?" I ask, hoping he doesn't say what I'm dreading he will.

"You fight like one of them."

He doesn't have to say their name for me to know what he means. I fight like a Fighter, and that is not a good thing.

"I know," I tell him, honestly. I haven't dared to tell anyone else this. I know I fight like one of them, now more than ever. I focus on attacking more than defending and fight like I'm training to kill. I've been close to seriously hurting Defenders I've sparred with. My father tells me I think like a Fighter, wanting to attack them so we can win. I've drawn pictures of their castle, and I am more fascinated by Alcmene and power than anything else in this small world.

"You want to fight. To end this war by attacking, instead of defending." He reads my mind. He doesn't look angry, like my father would have if had known everything going on in my mind. "I will tell you something I've never told anyone." He pauses, and the silence feels like it lasts for an eternity. He takes a slow breath before telling me, "I used to be a Fighter."

My jaw drops. There's no way that's true. He's been a trainer for the Defenders since before I was born, and he fights like one of us. How did he leave? How did he not get captured the minute he set foot in this castle? Did he know Alcmene? I don't have to ask these questions, because he automatically answers them.

He looks down. "I was born a Fighter but knew I didn't belong there. When I was old enough, about twelve, I ran away. I knew the direction of the Defender castle, so I packed my things, and with enough food for over a week, I traveled south. No one chased after me, knowing a kid wasn't worth sending out troops for. When I got here, The Council interrogated me for days to ensure I was really no longer with the Fighters. I gave up whatever information The Council wanted, and that's how they believed me enough to let me join the Defenders. They didn't capture me and torture me, like they are doing to Fighters now. But I was under surveillance for at least a year, and eventually, they let their guard down. I truly became one of them, and they recognized that. But The Council was still hesitant about me becoming a trainer. They didn't want me to teach trainees how to fight like the enemy, but I proved them wrong. I learned to fight like a Defender, and how to teach all of you. They finally accepted me completely. But when you came into training, I recognized your fighting style and even how you thought. You are exactly like who I used to be."

I try to process what D'andre just said. It doesn't seem real. I would have never guessed that he was a Fighter as a child. He's the opposite of them. He's caring, thoughtful, wise, and most of all, willing to protect us. He only wants to defend.

"Wow," is all I can get out.

He smiles. "I know it's a lot. But I wanted you to know. Besides The Council, you're the only one who does."

"Why? Why me?"

"There's something special about you, Ember. It just felt right to tell you."

I give him a small smile.

I ask him what I've been wondering. "If you lived with the Fighters, have you met Alcmene?"

He shakes his head.

"It may come as a surprise, but Alcmene is about your age, maybe only a year older. She wasn't alive when I was a Fighter."

That changes everything. Alcmene, a girl my age, is fighting for the throne? Isn't that way too young? I couldn't imagine holding the throne and so much power at my age.

"What about her father, the ruler? Did you know him?"

"I-" D'andre doesn't have time to finish what he's saying because an explosion sends us flying.

Chapter eighteen

EMBER

The ringing in my ears blocks everything out. After a minute of being completely disoriented, pain registers, and beneath the smoke and fire surrounding me, I see blood. My blood.

Smoke travels into my lungs, and I try coughing to rid it away, but it doesn't help. Am I dreaming? What's happening?

The worst pain comes from my leg. I look down to see part of my pant leg charred off, with a burn wound on the center of my thigh, the size of my hand. Blood trickles from my arms, where pieces of metal and glass from the explosion stabbed me. How did the Fighters make a bomb? They've never used them before. I didn't think it was possible with the limited resources this radiation-filled world has. I watch as the hole in the stone wall of the castle falls apart. This isn't good.

The searing, bubbling wound on my leg is killing me. It will leave a nasty scar. I rip the shards of glass and metal from my arms, holding back screams as more pain runs through me.

I see D'andre next to me, lying still. For a second I think the man I've known for years is dead, and my stomach drops. But then I see the slight rise and fall of his chest, signifying to me that he's alive but barely holding on. I crawl to him, wincing as I drag my leg along. The fire from the explosion spreads on everything in the training room that is wooden, cranking the heat up. We have to get out of here.

Fighters pour into the crumbling training room. I lock eyes with one who holds a throwing knife. In the explosion, my weapons were thrown across the room. I have nothing to defend myself, and I'm not so sure I'd be able to stand to try to fight.

Just as I think I'm as good as dead, the Fighter falls to the floor, an arrow sticking into his heart. My father stands beside me.

"Are you hurt?" I can't hear him, but I read his lips. He looks at my leg, now covered in angry welts, and the blood that runs down my arms.

"Cover us!" I yell as another Fighter runs into the room. My ears ring, and I reach up to find blood in my ear. I can just make out the sounds of screaming, and I try to push away the memories of my mother and sister dying the last time the Fighters attacked. I look at D'andre, and my skin goes cold.

A shard of metal from the training equipment is lodged into his stomach. His blood slowly drains out of him, creating a pool underneath us. My father stands guard at the hole in the wall, with an arrow ready to fly from his bow. He glances back at us with a worried look on his face. Blood covers his temple and hands.

The smoke starts to reach my lungs, and I choke as I reach D'andre. I keep the shard in his skin, afraid that if I pull it out, he will bleed nonstop. I apply pressure around the metal. Tears well up in my eyes. His blood runs over my hands, trailing down to the floor. It's not working. He can't die like this. He can't.

"Wake up." I cough, the smoke killing my voice. "Please." My eyes burn. His wound won't stop bleeding. *What the hell am I going to do?* My father kills a Fighter as he comes near, lodging an arrow in his neck. The Fighter staggers backwards, his hands reaching for his throat before he falls. He struggles for a few seconds before he stops moving. I'm not surprised that my father chooses to take Fighter's lives instead of capturing them. Nothing he does surprises me anymore.

D'andre opens his eyes. I feel a rush of hope.

"We have to get out of here." The ringing in my ears subsides a little, and I can just make out the sound of my own voice.

I see his eyes drift down to his wound, and he slowly shakes his head.

"Leave me. Even I know when I'm done for. Save yourself, kid," he chokes out before he lets his head rest back on the ground.

He starts to close his eyes again.

"Stop! I won't let you give up. Not that easily." The tears stream out of my eyes, and I almost forget about the pain from my own wounds or the men my father has killed. I only think about D'andre and his life, which is slowly leaving him.

"Save the others. Save yourself." Hot, sticky blood pools from his wound, leaving my hands colored a deep red. I'm afraid his blood will leave a stain on my hands that will last forever.

For the first time in my life, I have no idea what to do. How to save him. He's my mentor. He taught me everything I know. *What am I going to do?*

"D'andre, please." I plead with him to keep fighting, but I know we're running out of time. The Fighters are beginning to gain on us, and my father can't hold them off forever. The smoke is clogging my lungs. The fire will reach us soon.

"If you ever attack the Fighters, like I know you want to-" His coughing interrupts him, and specs of blood spurt out with each one. But he continues, determined to get his words out. "There are passages in the walls of the castle. The entrance to them is underground. There is a map in my room." I don't have time to process what he is saying before he grabs my hand. "Promise me." He tries to hold his head up to look at me. The blood starts to pour out faster. "That you won't fall onto their side. That you will never become one of them. If you do, they win."

I instantly know what he means. He thinks I'll turn into a Fighter. I fight like them, think like them. I get why he thinks I can *become* one of them.

"I-I promise." The crying on top of my coughing makes my words almost impossible to hear, but I know he understood them. He nods at me before his eyes close, and his head falls back.

"No," I sob, applying more pressure to his wound. It's no use. He's gone.

As I cry, the heat draws nearer. The fire. I have to get out of here.

"Goodbye. Thank you." My tears cloud my vision, and I limp out of the room after quickly grabbing my weapons, with pain running up my leg. My father follows close behind, and the ceiling caves in right as we pass through the doorway. D'andre's body is now covered in crumbled stone. I can't get the image out of my head. I wipe the tears from my eyes and the blood from my shaking hands. D'andre's final words run through my mind. The look in his dying eyes. My promise to him.

"Go somewhere safe. Your room, if it's still intact. Stay there, like last time. I have to go fight." My father hugs me tightly and places a kiss on my forehead before running off into battle.

Fire and explosions have spread throughout the castle, leaving the place in shambles. I can't tell where the rubble ends and the hallway leading to my room begins. I stumble in a random direction and see Defenders running and screaming. Trainees draw their swords, and that's when it hits me. Austin isn't here.

I run, joining the chaos around me. My tears stop falling and anger consumes me. I will take revenge for D'andre's death, if it's the last thing I do.

I grimace as the pain in my leg throbs. I need to find Austin. I rush through the castle as fast as I can. On the way to my room, I see the library completely up in flames. Everything I've ever known is getting destroyed in front of me.

My room is still intact, and I limp inside. I grab my weapons case and throw it onto the bed. A few of my throwing knives were lost in the explosion, and my rope was burned. I resupply myself, finally taking my sword out from the underside of my dresser. I try my best to hold it steady. My hands are stained with D'andre's blood. I empty my stomach in the corner of the room.

I hold my sword beside me. I won't hide. I have to fight. For my sister, for my mother, for D'andre. If I hide, I will never find Austin, so I have no choice regardless of my father's wish.

Another explosion wracks the castle, and I run outside as parts of it fall. The burning from the smoke in my lungs lessens as I step outside. I instantly smell blood. I gasp as I look around, seeing the world drenched in red. Bodies of Defenders I used to know surround the castle. I stop myself from throwing up again.

My focus lands on a Fighter who is throwing knives. I see the Defenders who are still breathing dash to get inside, avoiding his attacks. I take a deep breath before I run towards the Fighter.

I catch the Fighter off guard and get up to him close-range. My knife slices against his arm, leaving a small trail of blood. He winces and tries to attack. I deflect him, striking back. The Fighter jabs his silver-bladed knife at my shoulder, leaving me with a small stab wound. I grimace, but the pain is nothing compared to fighting through the pain in my leg. He kicks at my leg, noticing my obvious wound. I yell out in pain as I fall to the ground. As I see the Fighter's knife come towards my head, I roll over and sweep his legs out from under him. He falls, giving me time to swiftly recover. I stand up and quickly grab my rope. I tie him up before I run to take cover behind a rock near the entrance of the castle. I look around for Austin, but instead I see *her*. I've never seen her in person, but my father described her well. I can see the hatred in her eyes from here, and how all the Fighters seem to take her lead.

Alcmene.

She can only be here for one reason. The ruler of the Fighters fell, and she took the throne. My father was right. She must have planned the attack on us the minute she took power.

Blood covers Alcmene's hands and face. Defenders blood. She has long black hair that travels past her shoulders, down to her waist. She has no body armor, so she must be confident in her abilities. She is completely stained with blood. It runs down her hands, neck, and the sides of her mouth, giving the impression that she's ripped away flesh with her teeth. She stands over the body of a dead man. A sword lays by his hand. He must have fought back and failed.

Fear overtakes me. What if she kills me? The thought of death has never been so imminent before. With Alcmene fighting, the odds are all against me and my people. I see Alcmene throw a knife, which sticks in the back of a boy I once knew. I scream out in terror but cover my mouth to block the sound. The boy's name was Thomas. He was the boy I trained with on my first day. Gone.

Anger starts to cloud my mind, and without thinking, I'm running full speed towards Alcmene. But before I reach her, I feel a heaviness surrounding me, and an agonizing pain wells up in my eyes. My vision blurs, *darkens*. I lose focus, and I see her eyes lock with mine. I'm slammed to the ground less than a second later. Whatever feeling I was having is over, and I struggle to breathe from the impact with the hard ground. My mother's dagger falls from my hands. I try to fight but stop when I see who holds me down.

"Dad? What are you doing?" I push him away from me, anger easily showing in my voice.

It's hard to hear my father over the sounds of the screaming, and my ears still ring, although the sound isn't as deafening now.

"Are you trying to get yourself killed? You can't win against her. No one can." I look back at Alcmene, her attention now on two other Defenders. She easily slices their throats, *smiling* and *laughing* as she kills the people I once knew. She's even crueler than I thought. Crazy, even. The tears begin to pour out of my eyes again. My father grabs my dagger before practically dragging me behind a large piece of rubble. It shields us from the attacks, for now. I know we won't be protected for long once Alcmene and the other Fighters start moving towards the castle.

"What should we do? She's killing our people, Dad." My throat burns as I speak. I imagine the Defenders Alcmene just killed, the pain they felt as she cut their throats. The younger ones, who left this world much too soon. All with a smirk on her face.

"Go back inside. I need to get more arrows. Try not to let them in." My father slings his bow over his shoulder. I grab my dagger from him before he runs inside. I follow behind him. He runs in the direction of his room, but crumbled stone blocks his path. The castle is falling apart in front of our eyes. My home, slowly withering away.

"Shit," he mutters. My father pulls a knife out of his holster, giving up on his arrows, before looking at me. "Stay inside. I can't lose you."

He gives me a quick hug before he darts back outside.

I listen to my father, blocking doors and windows to keep Fighters out. I search everywhere for Austin without luck. I silently pray that he is still alive.

I run into D'andre's room, which is still intact. I need to find the map he was talking about. If I find it, it could be the key to planning my own attack on the Fighters if we make it through this battle. I rummage through his drawers as the screaming continues, and I try to keep his face out of my mind. His blood. I finally find the map hidden in a book inside one of his drawers. The drawing is old and was surely made with a shaky hand. Did he draw it before he left the castle as a kid? I wish I could ask him. I secure the map to my belt and let out a cry of relief when I see a twelve-year-old boy with curly brown hair run outside. Austin.

"No," I whisper to myself as I see him run to the battle. I lost D'andre. I won't lose him too.

"Austin!" I yell, trying to get his attention. He will never be able to hear me over all the noise.

I race after him, my leg burning. Right before I catch up with him, I feel a knife soar past my head, just missing me by less than an inch.

"Go back inside!" I yell to Austin. He looks at me, knife in hand, terrified, but he obeys. That's when I see who threw the knife. I prepare to attack, even though I have no chance of winning.

"Don't move," Alcmene says to me as she holds up another knife, ready to throw. She missed on purpose. Why didn't she kill me? I listen to her, and I don't move a muscle. Her voice is deep and rough. From this close up, I can tell that none of the blood covering her body is her own. She doesn't have a scratch on her.

As I look around, I see bodies scattered around, even more than there were minutes ago, turning the land dark and formidable.

"Why don't you just kill me now?" I ask her as she steps closer. Her dark brown eyes glare into mine, and I become paralyzed against the castle wall. A scar trails down her bloody face, starting right below her eye and ending at her jaw. It's old. She must have gotten it a long time ago. She looks older than eighteen. Anyone can see that she looks like a ruler. A terrifying one.

I see Fighters attacking the Defenders as I look past her. More dead bodies are soon to come, more blood to be spilled.

"That you will soon find out," she laughs.

What the hell is that supposed to mean? I force myself to look away from Alcmene's strong glare, and I notice a figure behind her when I do. She notices my eyes shift to the left, and barely moving from her position, she throws the Defender to the ground. Only then do I realize it's my father.

"No!" I move towards him, and Alcmene throws another knife at my head. It nicks my ear, and I freeze. She has at least half a dozen more throwing knives strapped to her side. She takes one from her holster and stabs it into my father's leg. He cries out. I scream, and try to move to help him. But when I see her raise another knife towards me, I stay in place. I wince as he yells in pain, clutching his bleeding leg. I so desperately want to run to him. Alcmene holds a knife to my father's throat, and a fear I've never felt before runs through me. I imagine him dead, buried beside everyone else in my family. I wouldn't be able to live with it.

"Stop! I don't care what you do to me; just don't kill him!" Although my father has betrayed me and what the Defenders stand for, he's my father. I would fall apart if he died, too. I'd have no one left.

She turns to face me, still holding a knife to my father, who breathes heavily but remains still.

I see Alcmene smirk slightly. "Give me your rope." Her brown eyes stare into mine, and her pale, blood-stained hands touch my shaky ones as I give her the rope. She ties my father's hands and feet together as the fighting continues around us.

"What do you want from him?" My father is the only Defender she's tied up, instead of killed. It doesn't make any sense.

She rips the knife out of his leg, letting more blood spill out. My father groans, trying to move his hands to put pressure on the wound, but he can't reach it against the tight rope.

"Why do you think I would tell you?" She laughs, flipping the bloody knife from my father's leg in her hand, letting blood spray off it.

Before I have any time to react, Alcmene pins me to the ground and leaves me tied up beside my father.

Multiple Defenders charge at Alcmene, and she takes her eyes off my father and me to attack them. Over five Defenders are attacking, but she takes them down like it's nothing, one by one. As she's distracted, I try to grab my dagger from my holster. My hands burn against the rope behind my back as I struggle to reach my knife. Once I have a grip on it, I slowly take it out, and begin to saw at the rope. I keep my eyes on Alcmene to make sure she doesn't turn around. After taking down the Defenders who charged at her, she travels a little farther to kill more. I try not to look at the bodies that continue to fall.

As a minute passes, I feel the rope fall apart in my hands. I'm about to break free when my father looks at me.

"Leave me," he mouths as Alcmene is about to return. I don't want to. What would she do to him? But I know I have no choice. I won't have time to cut him free too before Alcmene turns around. I mouth the words, "I'm sorry," to my father as I run.

I head through one of the entrances to the castle that isn't blocked by rubble. I choke on smoke as I rush inside, not daring to look back. I see Fighters and Defenders engaged in gruesome combat. My father would want me to hide, stay safe. But D'andre is dead, and I can't hide while the people who killed him attack everyone else I know.

I see a Fighter, and without thinking, I strike. He falls to the ground, and blood starts flowing out of the stab wound I made in his stomach. He tries to fight back, but the blood pouring out of his wound stops him. He clutches it, screaming in agony. I can barely hear it because my ears are starting to ring again. My rage does nothing but intensify. These people killed D'andre. They captured my father. They killed my mother and sister. Why shouldn't I kill one of them?

I feel the same heaviness that surrounded me earlier when I charged at Alcmene. My eyes start to sting, and my vision darkens, zoning in on the helpless Fighter before me. I hold my dagger up, ready to deliver a strike that will end his life, and that's when I feel burning in my chest. It's an excruciating pain that courses through me, starting in my chest and running up to my eyes. I drop my dagger when my hands begin to feel like they're on fire. I look down to see black veins trailing up my wrists and fingertips. I stare, my eyes wide with fear. I blink, hoping whatever this is will go away if I will it to. Like it's only a reaction to the sudden shock of this battle. But the pain and black veins don't go away. In fact, it gets worse. Black smoke comes out of my hands, darker than any night sky. That's when I really believe I'm losing my mind. But the Fighter beside me sees it too, and his jaw drops. He struggles to crawl away as he holds his bleeding wound.

Everything hurts so badly that I want to let myself pass out. But the Fighter's screaming and crawling grabs my attention. Instead of succumbing to this agony, I have the overwhelming urge to end his life. It's against who I am. I thought I was better after I killed a Fighter a year ago. I told myself I wouldn't do it again unless it was necessary. This isn't one of those circumstances. The Fighter pleads and cries as he bleeds. I raise my hands toward him anyway. The smoke hovers just above the veins that traveled to my palms. I can hardly see through the searing pain in my teary eyes. But just as I'm about to strike, someone grabs my shoulder. I whip around, preparing to attack, but I drop my hands when I see Austin standing before me. As quickly as the burning and smoke came, it's gone. If Austin saw whatever horrifying thing was happening to me, he doesn't show it. It all happened so fast I can hardly tell what went on myself.

Austin is covered in blood, which I immediately realize isn't his. He holds a knife in one hand and a rope in the other.

"You were going to kill him," Austin's voice trembles. "We're not like that, remember?" His voice is hoarse and his eyes red from tears. Suddenly he's not the young warrior who threw himself into battle. He's the little kid forced to fight in a war he shouldn't have been a part of. All I feel is guilt. Guilt for the sobbing Fighter lying on the ground in a pool of blood, and guilt for Austin seeing me like this. I was going to kill a Fighter when he had no chance of fighting back. I was going to show him no mercy. What kind of person does that make me? It makes me no better than *one of them.*

"Go," I say to the Fighter, my voice barely above a whisper. He looks at me like I'm crazy. Fear still lingers in his eyes before he crawls away. I know there's no use capturing him. He is weak and his wounds may kill him anyway. I pick up my dagger and feel relief when I don't see it covered in darkness anymore. I find more rope upon the wreckage, and Austin and I move towards the front of the castle. I won't kill the Fighters unless I have to.

I hold my dagger steadily in my hands, wiping my thoughts away. The castle starts to fall further apart. Austin and I capture the Fighters who trail in, before the ceiling above us caves in. I hold back tears over the Defender's who didn't make it out in time.

As the smoke clears somewhat and we're outside among the dead bodies, there is nowhere for Austin to hide. I want him to be safe, but his only option is to fight. I won't let him attack a Fighter alone.

Alcmene and my father are nowhere in sight. She must have taken him or killed him. I want to break down, travel to my sister's spot in the woods and cry and scream until I'm numb. But I can't fall apart now.

As I fight, my hearing gets slightly better, but that only makes things louder. The screaming, the chaos. The smell of blood clogs my throat. Bodies pile up, a good amount of Fighters in the mix. We are holding our ground well. I capture multiple Fighters with Austin.

With Alcmene nowhere to be seen and the large number of casualties increasing, the Fighters begin to retreat. I fight off whoever I can before they are gone completely. I turn around to face the castle, now reduced to a pile of stone from the explosions. Austin isn't beside me anymore, lost in the running Defenders as they race to heal their loved ones.

My home is gone. Everything I've ever known, is now nothing. The paintings my mother made that lined the walls, gone. Many Defenders I once knew, dead. My father, taken or killed by Alcmene. And I couldn't stop any of it. Just like I couldn't stop my mother and Meadow from being taken from me. I promised myself that I wouldn't let history repeat, but here I am, without a family or a home.

With the loss of the adrenaline I had in the battle, the pain from my wounds becomes unbearable. Bodies line the burned grass. We lost hundreds. I give in to the pain, wanting to wake up from this horrible reality. My last thought before I collapse is Austin, who is nowhere to be seen.

Chapter nineteen
ALCMENE

It's a five-day walk back to my castle. I travel with the remaining Fighters. They all keep their distance from me as I shout at them throughout the trip. They were useless out there. If I had gone alone it would have been just as effective. So many pointless deaths. The Fighters drag Ember's father along. It didn't take long to get her name out of him. I hate myself for only capturing her father and not them both. I also had Ember in ropes, but I didn't want to just stand by and guard her. My anger over Leviathan and my father urged me to kill more and more Defenders. In a way, I had to. So I lost her.

Once we arrive back, I sit on my throne for at least an hour, contemplating what to do next. Anger boils inside me. The Fighters are even more pathetic than I thought. Now the Defenders know we aren't unbeatable. At least we destroyed their castle, leaving them with no shelter. It's the perfect time to find them and strike again. But first, I have to train the incompetent Fighters better than my father did, and it will be a while before we have the strength to attack once more. In the meantime, I have to interrogate a prisoner.

I get off my throne and grab various weapons when I hear a knock at my door.

"Enter," I command, anger evident in my tone.

I don't know who I was expecting, maybe an injured Fighter or someone with a list of problems I don't want to fix, but not her.

"Amara. What do you want?" I twirl my dagger in my hands.

"Is that any way to greet a friend?"

Friends. Is that what we are now? She came back after three years, helped me kill my father, and didn't look at me like a monster when I took the throne. But three years is a long time. On the way to the Defender's Castle, she asked if she could become my second. It only reinforced the fact that I know she's trying to befriend me for power. I want Amara to stay because she wants to be my friend again. Or more than that. Not for the glory that she thinks comes with being the second to the throne. I told her I would have to think about her proposition. We haven't talked about it since. She seemed to avoid me on the way back to the castle.

"What are we going to do?" she asks when I don't respond.

"We?" I laugh. "It was all me in that battle. I will have to train the Fighters until they can match up to the minuscule training the Defenders have had, and then we will strike again."

She nods. "Okay. How long do you think that will take?"

I shake my head. "Why are you really here, Amara?" There is no way she came in here to ask me these pointless questions.

"I-" She pauses, glancing at me with a look of concern in her eyes. "I just wanted to know how you were doing, is all. You ordered the attack so fast after your father's death. And you didn't talk to me after you killed so many Defenders. I was wondering if you're okay."

I hold back a laugh. "Okay is far from it. Go back to whatever you were doing and leave me alone. I don't need your stupid questions pestering me any further." I keep my voice steady, but it's obvious I'm angry. Why won't she tell me the truth? That she's trying to manipulate me for power? It would hurt less if she only admitted it. I hate how she's acting like she cares when I know damn well she doesn't.

Amara looks down and nods. She's not mad at me, only disappointed in how I've been treating her. Somehow, disappointment feels worse. "I'll leave you to it." She turns, her curly red hair swaying a little as she walks out.

I don't need any more distractions. I have a prisoner to interrogate.

I stock up on throwing knives before heading down to the cellar. When I make my way down the stairs, I see Ember's father standing up against the bars. It's unusual. Almost all of the prisoners I've dealt with have been slouched in the corner, staying as far away from me as possible.

"Liam, it's a pleasure to finally meet you properly," I say as I run a knife along the bars. He doesn't seem afraid. Not at all. Something tells me Ember wouldn't be either.

"Alcmene. I've heard about you."

I laugh a little and turn to face him. I could have tortured him and heard this little spiel on the way home from his castle, but I had too many things to deal with. I let the other Fighters have their fun with him.

"Heard about me?" I smile. "And what have you heard?"

He looks me in the eyes. I so badly want to rip them out. If only Ember were here to watch.

"That you're pure evil. I guess I'll get to see if you live up to that." His confidence doesn't waiver as I glare at him. It's surprising. I've never met a Defender even half as unafraid. Usually, they would be begging for their lives by now, but there is not an ounce of fear in his eyes. Why? I'm sure he's seen or heard about the boy I left behind, burned and scarred at his castle a year ago. I'm sure he's heard the stories following that. He knows I can end his life in a second.

Everyone has fear, a weakness to exploit. For Ember's father, it may not be his own death, but Ember's, perhaps.

"Your daughter. Who is she?" His smile drops so slightly that I hardly notice it. Looks like I've found it. That was quick.

He stays quiet but doesn't back away from the bars.

"I'll only ask you one more time. Who is she?" When I saw Ember, I saw something I never thought I'd see again. Before her father threw her to the ground on the battlefield, I saw her eyes, solid black and filled with darkness. Later, after she escaped, I saw smoke coming out of her hands, and she almost killed a Fighter. I couldn't capture her before the ceiling caved in, and my Fighters began to retreat. But I knew then that she was special. Not like Levi exactly, but to some degree. And maybe her father can give me some answers, since I don't have her. He's the next best thing.

He says nothing. That will not do.

I take out my dagger, and in one quick movement, I stab it into one of his fingers that holds the bars between us. I rip my dagger out, letting a small amount of blood spurt from the wound. He jerks away and holds his bleeding finger.

"Trust me, I'll do far worse than puncture a part of your hand if you are reluctant to tell me what I want to know." He's farther away from me now. He presses his hand to his shirt, leaving a dark spot on the blue fabric, but he doesn't show any pain.

"What do you want from my daughter?" he asks, holding my gaze.

"Why do you think I captured the two of you? There's something *different* about her. I needed both of you to get the most information I could," I tell the Defender as he rips a piece of his shirt off, tying it around his hand. "But I had to settle for one. And now you'll tell me what I want to know, or you won't live to see her again."

He clenches his jaw. "I don't know what you're talking about. How is she different from anyone else?"

I smile. "So you don't know? Or are you just lying?" I step closer to the bars. "Every time you lie, I will cut a finger off. So, I think it would be in your best interest to tell me what you know about Ember. You can't lie your way out of this. I saw it with my own eyes."

He returns to the bars, and gets as close to me as he can. "Like I said, I don't know what you're talking about. Whatever you think you saw, you're wrong. There is no difference between her and any other Defender."

Getting close to me was a bad idea. I stab his hand clean through. When I rip my dagger out, a stream of blood comes with it. I spin the dagger between my hands, and blood speckles the Defender's face. Surprisingly, he doesn't scream. He just grunts and takes a breath as he rips more of his shirt to wrap around his hand. Maybe he's accepted the fact that screaming in pain will get him nowhere. It's unfortunate. I enjoyed hearing previous Defenders scream madly as I tore body parts off.

"I'm not lying," he tells me.

"I know." I laugh. I can tell when someone is lying. It's the easiest thing to see. And unfortunately, I know he's telling the truth. I lean against the wall away from the cell, away from him. I want some distance between us for my next puncture wound.

"You don't know about Ember's gift. What a shame. I'm *shocked* she didn't tell you," I say mockingly.

He stays away from the bars but looks at me with genuine confusion. "Gift?" he asks.

Does he really expect me to tell him?

I take my throwing knife out from my leg holster and fling it through the bars, into his shoulder. He stumbles but holds his ground. I already know what's coming next. The minute he rips the knife from his flesh, he throws it back at me. With perfect timing and a lot of training, I've mastered throwing knives in every aspect. So, when the knife flies in my direction, I wait until the handle is flipped just right, and I catch it without leaving a scratch. His eyes widen slightly. He wasn't expecting that. He still doesn't yell, but his breaths become shorter, and he winces as he holds his hand over the stab wound in his shoulder, applying pressure. Blood runs over the stone floor, adding fresh stains to the old ones.

"You can't tell me what I want to know, but maybe you can still be of use." I smirk, and for the first time, I see a hint of fear in his drained eyes.

Chapter twenty

EMBER

The first thing I think of when I wake up is the people we lost, followed by pain. I can't even cry, I'm all out of tears. My father may be dead. Or maybe he's being tortured by Alcmene. I hope he's dead. Because if he is being tortured, he will wish he was dead. Who knows what kind of twisted, cruel torturing methods Alcmene may be using on him right now? But I know that no matter how much pain he's in, he won't give anything up. That means she will have to kill him. My father will be of no use to her. At least he won't be in pain if she kills him.

I close my eyes and wish. I haven't made a real wish since I was a little kid, wishing to be the best in combat out of the Defenders. How naive I was then, never thinking about using the combat I was being taught. Back then, I did it for fun. But now, it's the only thing keeping me alive. This time, I wish to the stars that my father, as much as it hurts to say it, is dead.

Having him gone is a feeling different from those I felt when other people I love died. Maybe it's because some part of me believes he could return. Like this is all a dream I am about to wake up from. He was everything to me. He helped me through hell when my mother and sister died. He found light in every bad situation. And our last conversation didn't end well. I know I should be crying. I know I should be doing something, but I'm unable to move. I feel paralyzed. So many people died in one day. My home got burned to the ground in one day. One day changed my entire life, in the worst way imaginable.

"You're awake," I hear a voice say. I feel a bandage lift off my leg, where my burn is. I don't open my eyes, unable to face reality.

I feel pressure on my leg, where a new bandage is placed. I barely feel the pain anymore. The only thing I feel is anger, and the need for revenge. I was stupid, being angry at all the Fighters, when I only needed to be angry at one. Alcmene. She is the one who leads them. Without her, they may have never attacked us again. Alcmene killed hundreds of Defenders. It even seemed like she enjoyed taking the lives of people I once knew. Why does Alcmene want power so badly? Is that all she wants? But why does anyone want power at the cost of getting it?

"Ember." When I hear this voice I instantly open my eyes, repressing my never-ending questions. It's Austin. His face is bruised, indicating that he was punched at least once, and he has a bandage on his hand.

I look around and notice I'm in a tent full of medical supplies.

"The Defenders left alive were able to salvage some tents from the evacuation room. As well as food and medical supplies." I forgot that room even existed. A dusty storage area full of everything we would need if we had to evacuate because of the Fighters. I thought we would never need it.

"You were out for three days, on and off. I'm guessing you don't remember waking up screaming a few times as we dragged you here and set up camp." I don't. The last thing I remember is falling at the battle as the smoke almost choked me to death.

I sit up, and Austin stands next to me.

"I'm sorry about your dad."

I don't say anything because there really is nothing to say. No one will go after him. He will be left in the hands of the Fighters. In the hands of Alcmene.

I look to my left to see my belt on the floor. It holds my holsters and, most importantly, my mother's dagger. But I can't see it completely from where I'm sitting.

"Is my dagger in there?" I ask Austin. Out of every item in the castle, that is the one thing that matters to me most.

"It is, don't worry. I already checked."

We sit in silence for a minute. I silently pray that he will say something to end it. I can't be left with nothing but my thoughts right now. Not when they're so haunting.

"I've been thinking a lot about how you almost killed one of the Fighters when they weren't trying to fight back. At that moment, you really seemed like one of them," he tells me.

I look down. He's the second person who's told me that. I was just angry. I wouldn't have actually killed that guy. Right?

"I know you want us to plan our own attacks against the Fighters, and I used to think that was possible. But we lost a lot of people. We won't win if we attack now. I know you want to get your father back if he's not already-" he pauses, but I know what he was about to say. If he's not already *dead*.

"But we can't attack them to get him back, Ember. There's no way," he whispers, not wanting to admit the truth. He's right. If my father is being tortured at the Fighter's castle, there is no way we can get him back without getting killed on the rescue mission. He is on his own. *Unless*...no. That's too risky.

"We're having a memorial kind of thing in a few minutes for everyone we lost. We picked flowers and lit lanterns. People are planning to gather and talk about the people who passed." I really don't want to get up and face everyone. I don't want to see the grief-ridden looks on everyone's faces. I don't want to step foot outside of this tent. But I know Austin wants me to go.

"I'll go, but I'm not talking about anyone. I can't."

Austin sadly nods.

I slowly stand up, ignoring the searing pain running through my leg. Before I exit the tent, I put on my belt, feeling the comforting weight of my dagger at my side.

I walk out of the tent, expecting a nice wave of sun to hit me. Instead, gloomy clouds hang overhead, leaving us all in a sad dimness. Looking around, I see at least a hundred Defenders drenched in sorrow, as I was expecting. I see their tents, and the small amount of supplies we have. Going from a gorgeous castle to small, old tents is a strange feeling. I pass by people who sob quietly or hug one another with red eyes.

It's crazy thinking about how it was a normal day not too long ago. Sure, the factor of a possible Fighter attack always looms in the back of my mind, but I guess I never thought it would actually happen so suddenly as it did.

"How far away are we from the castle?" A part of me wants to see it. Although it's all burned to nothing, I think just being there will help me grieve.

"About a two-day walk. But we were going slow. I know what you're thinking, and no. You can't go see the castle. It's too dangerous. The Fighters may be waiting for us to return," Austin tells me.

He's right. We have to be more cautious now than ever. Venturing outside this camp will only lead to death.

Austin leads me to an area away from all the tents. Among the dampness in the air, and the horrible feeling surrounding our camp, this spot is pretty nice. It has flowers scattered across the land, and people are gathered around. Lanterns light up the despair on every Defender's face. One man stands in front of everyone.

"We all know why we're here today. To commemorate the people we lost. It was a horrible tragedy, but next time, we will be prepared. I hope some of you may speak on the fallen's behalf," the man says before he takes a step aside, offering the chance for others to speak.

For a second, no one moves. It's ominously silent and still until a woman walks to the center. Her eyes are red and puffy, her hair is a shriveled mess, and her clothes are torn and dirty from the travel here. She looks to be in her forties. It is obvious she lost someone.

She takes a moment to speak. Everyone watches her politely. "Three days ago I lost the one person left in my life. The one person who didn't die from the Fighter attack last year, or from an illness, or anything else. The one person who stood by my side through it all. I watched him die as I was held back by one of the Fighters. I lost my son." She doesn't cry. All her tears must have already been spilled. "And more than anything, I want the Fighters to pay. They didn't seem human when they held me back as they took the last breath out of my boy. They didn't seem human as they burned down our homes and killed our families. Then why should we treat them as such? Why don't we fight back?"

With that, she walks away to the tents. I hear a few Defender's murmur their agreement, but most stay silent. So I'm not the only one that wants to fight. Not the only one who's even thought of such a thing.

The man who spoke earlier clears his throat after a long silence. "Would anyone else like to speak?"

A couple more people volunteer. A man who lost his wife. A woman who lost her granddaughter. I manage to hold back my tears until a boy speaks about the father he lost. The boy is young, only around ten. He shouldn't have to go through this. None of us should.

Austin looks up at me. I'm glad he didn't lose his parents in the battle.

"Will you speak?"

I shake my head. "I told you, I won't. I can't." Even the thought of having to speak about D'andre makes my heart hurt. It makes me think of the moment before he died. Knowing I could have helped. Knowing maybe, just maybe, I could have done something to save his life. But it never came to me amidst the chaos.

The man who seems to be the head of this whole event walks up to me. "You knew the trainer, D'andre, didn't you?"

The word 'knew' stings. I only knew him now. He's not someone I know. He's gone, along with the rest of my family.

"Yes," is the only word I can get out. "Will you say a few words, if you don't mind?"

I can't. There's no way I can stand in front of these people and talk about him without breaking down.

"Yes, she will," Austin tells him.

I look at Austin, unable to say a word. But I know he sees the anger in my eyes, concealing my overwhelming pain.

"Don't worry, I'll be right with you," Austin says.

The steps up to the front of the gathering feel like the longest steps I've ever taken. My feet feel heavy, and with each step, it takes more effort to continue. Austin sees my hesitation.

"You've got this. Just imagine you're talking to me." Easy for him to say.

As Austin and I stand in front of everyone, he elbows me lightly.

"Say something," he mutters.

My brain hurts. I can't think of a single word. But I do think of D'andre, and all he's done for me. He was like a second father to me. He was a Fighter and was the only person who knew what it was like to think like I do. He was the wisest man I ever knew. And now he's gone. All that's left are memories. And memories aren't good enough. Eventually, we forget the good things that have happened, only remembering the bad. Soon I'll forget the smile on his face when I beat him in combat and only remember his grimace as he bled to death. These thoughts are how I form my first words.

"D'andre was my trainer, but that's not all he was to me. He practically raised me. He taught me so much. He helped me become who I am today. He was like a second father to me. One that loved me and cared for me. I just hope that the image of his death will leave my mind one day. I want to remember who he was, and not how he died." The last words are hard to say.

"He knew more about me than I knew myself. I loved him, and as long as I live, I will hope to avenge his death." Without turning around, or looking back, I head straight back to my tent, practically running to get there. Hot tears stream down my face as the wind blows them away. I told Austin I didn't want to talk.

I collapse onto my sleeping bag. I know it will be a while before I have the strength to get up again. In minutes, Austin is by my side. He wipes a tear from his eye. He knew D'andre, too. I've seemed to forget that over my own pain.

"You'll get through this. We all will," he mutters. I don't respond. I don't think words would come out even if I tried to. I just lie here, my head on my pillow, trying to brush the thoughts of D'andre out of my mind. But they don't go away. Neither do the thoughts of my father. Alcmene didn't kill him for a reason. He may still be alive now. And if he is, I need to save him. He and Austin are the only people I have left.

Chapter twenty-one

EMBER

I wake up to the sound of birds chirping. Austin is gone, although I don't remember him leaving. I must have been so sad and tired that I just collapsed into sleep. I know I have to get up, although moving seems unbearable. I have to train. If I have any chance at rescuing my father somehow, I need to sharpen my skills.

I grab a few throwing knives from my tent before I head outside. The sun is still rising when I walk out into the open air. Almost all of the Defenders are in their tents, but a few sit by the fire pit to watch the sunrise. One of the Defenders hears me approach and turns to look at me. It's someone I've seen around before, but I can't quite remember his name.

"Ember," he says. He gets up and grabs an empty water barrel near the fire. "Would you mind filling this for us?" he asks, handing me the barrel. A walk could definitely do me some good.

"Sure." I take the barrel down the short walk to the pond. I haven't been to the pond in years, but I remember my father taking me as a kid. We would swim in the water and he would teach me to skip rocks along the surface. But once my father became more wrapped up in council meetings or apparently torturing Fighters, we didn't take trips down to the pond anymore, and he didn't want me to go alone. So I never did. I stayed inside the castle walls most of my life, or at least along the outside edges. A trip further was a rare occasion. But now, as I look at the pond in front of me, I don't feel happy to be outside the castle. Maybe under any other circumstance, I would be. But not like this.

The water is crystal blue, and the sun lights up the side closest to me. Flowers bloom along the sides of the pond, and beautiful white water lilies spot the surface. After being stuck in the gloomy campsite, it's a bright change of scenery. I sit down next to the water, leaving the barrel next to me. I look out at the sky. The sun has fully risen, but the streaks of pink and orange stay. I think of the Fighters, many miles away. Alcmene could be staring at the same colors in the sky right now, but in a whole different place. On the opposite side of the war. It's weird to think of it.

I hear footsteps behind me. I can already tell who it is by the sound. I keep my eyes on the shimmering water as Austin sits down.

"I heard you went to fill up the barrel an hour ago. Are you alright?" I guess I've been staring at the water for longer than I realized.

"I'm fine."

"Right," Austin adds almost sarcastically.

"Ever been swimming here?" he asks.

"Yeah. When I was little. Feels like forever ago now. So much has changed." Everything has changed in the worst way imaginable.

Austin nods sympathetically. "My parents brought me once. But I was too young to remember." It's hard to believe that Austin is twelve and fighting in this war like it's his destiny. He deserves to be a kid, not a soldier. But I never got that chance either.

I look back in the direction of the castle. “We need to do something. We can’t just sit around and wait for Alcmene to attack us again,” I say.

Austin takes a breath. “You’re right. But how will you convince everyone that we have to plan our own attack? It goes against everything we all stand for.”

“How about this?” I look at Austin. “We plan out an entire attack, one that will not only allow us to win the war but will also allow us to free my father.”

Austin looks out at the water, thinking. “We’d have to be really convincing.”

I nod. My father has told me that The Council hardly ever accepts any ideas brought to them. It will be almost impossible to convince them, but I have to try. Now that I know some of the Defenders may want the same thing, it might not be such a crazy thought.

Austin and I walk back to our camp. The path has woods on both sides. I haven’t really been anywhere near the forest since Meadow’s death. But I can see why my sister liked the woods so much. The birds' light chirping, the sound of rustling leaves in the breeze, and the smell of pinewood make everything calm. I would be happy staying on this path or sitting at the pond with Austin all day. Maybe I’d be able to relax and forget about my father being gone. Or the fact that I’m alone in this war. But I don't have time to relax. I need to train the other Defenders. I need to make a plan.

Austin and I soon arrive at camp, and I place the filled water barrel near the fire before we look for paper to make a plan. We find some in a supply bin next to a cluster of light brown tents. We go to my tent, and I clear off a work table filled with bars of food and medical supplies. Austin hands me a pencil, and I lay out the piece of paper on the table.

"Time to get planning."

Chapter twenty-two

ALCMENE

"In only a few days' time, I will go alone to the Defender's old castle. From there, I will track them down and find Ember. I'll convince her to trade herself in for her father when I do. Otherwise, I will take his life," I tell Amara, as I point to different markings on a paper with my plan.

"Why go alone? Why not have all of us surround their camp, then trade him?" she asks.

"I will not risk us getting attacked. Not before the Fighters are more adequately trained. Once Ember is among us, I will begin their training immediately. Besides, I think Ember will be more inclined to listen if it is only me holding her father at knifepoint." I remember the terrified look on Ember's pretty face as I made eye contact with her for the first time. I crumple up the paper and discard it, memorizing every step beforehand.

"What if you can't find their camp? What if Ember won't give herself to you?"

"So many questions, Amara," I snap. She purses her lips. "I've thought about the possibilities, as I always do. There is no need to question me. There never is." I begin to walk over to my throne. I hear her footsteps follow.

"You didn't think about the endless possibilities when you impulsively sent us into battle." I hastily turn to face her, anger burning like fire in my eyes.

Without thinking, my knife goes to her throat. "You have no right to second guess my decisions." She doesn't move as my knife touches her neck. She knows I won't kill her, but hurt flashes in her eyes. She's surprised at who I've become. I know she isn't afraid, but I almost wish she was. It would be so much easier if she feared me like everyone else. "Because of that attack, we're a step closer to capturing Ember." I lower my knife.

"Why do you want to capture Ember so badly?" she asks in an accusatory way.

I scoff. "You will find out when she's my second in command."

Amara looks at me in shock and sneers. "You want to make a Defender your second? Are you kidding me?" She laughs almost maniacally. I so badly want to cut out her throat.

"When Ember arrives, you will see why." She continues to look at me with utter disbelief, but I catch something else. A hint of what appears to be jealousy. "And you thought *you* would be my second. That's why you're acting like this."

Amara's jaw tightens. "Maybe I thought I would be. I thought we were beginning to become friends again. But I guess not." Her enchanting green eyes stare into mine. "I helped you kill your father. I've been here for you. Doesn't that mean something to you?"

I scoff. "Are you serious? You're here now, but you weren't for three years. Three damn years, Amara! I needed you, and you weren't there!"

She walks up to me, lightly gripping my arms with her soft hands. Heat runs through me, and I hate myself for it.

"I'm sorry I abandoned you. I've regretted it every day since. After my brother killed himself, I didn't have the strength to reform our bond." She moves her hand to my cheek, running her thumb across the scar my father gave me. The scar that will forever tie me to him and his abuse. I feel my heart skip a beat, and suddenly, it's harder to breathe. "I won't leave you again. If you want me here, I'll stay. I promise." She's too close to me. Everything from our past flies through my mind. Every feeling I had, one sticking out among the rest. As she touches my face, I feel what I felt three years ago again. I never really acted on it back then. She was the one who kissed me, right before she left. But I could do it now. She's so close. I look at her lips and lean in, but as soon as I realize what I'm doing, I turn away from her. The warmth I just felt sputters out like a candle. Her hands fall away. I can't feel this way for her. Not again. Wanting someone will only make me weak. For all I know, she's using me for power. Why else would she come back after all this time? I want to tell her to leave, just as she did before. It would be easier that way. But the words that come out of my mouth are the opposite of that.

"Stay."

Amara simply nods, looking at me with some form of gratitude. I never thought she'd reenter my life after she left three years ago. But here she is, promising to stay. I want to thank her or at least tell her I understand why she left. Now more than ever, since I've lost a brother of my own. But I don't.

"That doesn't mean you can be my second." Her slight smile drops, as I knew it would. But I had to say it. The only person who can be my second is Ember, because of her power, and soon Amara will see that. Everyone will, once they find out.

I walk over to my throne, thinking of all the times my father sat here before me.

Amara asked the questions I have been contemplating while making my plan. I have thought about the fact that I may not find the Defender's base. And if I can't manage to find it, the whole plan will fall apart. But knowing the stupidity of the Defenders, I'm guessing they'll leave me a trail straight to it. And the other question, what if Ember doesn't trade herself in? Well, that one's easy. Ember *will* trade herself in because her father's life will depend on it. And Ember must know that I'm not one to bluff. If she doesn't come with me, I truly will slit his throat in front of her, and then I'll manage to capture her anyway. But that would be the hard way. And I'd rather capture Ember the easy way, without alerting the entire camp.

Ember's father will come with me on the trip to their base, so I can't starve him completely before I bring him, but I can at least make his life as miserable as possible. I take my dagger out of my holster, holding it tightly, remembering the day Leviathan gifted it to me. I gather the rest of my weapons and go down to the cellar, excitement surging through me. Torturing helpless Defenders never really gets old.

Chapter twenty-three

EMBER

Austin and I sit in my tent and brainstorm ideas for a plan. It has to be well thought out since we will be presenting it to The Council and the rest of the Defenders. But even if The Council declines our proposition, I know I'll end up going after my father anyway, even with no one by my side. I have to. And I need to kill Alcmene. If there is any hope in ending this war, it will start with her death.

"If we attack the Fighters head-on, we will lose. They have more soldiers than us and Alcmene will be in the mix." Austin nods.

"We need to get in and destroy Alcmene from the inside without alerting anyone else. But how?" he asks. In order to get into the castle without being caught, we can only bring a few people. I don't know if we'd win against her without an army.

"If the castle is similar to ours, they will have many entrances, but they will all be guarded heavily," I tell Austin. He sighs and lays his head on the table in his hands.

“One kill,” I say. “One kill, and the war is over.” It sounds so simple, yet it seems impossible. She will have guards everywhere, and she is an expert in combat. Who knows what she’ll throw at us? Without my father or D'andre, I'm the only match for Alcmene. If we can't capture her slyly, I will be the only one willing to face her directly, and I don't think I'd win. My chest tightens at the thought of her slitting my throat, destroying any chance of the Defenders winning the war after my death. My father, if he is still alive, will be locked in chains forever or slowly tortured to death by her hands.

I begin to tumble into my dark thoughts, thinking about all the people Alcmene has killed. When I think of D’andre, a saving idea comes to my mind. My eyes must light up because Austin asks me, "What is it?"

“Before D’andre died, he mentioned passageways within the walls of the Fighter castle that were hardly ever used. The entrance to them is underground. There may not be too many guards down there, or at least an amount we can handle. I had his map before I passed out in the battle. Do you know where it is?”

Austin's head pops up. “It’s in my tent. It looked important, so I kept it while you were sleeping for a couple of days. I couldn’t make out what it was.” Austin runs outside. I wait for a few minutes before he comes back with the map. He unrolls the old parchment on my table, and the faint lines run in all different directions. I can barely recognize the Fighter castle, but it’s there, a red dot at the North of the map. I look around the castle, and D’andre has drawn places where guards are, as well as lines indicating tunnels. I'm sure the guard posts aren't very accurate anymore unless they haven't changed their layout in decades. But the tunnels wouldn't change with time. It's hard to decipher with the fading ink, but I can see the tunnel that marks the entrance to the passageways. Southwest of the Fighter castle, about four hundred meters out in the forest, there is a trap door with a ladder that goes underground to the tunnel. We would have to find it in the middle of the enemy's woods, only using this crumpled, fading map. But it's a start. Alcmene will never guess that we have this knowledge. She won't be expecting it.

"The map shows us the entrance to the tunnels, but we can't see the paths inside the castle walls. We will have no idea which passageways to follow once we're inside," I tell Austin.

He furrows his brows at the map, before looking up at me.

"Then I guess we will have to figure it out when we're inside."

"But we could go down the wrong way, and end up in a room full of Fighters. We could be ambushed. How are we going to find Alcmene's room?" I ask.

"We figure it out," he repeats.

If The Council accepts, I will go with a few willing Defenders and travel through the passageways, listening for any sign of where Alcmene may be. We won't get caught if we stay in the walls until we find her. But this plan relies heavily on luck, and I'm not so sure it won't end in me dead.

If I manage to kill her, the Fighters will hopefully surrender now that their ruler is gone, and we can live in peace. I can get my father out of there and leave unharmed. But the thought of facing Alcmene makes my blood run cold.

I try to convince Austin to stay behind if The Council approves the attack plan, but he doesn't listen.

"I want to fight," he exclaims. I sigh. He is all I have left. I can't lose him. I won't let it happen.

Austin and I take a few minutes to make sure our plan is perfect before we make our way to The Council's tent.

We both take a deep breath before entering the tent which will determine the fate of all of our people. "This is it," Austin says, "you have to convince them."

I nod in response. He follows me inside the large, green tent.

Inside, we see a table similar to the one in the old council room at the crumbled castle. Five council members sit at the table, looking down at an array of papers. There used to be seven councilors. I never knew any of their names, but I instantly realize who's missing. My father talked a lot about his best friend. A tall, dark-skinned man with a full beard. Dark brown eyes, and a bright smile, although his past was anything but bright. As I look at the Council members, that man isn't here. Neither is my father. His friend is dead, died in the battle. If I'm able to get my father back, if this plan goes through, he will break knowing his lifelong friend is gone.

A woman sitting at the head of the table looks up at us. Based on where she's sitting and by how she holds herself with elegance, I can tell she's the leader. She has long blonde hair and ocean-blue eyes. Her hands are placed neatly on the brown table, and her left index finger has a smooth wooden ring on it. She has dark circles under her eyes, and a look of grief I instantly recognize.

My father once told me that being the head council member doesn't mean much. The only difference between her and the other members is that she has two votes instead of one whenever voting is permitted. She can't hold much more power than the others, because power changes people. We don't want one ruler like the Fighters do.

"You are council member Liam's daughter, correct?" she asks. The other council members take their eyes off their papers to look up at me and Austin.

"Yes. And this is Austin." I gesture to him. He stiffens and fidgets with his hands. He's nervous. "I am training him." The council member nods.

"I am head council member Reina." She looks at me. "Now that our previous trainer is no longer with us, are you taking over the training position for the Defenders? Your father told me that you are very talented in combat."

My throat burns at the thought of D'andre and the smoke. The blood that took forever to wash off my hands.

"Yes. If you would allow it," I tell her as I clear my thoughts. It's what D'andre would want. However, the thought of replacing him makes my heart hurt.

She looks to the other council members, and they all nod as her glance passes over each of them.

"You will be perfect for the position. You have our blessing to train the Defenders."

I smile. "Thank you." I can tell that Austin feels more comfortable as he loosens up by my side.

The Council sees the folded map in my hand. "What do you have there?" one of the men closest to Reina asks.

Austin and I share a glance. This is it. I take a few steps toward The Council, and hesitantly unfold the map on an empty section of the table. The council members look at the map as I begin to speak. I don't mention D'andre drawing the map. I'm sure most of them know he was a Fighter, but some of The Council may not, and it's not my secret to share.

"Austin and I have come up with a plan that could end this war for good."

A few council members look at us skeptically. Reina looks at the map with an unreadable expression. I watch as her eyes glance over the words I've written in the margins.

"You want to attack the Fighters." She furrows her brows.

"Yes. I have thought a lot about this plan, and I believe it would be best to attack the Fighters ourselves, instead of waiting for them to attack us. I know it is against everything we stand for, but if the plan works, we will finally be at peace. We lost so many of us in the last battle. I'm afraid if another one comes, none of us will live through it."

The entire council looks at me warily. Some have anger in their eyes.

"You're right. This goes against everything we stand for," a smaller woman near the end of the table says. I almost bring up how members of The Council tortured Fighters under the council room, but I shut my mouth before I have the chance. Verbally attacking The Council will do me no good.

"But what if it brings about peace? No more death," someone adds.

"How many would end up dying if we attacked the Fighter's main castle?" Reina asks, silencing the group.

"I believe we can get into the castle and kill Alcmene with only about four or five Defenders."

Her eyes widen. "How can we win if we bring so few people? It isn't logical. They would die for nothing." I start to fidget with the hem of my blue sleeve. Reina quiets the group as they start to argue. She narrows her eyes at Austin and me. "Tell me your plan. Every detail."

I tell her all about the tunnel that will lead us to the hidden passageways inside the castle. I don't tell her how I found out about them; luckily, she doesn't ask. A few of the council members mumble things I can't make out while I explain the plan. I keep talking through my nervousness. Austin remains silent.

When I tell Reina that I will kill Alcmene alone, she questions me. "How do you plan to do that?" she asks as she rolls her ring on the table.

"I've seen how she fights. I can stand a chance against her. And the other Defenders will be in the walls nearby, safe. They will help if I need them to." She nods, and I finish sharing the details.

"Like all matters discussed here, this will be put up to a vote." I knew this was coming. Austin looks at me with worry. It's all down to this.

"All in favor of this plan, raise your hand." I watch as my hope crumbles to nothing. Two council members raise their hands, but out of the five, it's not enough.

"If you attack the Fighters and fail, they will only retaliate harder. Our best option is to build our defenses, and prepare for the inevitable. I'm sorry, Ember. Liam would be proud of your efforts," Reina says. My jaw tenses when she mentions my father. I should have known this would happen. I shouldn't have gotten my hopes up in the first place. In 100 years, we've never attacked the Fighters. Why did I think I would be the one to change that? I'm not even on The Council. I have no say in anything that goes on in this war. I'm just another soldier in the battle.

I take my map back before Austin and I march out. This decision only means one thing. I have to rescue my father and kill Alcmene on my own. Soon.

I go to the pond with Austin, so we can talk without worrying about people listening in.

"I'm going with you," he says.

I meet his eyes. "You're not. I have to do this alone."

"But Ember-"

"No. Be with your family. Be a kid. Don't worry about me. When I return home, we may actually be able to live in peace. Like we've always talked about." I won't get my hopes up this time. But living freely would be a dream. War has always cast a shadow over my life. I want more than anything for it to be gone.

Austin's eyes water. "I don't want you to die."

I let out a slow breath. "I won't," I tell him. I really hope I'm right. Going against my worst enemy all alone isn't in my favor. I can only hope that my training and drive to win this war will allow me to beat Alcmene. I think of the blood dripping down her face and hands and shake the thought away.

"When are you leaving?" he asks.

"In a few days. I'll pack some supplies and train a little, say my goodbyes, and leave." In reality, I'm going to pack my bags tonight. I can't risk Austin trying to come with me. He can't know when I'm going. I will leave behind everything I've ever known first thing in the morning.

Chapter twenty-four

ALCMENE

I've been walking with Ember's father for four days. We are almost at the Defender's crumbled castle. Only a few more hours. Fortunately, he hasn't said a word this entire trip. He didn't even complain when I refused to feed him the first two nights. Most prisoners would be begging for even an ounce of food by now. But, as I've learned, Ember's father is different. He doesn't want to show his weakness, although I know he has it. He wants to keep his strength and dignity more than anything. But no matter what he does, I will always win in the end. He doesn't know my plan yet, or he would have fought more as I dragged him out here. He probably thinks I'm taking him somewhere to kill him. Who knows. But once he figures out I'm going to trade him for his daughter, I know he'll fight his restraints. He'll do anything he can to protect her. That is his weakness. But for now, as we head towards the castle, he doesn't try to fight. He walks in front of me, knowing that if he makes any sudden movements I will end his life faster than he can react.

Ember's father never ended up telling me anything useful. He didn't know about his daughter's power and he didn't give up any information about anything else. As he walks in front of me, leading the way, he limps slightly. It probably would have been smart not to throw a knife into his leg before this trip, but his lack of information angered me.

We walk for a few more hours. Every time he slows down, I press a knife to his back, and he continues at a faster pace. Eventually, after what feels like an eternity, we reach the castle. After the multiple explosions the castle endured, nothing is left but an enormous mound of stone and dust. The smell of rotting bodies hits me. There are hundreds of deteriorating corpses around us, each one in worse condition than the next. Some bodies are piled on top of each other, like they were trying to protect one another from the explosions. Some lie alone, dried blood covering their wounds with flies buzzing above them. Each death has its own story. Some mothers lie with their children. Together until death. Soldiers lie near each other, protecting their people until the very end. I know seeing all this horror should leave me feeling gutted for what I've done, but I only feel emptiness. After I eventually use Ember to finish off the last of the Defenders, we will finally win. Levi will be fully avenged, and maybe I'll be happy again. Nothing else matters.

Ember's father stops in his tracks. I stand beside him, and I can see his eyes start to well up. I know he's doing everything he can to try and fight the tears. He walks up to one of the corpses. The body is badly deteriorated, but I can just make out the face of a man. He stops trying to fight his emotions, as he falls down to his knees, grabbing the hand of the dead man.

"My best friend," he sobs.

"Enough of this." I walk over to him and grab him by the collar. His hands reach for the man, but tied together, they don't reach far. I look across the land, and easily find footprints and blood leading in a single direction.

"Wow. You're people are even bigger fools than I thought. They're going to lead us right to them." I feel him tense up before trying to pull away. I reach for my knife, holding it to his throat.

"What did I tell you about resisting?"

"You won't kill me. You need me," he scoffs.

Clever man. "You're right." I move my knife up to his face. "I won't kill you. But that doesn't mean I won't take an eye out." I let the knife cut the skin just to the right of his eye. He doesn't move but he tightens his jaw. "Let's go then," I say, grabbing his shoulder and throwing him in front of me. "Follow the trail." I keep the tip of my knife on his spine.

The trail goes on and on. We walk for hours, and I get sick of dragging along the exhausted prisoner. I set up camp and tie him to a tree. I make a fire for warmth as the night air sends chills down my back. I double-check his knots before I drift to sleep.

When I wake up, I untie Ember's Father, and we continue walking. It's the same as it was all the days before. He walks slowly in front of me with my knife at his spine. Eventually, we make it to the Defenders new camp after two more aggravating days. It's nightfall when we get there. Hundreds of tents line the camp. Supplies scatter the area, along with a fire in the center. Finding Ember's tent without running into another Defender will be practically impossible. Unless she's not in her tent.

"Where would Ember be, if not in her tent?" I ask him. He doesn't answer. I slam his back into a tree, moving my dagger to his eye. I pierce the skin centimeters away from his right eye, sending a small stream of blood trickling down his face.

He continues to stay silent. "Why do you need her?" His voice comes out rough from the lack of water I've allowed him.

"I won't go over this again. Tell me where she would be." He doesn't talk, so I slice into his eyelid, splitting it in half. He cries out, moving away from my dagger. I reach for him, and he tries to kick me, but I'm too fast. He's on the ground in an instant, his tied hands hitting the grass before the rest of his body. "I'll only ask one more time or the eye comes out."

I bring my knife close to him again, already stained in his blood.

"The pond," he grumbles.

"That wasn't so hard, was it? Just two words, and you wouldn't have a spliced eyelid." I pick him up and tie him to a tree, reinforcing the knot multiple times. There's no getting out of it. I will leave him here until I have Ember, where I'll trade him for her.

Ember's father points out the direction of the pond, and I promise him that if he told me the wrong direction I will kill him when I get back.

By the time I get to the pond, it's almost completely dark. To my surprise, Ember is actually here. I bet her father didn't really believe she would be. Too bad for him.

I keep a good distance away, where she won't spot me just yet. Ember sits at the edge of the water with a small, brown-haired boy. I see something in the boy's hands, but I can't tell what it is from here. Ember's face is lit up in a smile. Little does she know, she won't be smiling for long.

Chapter twenty-five

EMBER

Austin tries to catch a frog to take our minds off my departure. He smiles like he's just won the lottery when he manages to catch one after half an hour. It only reinforces the fact that he can't come with me. He's still a kid, finding joy in the smallest of things. He's old enough to be a soldier, but he's not old enough to die at the hands of Alcmene if I can't kill her.

After a little while longer, the sun has completely set. I have to pack plenty of food and supplies for my journey ahead. It is a long walk to the Fighter's castle.

"Almost ready to head back?" I ask.

"Sure." We stand up, ready to leave, when I feel a presence behind me. Before I have time to turn around, I feel arms wrap around my shoulders and sharp, cold metal at my throat. Austin drops all of his supplies when he sees the knife at my neck. I don't have to turn around to know who it is. I can already tell.

"Alcmene." My plan is ruined. Alcmene is here now, of all times, and she has the advantage. There's no sneaking up on her through the castle's passageways anymore. I tense at the knife at my neck. She could kill me faster than I could blink.

I think of all the lives lost in the battle that destroyed my home, and anger surges throughout my body. She is responsible for everything. I know I can't try to fight her. She's too quick. Too well trained. I have no element of surprise on my side. Austin stands in front of us, motionless.

"You're going to come with me." Her voice is sharp. She tightens the grip on her knife.

I push away my fear. "Or else what?" I ask.

"Or I will kill your friend where he stands. Followed by your father." So my father *is* still alive. Or at least that's what she wants me to believe.

I see Austin's hand move ever so slightly. He's trying to reach for his knife at his back. I shoot him a look, pleading for him to remain still. He hesitantly retracts his hand back to his side.

"Go back to the tents, Austin. Let me go," I tell him desperately. If he doesn't leave, Alcmene will kill him, or worse. I can't lose anyone else. He shakes his head. My heart drops.

"I'd listen to her if I were you. And don't try to wake the other Defenders. They'll never catch up to me." I feel her knife pierce my neck slightly. Alcmene's breathing is jagged, like she's afraid that whatever she has planned won't work. A small stream of blood travels down my skin. I don't let the pain show. "You're just like your father," she whispers, her breath hot on my neck. I struggle to break free, although I know it's no use. She tightens her hold on me. I look at Austin, silently begging for him to leave. He frowns at me. I know he wants to help, but he can't, and he knows it. After a few seconds, he finally nods.

"Fine. I'll go." His voice is shaky, and I know his tears are about to fall. I mouth the words, "I'll be back," before he turns and begins the walk back to camp.

When he's gone, Alcmene demands I hand over all my weapons. I try to hide my mother's golden-handled dagger, but she finds it. It hurts more than anything when she takes it from me.

Alcmene takes me into the woods. Once she gets her knife off my throat, I'll have to try to escape somehow. We seem to head in random directions, spiraling through the trees, leaving me disoriented. She doesn't want me to figure out how to return. I walk in front of her, as she pushes me forward, never taking her knife off me. I catch a glimpse of her face. Her scar seems to gleam in the dim moonlight, and her expression shows a determination I've never seen.

We walk for at least twenty minutes, swerving past tree branches and raised roots. It gets so dark, even seeing a few feet ahead is difficult. I trip multiple times, and Alcmene drags me back up, her grip on my shoulders increasingly rougher. Her nails dig into my skin. Eventually she shifts to walking on my side, so I can follow her lead a little better. She walks briskly, like she's been through these thick woods a hundred times over.

When we stop, I see my father. I never thought I'd see him again. I was almost certain Alcmene was lying and killed him at the castle. He is tied to a tree in front of us, his clothes torn and his face pale. Dried blood covers his skin and drips down his eye. She must have tortured him, which is what I feared she would do. It looks like he can hardly stand by the way he slumps against the tree. I think I'd rather die than suffer. I know he would too.

My father looks up at me, blinking multiple times, almost as if he thinks he's in a dream.

"Ember," he chokes out, his voice so hoarse the word is barely audible. Alcmene takes the knife away from my neck but holds it securely as she stands between us.

"I'll give you two options." She looks at me. "Option number one, you give yourself over to me completely. You come with me to the Fighter castle without putting up a fight. I don't want to have to drag you all the way there. Or two, you try to fight me, and I kill your father, then I kill you." There's nowhere to run. She knows these woods, she would catch up to me almost instantly, then I would die along with my father. But how can I just turn myself over to her? My people need me. Austin needs me. I look at my father. I can see pain in his eyes.

"How can I trust you won't kill him anyway?" She idly flips a knife in her hands like she's bored.

"I won't," is all she says, looking me in the eyes for the first time since she's captured me. I shouldn't believe her. She's a maniac who murdered countless people with a smile on her face. But when I look in her eyes, as terrifying as they are, I know she isn't bluffing.

I know I can't get out of this. Not right now. But maybe If I agree to go with her without a fight, I'll be able to escape during the night on the trip to her castle or something. I can't try to run now. What my father did to the Fighters; starving them, beating them, was unforgivable. But no matter what he did, and no matter how long he lied about it, I won't let him die. I can't. He's my father.

"I'll go with you." My father's expression drops. He tries to speak, but no words come out. I see a small smile form on Alcmene's lips.

She takes a throwing knife from her chest holster and throws it a few feet away from my father. "Get the knife and cut yourself loose. Don't try to come after us. I'll kill your daughter if you do."

I catch one last glimpse of my father, guilt and sorrow written all over his bruised and bloody face. I don't get to say goodbye to him. Alcmene ties my hands together behind my back and drags me away before I have time to say anything. As she pulls me through the forest, almost ripping my arms out of their sockets, I realize I may not live for much longer. Alcmene traded my father, her only hostage, for me. She wants me for some reason, and it could very well be to kill me in front of her people.

Alcmene drags me through the thick woods for at least a few hours, never growing tired. Her black hair, as dark as the sky, brushes my bleeding neck every so often, and her knife inches me forward at a faster and faster pace. I hate how close she is to me. I keep thinking about her slaughtering Defenders at the battle. I remember passing out, overwhelmed with pain and loss. Waking up in a tent a few days later was horrible. All I wanted was revenge. And now here she is, and she's here alone. This is my chance to get back at her for what she did to my people. But killing her now is a suicide mission. As much as I want to rip her throat out every time she touches me, I know I can't.

Thankfully, after hours of our close proximity in the humid forest driving me mad, we stop at a clearing with a small pond. I've never been anywhere besides our old castle and our new campsite. Seeing this part of the world is all new to me. I just wish I was seeing it under different circumstances. In a normal scenario, I would look around and take in all of the beautiful surroundings I've never seen, shining under the light of the moon. But I can't at a time like this. Now, the only thing I can focus on is Alcmene's breath on my neck and her knife at my back.

Alcmene throws me down next to the pond. I hit the ground hard, unable to soften the blow with my tied hands.

"Don't move." I wouldn't dare.

I watch as Alcmene takes two metal canteens out of her backpack and fills them with water. Every so often I catch her glancing at the stars with a grim look on her face. Something is different about her since the last time I saw her. At the battle, all I saw in her eyes was fury. Pure hatred. But now, as she looks at the stars, I see something else in her eyes. So subtle I hardly notice it, but it's there. *Pain*. She shoves the canteens into her black backpack before tying me to a tree at the edge of the clearing. She begins to collect firewood. I watch her movements. Everything seems so routine. She must have set up camp like this a hundred times. Alcmene gathers wood in her arms and occasionally throws piles of it near me, but she never goes far into the woods around us. She keeps me in her view at all times. After gathering a decent amount, she unties me from the tree and, to my surprise, unties my hands.

"Be useful and make a fire."

I look at the wood she has piled in front of me. I don't have a match or anything to light it with. "I don't know how. Not without a match." Even if I did know how, I wouldn't give her the satisfaction of being her slave.

She scoffs. "Of course you don't. Yet again, the Defenders never fail to disappoint me with their growing stupidity." I never needed to light a fire without a match at the Defender castle. I never left the perimeter.

Alcmene separates the wood into piles and gestures for me to sit. She doesn't seem worried that I'll try to run away or attack her. I'd die if I tried right now. She'd outrun me in a minute. And she's the one with all the weapons. But I need to figure something out. I can't let her take me to her castle, where my life will surely meet its end.

I sit beside her, trying to keep as much distance between us as possible. I'm worried if I'm too close, I'll snap and try to strangle her with my bare hands. I wonder if D'andre would hate me for it if he were here to judge. Defenders are taught not to kill, but she deserves to die. She killed so many of us. She wouldn't hesitate before killing me.

"What do you want from me? Why don't you just say it?" I yell. She barely looks in my direction. The whole way here she remained silent. Every time I tried to speak to her, she pressed her knife deeper into my back. I'm sick of being in the dark about why she captured me.

"You will find out eventually. Or, if you keep talking, you won't. I'll slice your throat open before you get the chance to figure out why I traded your father for you." She keeps a steady tone. It seems as though she doesn't have a care in the world for what she's done to the Defenders. I think back to my talk with my father from a while ago. I wondered why Alcmene would want power. Now I want to know why exactly she killed hundreds of my people. Why she captured me. What is her goal in all of this? There was pure hatred in her eyes when she killed the Defenders. And pain that I saw in them today. I can tell there's something more to Alcmene than just wanting power. But what?

"Why are you doing this? Any of it?" I feel the urge to charge at her, to let my anger out and kill her myself.

Her eyes darken as she stands up abruptly, closing the space between us. I feel a familiar cold metal at my throat. "I told you, darling. Don't speak again," she taunts me. The scar down her face is even more prominent in the fire-light. I wonder how she got it. How would anyone get close enough to her to cut a line down her face? She killed the Defenders in battle before they got within a foot of her.

She sits back down and starts to pile wood into a small pit made out of rocks. She takes two sticks and begins to rub them together, her hands moving down to the bottom and then back up. By the looks of it, she's done this many times before. She begins to speak.

"To make heat, you need friction." I wonder why she's taking the time to tell me this, but I don't really care. I let my mind drift elsewhere as she continues. Austin is alone right now. Our plan may never be brought to light now that I'm gone. My father is alive, but this may be one of my last days breathing.

Alcmene moves the sticks together for a while, and I begin to believe she will never make a flame. But after another minute, I'm proven wrong. A small tendril of smoke rises from the bottom of the sticks, and she quickly brings them to the tinder in the rock pit. Soon, with a bit of effort, the tinder lights. In an instant, she is blowing on the flame, increasing its size. She adds more wood until the fire is big enough to lay the canteens of water beside the flames to boil. She keeps an eye on me, but I don't move.

"After these boil, we will leave. We will rest for a night after two days of walking. If you can't handle that, I'll start cutting off fingers. There's no way I'm dragging you all the way there. You'll have to cooperate and walk," she demands, never taking her piercing glare off me. I nod in response.

The only opportunity I have is in two days when she sleeps. I have to kill her then. But I'm guessing she will wake at any sound of movement, and her weapons will be at her sides, ready to fly my way. But the way I see it, I only have two options. I could die in two days trying to escape, or I could die the minute I enter her castle. The first option gives me a chance of living, so that seems like the right choice.

Chapter twenty-six

ALCMENE

After the water boils, I take a long sip from my canteen. Ember stares at me, silently begging for water. She doesn't look surprised when I don't offer her any. She can last another day without it. I put my canteen in my backpack before approaching her. I tie Ember's hands together again, but in front of her this time.

We continue our walk to my castle. Awaiting us will surely be a furious Amara and a load of Fighters I have yet to train. I still don't understand why Amara is acting like she cares about me; about my mental well-being after I murdered my father. Whatever the reason, her constant badgering has become an annoyance lately. I don't have anyone to depend on for the first time in my life. I don't want to become attached to Amara in any way. I can't. Not now that I'm in charge.

It is pitch black now, the stars and the moon's light barely helping me see. But I can scale the woods just fine in the dark. It's

Ember who's the problem. I thought about bringing a lantern, but lighting repeatedly due to the strong wind would be a nuisance. And once we got closer to my castle it would have been pointless in the crashing storm. It'll be a few more hours before the sun comes out, and Ember will just have to manage.

Soon we are out of the forest and onto mostly flat, grassy terrain. Ember trudges behind me, certainly waking any animal nearby. I walk soundlessly in front of her, holding her wrist to keep her close.

"Keep up. I told you I won't drag you. If you become a problem, I will dispose of you." She takes her eyes off the ground to look at me.

"You won't kill me. You need me for some reason."

I smile. She's not so dumb after all. I glance back at her. "Right. But don't think I won't torture you or your people." I point to a holster at my side, which holds a small signal flare. A large one is in my pack. "One signal to the Fighters and they'll attack your new base." Her eyes widen slightly.

I told Amara to watch out for my signal in case I needed her to send Fighters after me. She assured me that she would stay on lookout for the smoke of a flare in the sky. Even though we were arguing a few days before I asked her for the favor, I knew she wouldn't let me down. Besides, there was no one else to ask.

Ember and I continue traveling. There is still open land ahead, with trees on either side of us. I know this path well, but Ember doesn't. I look back at her once in a while and see her looking around in awe at her new surroundings. It all seems pretty bland to me, but I'm guessing she's never really left her castle. Levi and I took trips sometimes (mostly during the night when our father was asleep) to travel beyond the castle walls. The first time we went out, I was just as amazed as Ember by everything. It's crazy to think that only a small part of our world is livable. Only a small part has forests and ponds and green land. The rest is dried up and destroyed. Completely uninhabitable. But that doesn't mean that what's left of the world isn't beautiful. Especially the forest. It's so freeing compared to the suffocating castle. Even without my father roaming around, I still hate the place. All that is left are memories of Levi, and sometimes they're too much to bear.

Although Ember is my prisoner, she seems pretty calm. She trails behind me slowly, without speaking or trying to attack me. Smart.

Eventually, after walking in a straight line through the open grassland for a while, we hit more forest. I push Ember in front of me, since monitoring her through the thick woods will be easier that way. I reorient her in the direction we'll be traveling, and she moves away from my touch. She's moving slightly faster now that her hands are tied in front of her, but she's still aggravatingly slow.

We continue walking, and I chuckle whenever she trips over a tree root. The trees tower above us, allowing us shade from the rising sun. If I'm honest, I miss seeing the sun at my castle. It is almost always raining and storming. But I'm comfortable in the environment after all these years, and I've learned to flourish in it.

The sound of birds chirping fills the forest. Ember looks up at them and falls over a rock while doing so. She lands with a hard *thud.*

I groan. "Get up. We're already going to get there a day later than I planned because of your painfully slow pace."

"I can't. Not with my hands tied."

I sigh and walk over to her on the ground. Her face is planted in the dirt. I laugh. I stand next to her and bend down to grab her shoulder, when I see her hand slowly move towards one of my waist holsters.

"Do you really think I'm that dumb?" I swat her hand away and kick her in the ribs. She yelps, not expecting the sudden pain. After a second, she easily rolls over onto her back, then stands up. Her face is covered in dirt.

"Try something like that again and I'll do much worse." She doesn't say anything, but she turns around to face the direction of my castle. At this rate, it'll take us another three days to get there.

We continue through the forest until eventually, we get to a pond.

"Can't we stop here for a while? We've been walking for over a day."

"Get used to it," I reply. I grab her tied wrists and push her further in front of me.

"Just tell me what you want from me," she says, looking back to meet my eyes.

I remain silent. I will tell her eventually, but not now. I need to be sure of her power first. But if she really has a power, why hasn't she used it to escape by now? Levi would have easily been able to get out of this kind of situation. Unless she doesn't have full control over it yet.

Levi unlocked his power with rage. Ember has been angry at me for what I've done plenty of times. She should be angry enough to unleash it by now. Although Ember hasn't been screaming at me, I can see fury in her eyes everytime she looks at me. Pain. I know she wants to kill me more than anything. So why isn't she trying harder? We made a deal, but I didn't think that would actually stop her.

Levi's power was his strength. Maybe Ember's is different. Maybe it's not activated by rage at all. Another emotion possibly? Or this is all just ridiculous and I've captured Ember for nothing. I saw her eyes change, and some kind of dark smoke that could have very well been a hallucination due to the circumstances. And now I'm doing all of this to justify what I thought I saw. I wonder what Levi would think of all this. After all, maybe I'm going crazy because of him. Ember having a power like Levi's might just be something my mind is making up to fill my void of pain.

I shake my head and snap out of my thoughts. I've come this far. Whether Ember has a power or not, she's mine now.

Ember walks at an even slower pace than before. Suddenly, I understand why.

"You'd rather die than make it to my castle, wouldn't you? You're afraid of what will happen to you there." I smirk. She abruptly stops and turns to face me.

"I'm not afraid," she tells me. Her voice is calm, but I can see rage bubbling up in her eyes. I so desperately want her to let it out.

Her eyes glance down to my weapons. Three throwing knives are at either side of my waist, as well as Levi's dagger. I have another knife strapped to my leg and more in my backpack.

"You and your knives don't scare me. Neither does your castle." Her voice is strong like Levi's was whenever he stood against our father. She's trying to sound threatening, but it's not working. Ember steps closer till we're merely inches apart. She's a bit shorter than me and tilts her head slightly to stare me down. Her braids are loose and frizzled after trekking through the woods, and cuts from branches dot her face. Her eyes shine as she looks at me. There is a beauty to her that is somehow intriguing. How confident she is. How most Defenders would give into exhaustion by now, but she doesn't. How her eyes are full of light, even in this world of darkness.

"You won't get to torture me. I'll outsmart you before you get the chance. I'll be gone before you know it." She glares at me, but I don't dare look away. She needs to realize that I will never cave. And she'll never outsmart me. I'll always be one step ahead of her.

"You think you can get rid of me?" I take a knife from my side, undo her restraints, and hand it to her. She furrows her brows. "Try," I demand, taking out a knife for myself. Ember smiles, but the look in her eyes tells me all I need to know. She's putting on an act. She knows she won't win, and that will be her downfall. The moment you lose faith in yourself is the moment you lose the battle.

She swipes at me but I'm already out of the way. I slash at her shoulder, easily slicing into her flesh. She grimaces, but doesn't slow down. She swings her knife towards my face, and I dodge it, slicing mine just above her right cheekbone. My knife leaves a small line of red in its wake, but not deep enough to scar. I don't want to kill her, so I don't try to inflict too much damage. At least no damage that will cause her to lose too much blood. I meant it when I said I didn't want to have to drag her to my castle. She comes at me faster now, but her rage makes her act on impulse. She thrashes with her knife carelessly, barely trying to aim. I grab her wrist, stopping the attack, and bring my knife to her neck. She stands motionless.

"Don't let your emotions ruin your precision." I keep the knife to her throat, but use my other hand to take her weapon. I put it back in my holster. She scoffs.

"Don't try to give me a lesson. I know how to fight." She wipes the blood from her face and applies pressure to her shoulder.

"Yeah, right." She has skill, no doubt, but her close combat techniques are not why I captured her. Her power is. So why didn't it surface during our fight? That would have been a great opportunity for her. I don't get it.

"I will get back to my camp eventually. And I *will* win," Ember says, fire never leaving her voice. I smile. She sounds like me, full of a relentless determination. But in her case, it's foolish. She will never win against me.

"Mhmm. Good luck with that," I laugh. It's obvious she's had more training in combat than most of the other Defenders, but there is still much she needs to learn. With me as her instructor, she'll be ready to be my second in command in no time. As long as Amara doesn't have her head for it. But if Ember doesn't have a power, she's just as useless to me as everyone else. I hope I'm right about what I saw during the battle. Otherwise this would all be for nothing. "We're wasting time. Keep walking."

Chapter twenty-seven

EMBER

I've never walked for so long in my life. I guess I've never had any reason to. My legs are about to give way at any minute, and I feel like passing out from overwhelming fatigue. Alcmene strides behind me. Besides the dark bags under her eyes, she seems perfectly fine. She must be used to it. She doesn't break a sweat even with the heavy bag on her back. It's been several hours since Alcmene and I last talked, or rather since we fought. It was stupid of me to do so. As much as I hate to admit it, she was right. My anger won't help me. It will just make things worse. I wonder if she's had personal experience to figure that out. I wonder what she's been through to make her this way. So heartless. I wonder so many things about her.

What I do know is that I will have to outsmart her somehow. Sooner than later. Once we get to her castle, she will be even more familiar with her surroundings. I'm sure she will have every escape route bolted shut. I know about the secret passageways in the walls now, but I'll never have the chance to use them. She'll have her eyes on me at all times. I think back to when I discovered Fighters being tortured under the council room floor, in a cold cellar. I can imagine the Fighter's castle having something similar. A prison where no one can hear my screams. Although I'm not so sure Alcmene will torture me. Wouldn't she have done it by now? I don't understand what she wants from me.

Alcmene catches me slowing down. "Don't stop now. We have a long way to go." She makes sure to drag out the word 'long' when she says it. I can't imagine my legs hurting more than they already do. The last day of walking will surely be the worst. There's no way I won't pass out before then. We trek through the forest on no particular path. We climb over fallen trees and broken branches. For me it's like scaling through an obstacle course, but for Alcmene, trudging through the forest is like a walk in the park. She steps without making a sound, like a hunter going after its prey.

Every once in a while we get to a creek we have to cross. To my surprise, Alcmene doesn't let me die of dehydration. She fills her canteens and allows me small sips of water periodically, but definitely not as much as I need. My lips are chapped and my head is pounding.

When I look back at Alcmene, she stares blankly ahead, seemingly lost in thought. It makes me even more curious about what she's been through and what she's thinking about every time she stares up at the stars, or off in the distance. There must be some reason why she ended up this way.

Another hour or so goes by, and the forest goes on. I used to sit at my desk in the old castle before training, dreaming of the day the war would end. I'd dream of walking through the woods without a care in the world. Now, I so desperately want to get out of the forest more than anything. Away from the towering trees. Away from the woman who's taken more lives than I can count.

"Is there any more open land before we get to the castle?" I ask, my voice hoarse after not speaking for several hours. I'm sick of tripping over raised roots and pushing through drooping tree branches.

"We'll get out of the woods soon, but you won't like it." She smiles slightly as she sharpens her dagger while we walk. It's the dagger I see her use most often. The handle is silver in color, and the blade is made out of some sort of dark purple rock. It's sharp. I can imagine the blade covered in blood as she killed my people. My own precious dagger is by Alcmene's side with her own. If I die by her hand, my mother's dagger will never be passed on again. The line will end with me. The thought makes my chest hurt.

"What won't I like?" I reply, trying to let the memories of my mother leave my mind.

"You'll see." I'm way too impatient for Alcmene's games.

We walk for a while longer, my legs shaking and my eyes fluttering closed often from exhaustion. The rope tying my hands together leaves burns around my wrists.

When we leave the woods, I see why Alcmene said I wouldn't be happy. All around us are steep hills the size of mountains, and there's no way around them. The forest was torture already. I don't know If I can handle going uphill for hours on end.

"At least a day's worth of walking up and down these hills. Then more forest, and we're there." She slides her newly-sharpened knife back into its holster. The sun is going down, and Alcmene's steps only get faster. I'll never be able to keep up once it gets as dark as last night. "They call these hills The Fractured Slopes," she tells me. I wonder who the 'they' she's referring to is, but I don't ask. The minute we start walking up The Fractured Slopes, my legs collapse.

"I told you when I boiled the water that we would walk for two days before stopping. We still have a few more hours until that point." Alcmene lifts me by my shirt collar and throws me in front of her. "Walk," she growls.

Somehow I continue trekking until the sun sets. We finally make it to the top of one of the hills where the ground is more or less flat. Alcmene sets her bag down and holds her dagger firmly.

"Sleep. I will, too. But know that if you move even a little, I'll wake up and slit your throat."

I nod. Although I'm more exhausted than I've ever been in my life, I know I have to wait until she falls asleep. This will be my only opportunity to try and kill her before we arrive at her castle.

Alcmene settles down on the grass, maneuvering her backpack under her head. I watch as she closes her eyes. Immediately she looks less angry now that her eyes aren't burning holes into my back. I watch her long hair blow gently in the wind for a minute, before I fix my gaze on the sky. I watch the stars twinkle and shine, for what feels like forever, until finally, Alcmene's breathing slows. Her dagger is still in her hand. If she wakes up, she'll thrash at me. I have to be careful about this. I slowly get up, my legs instantly feeling sore. I clench my jaw after every step. I hardly breathe, worrying Alcmene will hear it. I step carefully, knowing the smallest crunch of grass could wake her up.

I'm standing over her now. Her black hair spills over her face, covering one of her eyes. I can still see her scar poking out. It looks like it came from a knife. The line is slightly jagged near her jaw, like the knife was twisted. I can only imagine how badly that hurt. I watch her chest rise and fall. Her hands lie on her stomach, her dagger clasped between them. Even with a dagger in Alcmene's hands, she doesn't seem threatening while asleep. She just looks like a teenage girl, sleeping peacefully atop a huge hill underneath the glimmering stars. Not the leader of the Fighters and a mass murderer.

I reach down to grab my dagger from her ever so slowly when her nails dig into my hand. I jump backward and she's already on her feet.

"I thought you needed the sleep." Her nails draw blood. I try to pull away, but she doesn't let go. "You won't be able to kill me. Not that easily anyway." She pushes me to the ground before sitting back down against her backpack.

"Go to sleep this time," she insists, annoyed, before closing her eyes again.

I know that trying again will be useless. I grumble and lay my head on the ground, reluctantly giving in to my exhaustion. I am met with a horrible dream.

I lie in my bedroom, drowning in grief over all the losses I have endured. I want to do something. Anything to avenge their deaths.

My father is outside my door now. I bid him away with a shout. He doesn't listen, and pushes my door open. I'm not in control of my emotions. I want revenge for my mother and sister. For D'andre. I want them back. Pain consumes me, burning like fire on my skin and inside my body. The veins in my arms turn black and spread to my wrists and then my hands. I can't control it. Smoke rises from my palms, and it feels like I'm holding molten lava. It flies from my grasp, consuming my father, adding him to the list of the fallen.

Then it turns on me, pouring into my throat and crushing my lungs. I fight for a minute before deciding it's no use. I succumb to the agonizing pain and let myself join everyone I love.

I wake up in a pool of sweat, instantly flinging myself onto my feet. I catch my breath as it spirals out of control. I look down at my hands, imagining the black smoke emitting from them, accompanied by the searing pain. I flip them both ways, but nothing is there. Just dried blood and calluses.

"That was quite the dream you had," Alcmene taunts. She doesn't ask what I dreamt about but stares at me with a curious darkness in her eyes. She's trying to read me as she always does, but this time, she doesn't know what I'm thinking.

I groggily stretch my sore legs, and we continue our walk to the castle. Every half-hour or so, I check my hands. I continuously find nothing. Alcmene seems to be paying closer attention to me now. Every time I glance behind me she is staring straight at me. She isn't spacing out like she did back in the forest. She wants to know whatever I'm hiding. To be honest, I don't know myself. Something happened to me at the battle, and now it's haunting me through nightmares. D'andre told me there was something special about me. Is this what he meant? Did he know? How could he have known? To him, I was excellent at combat. I was his prodigy. His friend. He couldn't have known about this. He thought I had a lot of skill, and so did I. I was great out of all the Defenders, but Alcmene can beat me at her worst, so I can't be so great after all. It makes me wonder how long she's been training. What's training like at the Fighter's castle? Who taught her? The questions build and build. There are so many things I've wondered about her. Even from the first day my father told me about her, I had questions piling up. Looking back, that day feels like it was forever ago. I was safe back then. I had a home back then. Hundreds of my people were still alive. D'andre was alive.

Alcmene may torture me when we get to the castle, but I will never give in to whatever she wants out of me. There's nothing she could offer to make me help her. Not after what she's done.

We travel up the hills through the heat of the morning. My legs ache and scream for rest. I know I can't give in. Alcmene still looks as confident as ever, but she fidgets with her dagger as we walk. She's always messing with something, whether it be her dagger, backpack straps, nails, or anything else she can find. She's restless, but she tries not to show it.

Eventually, after a day's walk, we hit more woods. We keep walking and I struggle to keep pace with her. It starts to rain. Hard. Not only that, but a booming thunder strikes around us, and flashes of lightning fill the sky. It's dark out, even though it's only the afternoon. There's no point in trying to take cover from the rain. I'm already soaked in a matter of seconds.

It's only stormed a few times in my life at the Defender's side of the land. And when it did storm, it was short-lived. It rained occasionally, but never this hard. Because of that, our people had to travel long distances for water, sometimes even braving the dead parts of land.

Alcmene doesn't seem at all phased by the rain or loud jolts of thunder. I jump every time I hear it, but she continues walking like her ears are attuned to the noise. She lets the rain soak her. In fact she seems to flourish in it. She walks faster than before, still making no sound in the woods. She never snaps a twig.

"At our castle we have many sewers and a moat, trapping water or sending it underground rather than letting it flood the place. It never really *stops* raining around here." I barely hear her over the sounds of the storm, but I think I see a small smile run over her face as she looks up into the rain. Her smile transforms her face. It's the first smile I've seen on her that isn't evil or sarcastic. Her dark hair is even darker from the rain, and small rivulets of water drip down her face. I notice her clothing clinging to her curves, and as I feel my cheeks burn, I turn away.

Soon, after almost drowning to death, we reach the castle, or rather multiple castles. A huge black castle sits in the middle of two smaller ones. A huge arched window near the top reveals what I'm guessing is some sort of throne room. I think of my drawing, which wasn't too far off. Lanterns hanging on the walls allow me to see the lit-up structure among the dark sky. A gigantic moat surrounds the castle, collecting the pouring rainwater. A bridge goes across it, and guards stand at the entrance, holding sharp swords by their sides. I count at least ten of them at the bridge, and I can make out more by the castle doors. They all stare straight ahead, letting the rain pelt them like it's nothing. The two smaller castles have no guards, and are a quarter the size of the main one. I wonder why they're even there at all.

We walk across the bridge, and my heart pounds in my chest. I feel like I'm going to pass out. I couldn't escape in the wilderness, but now I have no chance. This is Alcmene's home. She'll know every inch of the place. There is no way I'll be able to get out. I'll die here, and I know no one will come after me. Austin will try, but he'll know he won't make it alone. My father won't sacrifice any of our people for me, as much as he loves me. Eventually, I'll be forgotten. Another corpse in the war among thousands. I begin to look around frantically, trying to come up with any way to escape before we go inside. But with my hands tied and guards surrounding us, I know there's no way out. Alcmene sees my distress.

"Don't worry," she laughs. "You're going to have the time of your life in my dungeon." I stiffen.

When we get up to the guards at the castle doors, they all bow in unison to Alcmene. Their heads bow so low that their hair skims the wet ground. She smirks slightly. I think back to one of the conversations I had with my father. I wondered why anyone would want power. Maybe Alcmene wants it just because she loves people conforming to her. She loves being bowed to and treated like the queen of the world.

She mutters a few words to one of the guards, which I don't hear while I'm lost in my growing fear and paranoia. Alcmene pulls me inside, and the gray doors slowly close behind us. Her grip on my wrist is firm, and her nails dig into my skin again. There's no going back now.

Chapter twenty-eight

ALCMENE

After a lot of protest, I leave Ember in the cellar behind bars. I know I can't torture her too much, because my end goal is for her to stay on my side. I am certain that I wasn't imagining it when I saw Ember's eyes change on the battlefield a while ago. Her power came out when she was dreaming last night. Black, wispy smoke rose out of her hands right before she startled awake. I should have been terrified when I saw it. But I wasn't. I was fascinated by what she was capable of. The power Ember holds is dark but beautiful. The smoke reminded me of the forest, dark and deadly but comforting in a unique way. What I don't understand is why Ember's eyes were black when using her power, while Levi's were white.

I walk into the throne room, change out of my drenched clothes, and lay my knives as well as my bag out on my table. I will have to organize everything eventually, but not now. I couldn't let Ember see any sign of weakness, but that walk was rough. All I want to do now is sleep.

Right before I blow my candles out, my door flings open and Amara storms in.

"You have no right to barge in here." I keep my voice calm, but I'm filled with rage.

"She's here, isn't she?" I know she's asking about Ember.

"Ember was deposited in the dungeon, yes. How does that concern you?"

Amara is terrible at hiding her emotions. Maybe she's not even trying. She had the same look in her eyes when I told her I wanted to make Ember my second. She's jealous.

She doesn't say anything; just stares at me with a telling glare.

I sigh. "I know you want to be my second. But you can't have everything, Amara." By the look on her face, my words hurt her more than I intended. But I can't deal with her right now. I just want to sleep the rest of the night away.

"I don't understand. Why would you want a Defender who wants you dead as your second in command? It doesn't make any sense," she fumes.

I rub my hands over my eyes. I'm too tired to dodge her questions. At this point, I don't see the harm in being honest with her.

"Ember has a power. I don't know everything about it yet, but if it's as strong as I think it is, it could turn the tide in the war if she joins us."

She scoffs in disbelief. "You think that random Defender has some sort of super power? Have you lost your mind?" She laughs and begins to leave the room. She never knew of Levi's abilities, so I can understand why she thinks this is crazy.

I grab her arm as she nears the doorway. She spins back around, drawing closer to me.

"I saw it during the battle." I say.

Amara looks into my eyes, trying to tell if I'm actually being serious. She touches my hand still on her arm, and sighs. "She'll never join us, Alcmene. Not after all you did."

"I know it will be hard. Almost impossible. But I have to try." I instinctively think of asking for Amara's help. I used to depend on her when we were younger. But times have changed since then.

She moves away from me. "Even if she does have some ridiculous power, it doesn't mean she's worthy of being your second," she argues.

"She is the *only* one who's worthy enough," I counter.

Amara's gaze turns dark. "I thought *I* was worthy. I meant it when I told you I wouldn't abandon you again! But you just don't seem to understand that!" she raises her voice. When she said she'd stay from now on, I almost believed it. But why would she stay for any reason other than to gain power and become my second? She's lying, and I'm so sick of it.

"I know why you're acting like you care. You're just using me because you want power. You want a spot standing by my throne. If you weren't using me, you would have shown up when I needed you! For years, I was alone! You said it was because of the grief from losing your brother, but I don't believe it!" I yell back.

"I'm not using you for power. That's not why I came back. And that is not what I want." Her voice is quiet now, and she looks into my eyes, her gaze softening. She places her hand on the back of my neck. I have the slight urge to lean into her touch, but I don't do it. I'm still furious with her.

"I care because I-" she stops mid-sentence, suddenly unable to speak. I think I see her gaze flicker to my lips, but it's so subtle I can't tell. She looks away from me, taking a deep breath. "I have to go." She drops her hand and quickly leaves the room.

Somehow, after all of my doubt, I believe her. All my life, I thought that anyone who wanted to get close to me was only using me. But with Amara, I know it's different, as hard as it is to admit it. I run my hand along my neck, where Amara's soft hand was a minute ago. I can't allow things to return to how they used to be. I've changed since the days Amara and I were best friends. More than friends. This will only end badly.

The storm brews outside the large throne room window. In a way, I kind of missed it when I was at the Defender's side. The storm always reminds me of home. I look at the large blood stain on the floor, where my father took his final breath. I remind myself that this castle isn't home anymore, not without Leviathan. I walk out of the room.

I wake up the next day, still feeling exhausted and sore from the hike here. My conversation with Amara clouds my mind. I probably would have made Amara my second if I never saw Ember's eyes change during the battle. For a brief moment, I feel a twinge of guilt. I shouldn't have acted the way I did over Amara's jealousy. It only hurt her more. But the feeling quickly washes away, and my usual anger and need for revenge replace it. Having Ember here gets me one step closer to fully avenging Levi by winning this war.

I just need to convince her to join me. Somehow. It seems like it will be an impossible task. How will she ever listen to me when every time she sees me, it looks like she wants to rip my throat out? It will be hard to accomplish, maybe the hardest thing I've ever attempted. But with Levi on my mind, I head down to the cellar.

I find Ember sitting against the wall at the back of her cell. Unlike her father, she isn't standing at the bars, but unlike other Defenders, she isn't cowering in the corner. She looks up at me as I enter, exhaustion drawing dark circles under her green eyes. Her clothes are dry now, but she still looks as miserable as she did on the walk here. No surprise.

"What do you want?" she chokes out, her voice rough and barely above a whisper.

I grasp the bars between us. Ember slowly gets up and moves a little closer to me. She isn't afraid, although she should be. Even the other Fighters cower in fear when I'm near. They know I killed my own father, and some believe I killed my brother too. The power I now hold is something new. Fighters have always been terrified of my father, but it's on an even higher level for me. I've never seen the Fighters so scared before. I have more influence and power than my father ever did, in only a short time. With Ember by my side, we would be unstoppable. We would win the war; most importantly, Levi would be proud.

"I want information," I tell her. I won't tell her that I know about her power just yet. I want her to think I'm clueless in the matter. Everything I do is for a reason, and this is the same.

"Why do you think I'd give you any?"

"You have no choice, darling." She clenches her jaw at the nickname. I almost laugh, but I hold it in. It's so easy to make her mad.

Too easy. “Remember, while you’re locked in a cell, I’m roaming free. I could easily send my people to attack your father and your little friend Austin.”

Her gaze darkens at the mention of Austin. “You wouldn’t. You would just lose again.”

A wicked smile spreads across my lips. “That’s where you're wrong. I am personally training each and every Fighter. Your new camp will fall in a matter of minutes.”

She looks away from me towards the floor. She takes a shallow breath. I can tell she is thinking about her people being slaughtered as her eyes begin to water.

“I’ll give you whatever information you want. Just don’t attack them.” That was easy.

Ember looks up at me. I take my obsidian dagger out of my holster. She instantly steps back from the metal bars.

“I’m guessing you won’t trust my word alone,” I tell her, holding the dagger up. She casts me a wary glance and furrows her brows. “A blood oath,” I say. “I won’t attack your people if you give me everything I want from you.”

She looks away from me, thinking. “What about after?”

“We’re at war, darling. I won’t promise to never kill your people. But at least you know they will be fine while you're incapacitated. And who knows, maybe in the meantime they will attack us *themselves.*” I smile at the ludicrous thought. Ember’s eyes widen. Something I said caught her attention.

“A blood oath has magic laced inside the origin. Breaking this oath will poison you from the inside out.” She laughs lightly, as if she doesn’t believe me. I smile. “I've seen it myself. It starts with your skin. It slowly peels away, little by little. Around your eyes first, then through your body, cutting deeper and deeper. Then the burning starts, and the smell of cooking flesh…" I'm about to go on when Ember stops me.

"I've heard enough. I believe you. I won't break the oath."

"Good."

I hold out my hand, and slice my knife in a diagonal line across my pale skin. As the knife pierces my flesh, a stinging pain runs through me, but I don't let it show. I try not to think about my father cutting my face years ago. A small line of blood flows out of my open wound. Ember steps closer and allows me to do the same to her, wincing as I slice her skin.

I press my hand to hers. She tenses at the contact. Our blood mixes together, and I start to feel a burning pain in my hand. I can tell it's not from the knife wound. The small cut is nothing but a dull ache. This pain is much, much worse. A smell rushes to my nostrils. Burning flesh. I rip my hand away as I hear my skin sizzle like cooking meat. I stare down at my hand, the flesh charred and flaky. Red welts start to appear on the surface of my skin.

"What the hell did you do to me?" I usually keep my voice as calm as possible, but I can't stop myself from raising it this time. Did she just use her power?

She looks at her unscathed hand with her eyes wide and mouth open in shock or fear. "I-I don't know." She stumbles away from me, near the back of the cell. I look down at my burnt hand, still feeling as though it's in a pool of lava. As far as I know, Levi's blood didn't do anything like this. It didn't do anything at all. His power was only his strength. Maybe hers is something through her blood? Something that burns people? Then what was the black smoke from earlier? I read her expression. She is just as shocked as I am, if not more. She has no idea how much power she may hold at her fingertips. Or in her blood.

My mother used to tell me stories about magic. She read books from the castle's library and claimed that some were true. She said there are two different kinds of magic. Light magic runs through the green part of the world, keeping it safe from the radiation. Keeping the flowers in the meadows blooming even with no sun. Light magic is good and generally safe. But dark magic is another story. It's the opposite. Rare but monstrous. It poisons and kills people. It can easily spiral out of control. I never really believed the stories she told me, as they were merely fairytales, something of children's imaginations. But after seeing my brother's power with my own eyes, it doesn't seem so far-fetched. Maybe Levi had light magic, as his eyes were white, and he only used his power to protect me. But that means Ember's magic may be dark. Horrifying. But is Ember truly evil? She must be to possess that kind of power. If she really has it, she belongs on this side of the war, ruling by me as my second. But what if she can't control it and kills us all?

Chapter twenty-nine

EMBER

Alcmene leaves the room as quickly as she came. I'm left alone, wondering what I just did. Alcmene's hand was left burned and red. Mine, however, is fine besides the cut from the blood oath. I sit against the wall at the back of my cell. I already miss sunlight. I haven't had anything to eat or drink in a couple of days. Maybe Alcmene will forget to feed me, and by the time she comes back, I'll be a rotting corpse.

I rip off a piece of my pant leg to wrap around my bleeding hand. I feel like throwing up when I remember I made an oath with the enemy and that her blood is now mixed with mine. It didn't feel like I had a choice, yet I still feel sick about it. But now that Alcmene and I have made an agreement, one that is unbreakable, I have to get her to trust me. Once she does, *if* she does, I will be able to kill her without sending hundreds of Defenders into battle. I have to be smart about this. I have to do anything and everything I can to convince her to let me out of this cell. Only then will I have the chance to bury a knife into her throat. When her blood spills, everything will end.

Doubts swim through my mind like endless waves. What if she never lets me out of this prison? What if she gets her answers out of me right away, then kills me before I have the chance to get my hands on a weapon? I look at my hands. My blood burned Alcmene somehow. I may not need a weapon at all. But she'll be wary of me now. There's no way I'll be able to get close enough to her to attack her with my blood. I think of the scar on Alcmene's face. Someone managed to get close to her before, so it can't be impossible. I just don't know where to start. How to get her to trust me.

I cringe at the thought of dying here all alone. If my plan doesn't work, I can only hope that Austin and my father will follow up with the attack I planned before I was captured. But that plan relied heavily on me. I was supposed to slip through the castle's passageways and kill Alcmene, with a few other Defenders as back-up. Without me, they don't have a shot at killing her. My father could step up and take my position in the plan, but I don't think he would leave our people and risk not returning. There is no way The Council would let him.

I look over to the empty, cold cell beside me. Blood stains the floor. Does that blood belong to my father? He was here for days, tortured and manipulated. I can only imagine how bad it was for him. I imagine him taking the beatings silently, never daring to give up whatever Alcmene wanted to know. Things have changed so suddenly. Now my father is back home, and I'm the one in a cage.

I feel like crying. Or slamming my fists against the wall until they bleed and break. If Austin and I never went to the pond the night Alcmene took me, she may never have gotten to me. But since I didn't worry about the danger of leaving camp at night, I was captured and Austin was left alone. No-not alone. He has his family. I just hope they will be able to protect him if need be. I need to kill Alcmene and find my way back to him. She will attack, maybe not now, but sooner than later, and it will be my fault if he dies. Not just him, but everyone. The blood of all the Defenders will be on my hands if I can't kill Alcmene.

I sit in the darkness, completely still. Time goes by, but I don't know how fast. Without the sun in the sky or the stars to guide me, the emptiness and darkness of this room makes it feel like time warps together into nothingness. I know I'll go mad if I spend a lot of time here. Seconds, minutes, hours go by, and Alcmene finally returns. She still doesn't have food or water with her. My lips are so dry they're cracking.

Alcmene somehow looks angrier than usual. I didn't think that was possible. Something must have happened in the time she was gone. Hoping that talking to her will eventually get her to trust me more, I decide to ask about it. Shockingly, she tells me.

"A Fighter, Amara. She's angry that you're here." She says nothing more. I wonder why a random Fighter is upset about my presence. I thought all of the Fighters would be glad that I'm behind bars. But I don't ask. I'm sure she wouldn't tell me any more than what was already said, and I don't want to push my limits.

"Now that the oath is sealed, you have to give me information on whatever I ask." Alcmene takes a seat in a metal chair across from my cell. Usually, she stands, trying to provoke me. Maybe she's realized it won't work. I move closer to the bars.

"Obviously, you're good at combat. Tell me about that. How you grew up learning to fight." I find it weird that she wants to know my backstory. I figured she would ask me questions about Defender battle plans or something of the sort. But I don't refuse. I clear my scratchy throat and do my best to make my voice heard.

"I started training at age twelve. I was taught by a man named D'andre." It hurts to say his name aloud. It hurts even more to look into the eyes of the woman responsible for his death. I debate telling her D'andre used to be a Fighter. I decide against it. She listens without interrupting me. As usual, she has something to keep her occupied. She sharpens her purple-bladed dagger as I speak. I try to remain calm, but every time I see that dagger, I think of the people she's killed with it. How she laughed like it was fun when she murdered so many Defenders.

"He taught me everything I know. And when he died..." I can't seem to continue.

"When he died, what?" She stops sharpening her blade.

I say nothing. I can't take my eyes off the dagger in her hands. She notices.

"I'm assuming I killed this man."

I tense up. "Not directly, but yes. The explosion killed him." I think of the shard of metal lodged in D'andre's stomach. The smell of his blood. Alcmene looks at me. I see no remorse in her brown eyes. I wasn't expecting any, but it still hurts when I find none.

"Why did you do it? Why did you kill my people, laughing while you took their lives?" She looks down at her dagger like it somehow has the answer. She has the same wounded look on her face that she carried when she gazed at the stars on the journey here.

"I don't have to answer your questions. That's your job," she says, with venom in her voice.

"Aren't oaths a two-way street?" I exclaim, gripping the bars.

She seems surprised by my question, before her usual snarkiness conceals her expression. "Yes. Technically they are." She looks down at her dagger again, then back at me. She holsters it and stands up, moving right up to the bars between us. She brushes her black hair away from her face. "I started ruling the Fighters for power, of course. My father held the throne, and I wanted it. So, I took the throne and the power that came with it. I sent my Fighters out to attack the minute I became the ruler. Then I killed hundreds of your people." She smirks, like she's taking pleasure in the lives she's ended. "I won't say I didn't enjoy killing them."

"So power is all you want?" It seems hard to believe.

"Power is all anyone wants. You can't tell me you wouldn't want hundreds of people obeying your commands, bowing at your feet, serving you. Worshiping you."

I don't say anything, but as I look into her eyes, I see pain in them. She's hiding something. There's more to Alcmene than meets the eye.

She sits back down quickly. "Tell me more about you."

I explain how I was a fast learner in training. I excelled quickly. She asks about Austin, and I tell her how D'andre let me train him. After his death, I felt like I had to be the new trainer for everyone.

She keeps asking me questions about my family. I don't know why. It seems to be completely irrelevant. But knowing her, she must have some kind of ulterior motive. After all, I need her to trust me as much as possible, so I tell her what she wants to know.

"Your father. Is he the only one you have?" I try to hold my anger back. The Fighters are why he is the only one I have left.

"Yes," I say through gritted teeth. She nods. I wonder what family Alcmene has left now that she killed her own father. Is there anyone left? Silence fills the room as she thinks of something else to ask me.

"I saw you during the battle. You almost killed one of my people when they weren't fighting back. That's not what Defenders do, right? They capture, they protect." The sound of her voice is like a pounding in my head. Every time she speaks, she reminds me of a snake. She's trying to get to me, through my family, through my values. She's manipulative. Poisonous. Just like my father said she would be when he first told me about her. I don't respond to her nagging question.

Alcmene stands up again, forcefully grabbing the bars between us, her knuckles turning white. "If that boy didn't stop you, would you have killed that Fighter?" she asks, anger rising in her voice.

I don't answer. I have been wondering the same thing since that day. Austin pulled me away, stopping me from almost ending a life and betraying everything Defenders believe in.

"Would you?" She grips the bars even tighter. She could come in and torture me right now. I know she has the key. But she doesn't. She keeps distance between us willingly. Why? There are so many questions I have about her. So many are unanswered.

"I don't know!" I shout. I tear my gaze away from her and try to drown out the sound of her voice. I would have killed that Fighter. I *know* I would've. By the look on her face, she knows I would have, too.

"You're just like me. Only you haven't realized it yet." Her voice returns to its normal cadence. Smooth and calm, like nothing she does matters to her.

I back away from her. As far away as I can get. I can't hold in my anger anymore.

"I am nothing like you! You murdered countless Defenders, and for what? For power? How is that an excuse?" She doesn't react. She must have been expecting me to yell. She always knows my next move. It's like she can get into my head and see what I'll say or do next before I do it.

"You killed people I loved! You are responsible for the deaths of my mother and sister! You even killed your own father! What is wrong with you?" Her slight smirk drops when I mention her father, but other than that she doesn't move or speak.

I step closer to her again. Her eyes never leave mine. Before I realize she's doing it, she reaches into my cell and grabs my hands, digging her nails into the backs of them. She pulls me towards her, and my head slams into the metal bars. I try to jerk away from her grasp as blood drips into my eye, but she doesn't let go. I wince as her nails pierce my skin, and drops of my blood fall to the floor. My head aches.

"My father deserved to die. More than anyone." Her voice is practically a whisper, and she digs her nails deeper into my skin as she speaks. I try not to let the pain show on my face. In an instant, she lets go and walks up the stairs without saying another word.

I wipe the blood off my hands, and the blood falling from a new wound above my eyebrow. I sit against the wall at the back of my cell. I inspect the gash on my palm from our blood oath. It will definitely leave a scar. If I do make it out of here alive, the scar will forever remind me of this place. And of *her*.

Although my encounter with Alcmene has left me starving and bloody, I smile knowing I've found a weak spot. Her father.

Chapter thirty

ALCMENE

I race upstairs, slamming the door behind me. I look outside my window. I can just make out the setting sun between the storm. I haven't slept in days, preoccupied with Ember's arrival and Amara's jealousy. Training has kept me up as well. Even though I don't really need training anymore, it helps keep my mind off things. Things like my father and Leviathan. Even my mother. They're all among the stars now. My whole family. Dead in the span of a few weeks.

I lie in my bed, trying to let sleep take me. I close my eyes, trying to drown out my endless thoughts. My dead family members always keep me up at night, but now something new haunts me. *Ember*. If she figures out how to bend her magic to her will and escape, I will be doomed along with the rest of my people. But if she doesn't, she is the key to winning this war. I know she has a darkness deep inside her. One can only wield dark magic if they have darkness within. She almost killed a Fighter who was begging for mercy. She wanted revenge for all the lives I took, by taking a life herself. A part of me wishes she went through with it, so she could see the darkness she holds. In a way, Ember and I are the same. We both have darkness inside us, swimming through our veins. The only difference is, I'm not afraid to let it out.

After hours of restlessness, I finally drift off into a short sleep.

The storm is still outside when I wake up, although it's not as bad. I send one of my guards down with food and water for Ember. I don't want her to die, but I'm also not going to give her food every day.

I look down at my burnt hand. It's no better than yesterday. The skin is peeling and red. I wrap a bandage around my blistered skin and the cut from the blood oath. I head down to the training room, procrastinating seeing Ember after yesterday. She brought up my father, which impacted me in a way I never thought it would again. I wasn't upset over the fact that I killed him, I was upset because of why I had to. Levi. He was always the reason for my happiness, and now the reason for my pain.

When I get to the training room, the room immediately clears. I smile. Being alone during training is one of the very few things I like about being the ruler of the Fighters. The thing I hate the most is being treated so differently from everyone else. Except by Amara. She never treats me like I'm some prized possession. But after we argued over Ember's arrival a couple days ago, I haven't seen her since.

I approach the target practice line on one side of the training room. At the end, there are six targets of different sizes. To my left is the biggest target, and the smallest all the way to the right. Black circles line the wood, framing one red circle in the middle.

I take out six throwing knives, laying them on a small table beside me. I hold the first one by the blade, lining up my shot with the largest target. I count my breaths, and on the second, I release the knife and propel it forward. It lands perfectly in the middle of the bullseye. Too easy. The rest of the shots are the same. Training is as simple as ever.

I think for a minute while collecting my throwing knives. If I end up convincing Ember to join me somehow, and she learns to hate me less, she could be like Levi. I could help her with her training like I did for him. And eventually I'd make her my second. I collect my last knife from the smallest target. I sigh, realizing Amara's right. Ember will probably never listen to me, not after everything I've done. And now, instead of spending time in the cellar trying to slowly manipulate and convince her, I'm spending my time here. It's just that when I'm in the cellar with her, my emotions spiral out of control so easily. Usually I'm composed through everything, but no matter what she says, it gets to me somehow. It should be the other way around. After all, she's the one behind bars.

Still procrastinating, I take another hour or two to do some weight training and archery. No Fighters come in to annoy me, which reminds me of something. I haven't gotten around to training my people yet. They are still as pathetic at fighting as the Defenders. I rush out of the room and command my guards to gather everyone in the throne room. As I take my place on my throne, a crowd forms. I find myself absently looking for Amara in the mess of people. I scan through the Fighters multiple times, but even from my high vantage point, I don't see her. I try not to let my disappointment show. One argument, and she disappears again. I should have expected it.

Everyone bows to me, and the chatter stops when I start to speak.

"Our last attack on the Defenders was…" I try to find the right word. "Unfortunate." I pause. "We lost many, and all we got out of it was the fall of their castle." I leave out the part about capturing Ember. That was our biggest win out of everything, if she holds the dark magic I believe she does. But I don't want everyone to know about her just yet.

"We didn't win the battle. But next time, we will win the battle, then the *war*." I don't have to raise my voice very high to be heard. Everyone listens intently, capturing my every word. My confidence radiates throughout the room. I find my guards standing up straighter.

"I will start training outside. I will make a schedule, training around a hundred Fighters at a time, switching daily. I know Anwir slacked on your training, and it has made you all weak. Weakness won't cut it any more." I glare at a few Fighters. "Once I'm through with everyone, you will all be ready to help me win this war."

The Fighter's nod, a couple brave ones thank me, and everyone leaves the room.

I make use of the tame storm to walk outside. I head to one of our fire pits, smothered by the rain. Out of the corner of my eye, I see a woman with curly red hair and a tight black vest walk up to me. I feel an ounce of relief.

"Amara, where have you been? I didn't see you at the meeting." I don't mention the fact that I thought she abandoned me again.

"I didn't think you cared where I went." She plops down beside me, so close that our knees touch. Any other Fighter wouldn't dare get this close, but she's not just anyone.

I didn't think I'd care about her as much as I did years ago, but I might care even more now. The feelings I had for her when we were younger never really left. It scares me.

She doesn't tell me why she missed the meeting, so I don't ask. Her eyes show tiredness in them. I'm guessing she hasn't been sleeping well, either. Amara stares out at the firepit, the one she burned her brother's body in.

"I still think about him. It doesn't hurt as much as it used to, but it'll always affect me," she says. I nod, but it doesn't feel like the pain of losing Levi will ever get better.

"Why did he kill himself?" I ask her, hoping the invasive question won't turn her away. I've never known why he did it.

"He seemed happy all his life, but a few months before he ended it, something was off about him. He distanced himself from me entirely, and when I did see him, he acted so differently. Cruel, even. I don't know exactly what happened. If something triggered his sudden behavior or if he had been hiding it all his life. All I know is that I shouldn't have let him get to that point. I should have tried to understand and help him more before he died, but I was too late." Her face is blank, and for once, I can't tell what she's feeling.

I look at the firepit, too. The memory of burning my brother will always be scarred into my brain. Just like the memory of him bleeding out in front of me.

I know Amara's mother is still alive. She must have been there during his burning ceremony, helping Amara to ease the pain of his passing. I didn't have that luxury.

Amara sees the pain in my eyes and touches my hand, slowly interlacing our fingers. I don't pull away, but I feel heat on my face. She chuckles.

"How is your mother?" The question comes out of my mouth randomly. The last time I saw Nyla, three years ago, she looked sickly. Before my father's time on the throne, Nyla used to be the ruler of the Fighters. She was the only ruler to ever step down willingly. Usually, rulers get taken off the throne by dying or fighting to the death for their place of power against a Fighter who challenges them. Nyla stepped down when Amara was an infant, but Amara never really knew why. She said her mother was always very secretive about it. Anwir only got the position because he won a battle against other Fighters for it.

"She's worse. I'm surprised she's still alive, to be honest. She's been sick for years." Her expression turns cold. I know she's always had a complicated relationship with her mother, but I never learned all the details.

I decide to change the topic.

"I'm sorry about your brother." I squeeze her hand lightly. Saying sorry has never come easy to me, but saying it this time, I mean it.

"I'm sorry about yours. And I'm sorry for leaving you and for acting so insane about Ember's arrival and her supposed power."

"That's a lot of things to apologize for." I laugh, letting go of her hand. We sit in comfortable silence for a minute before she speaks.

“Obviously, I wasn’t at the meeting, but I heard you’re going to be training the Fighters. That’s a hard job to do alone,” she says.

“Why? Do you want to help train them?” I joke, but she takes it seriously.

“If you’d have me.” I look away, thinking. I know Amara is a skilled Fighter. She made it out of the last battle alive, which I can't say for a lot of the other Fighters. And she's better than me with a bow and arrow. She could teach the Fighters a thing or two.

"I don't see why not.” I say. She smiles. At least it will take some of the weight off my shoulders. Hopefully it’ll get me out of training the Fighters every day. And it will give me more time to convince Ember to join me. I’ll need all the time in the world.

Chapter thirty-one

EMBER

Alcmene hasn't come down to the cellar in at least two days. It's hard to keep track of time, but that's my best guess. I haven't been given food since then, and only a small amount of water. I look down at my hands, pale and dry. The long, diagonal cut along my palm reminds me of my plan to end this. But killing Alcmene feels like a far-off dream. She will always be one step ahead of me.

I haven't seen the black smoke come out of my hands again since the day of the battle. It makes me wonder if it's all in my imagination. But the burn on Alcmene's hand from my blood makes me think otherwise. She claims she needs me for information, but what can she possibly get out of me? There must be something else she wants. I know she doesn't want power. The look on her face when she said it indicated a lie. She wants something from me that only I can give. She released my father for me. Surely that means something. I look down at my hands again. Does she know about the smoke? Has she figured it out from my burning blood?

I sit idly up against the wall for a while, trying to get some sleep. When I finally start to drift away, Alcmene comes in with food and water on a silver tray. My stomach grumbles. When she gets closer I can see the food; It's a small amount of mush, which appears to be oatmeal. I guess it's better than nothing. She says nothing but digs the key to my cell out of her pocket. That is when I get an idea. Turning away from her, I reopen the wound on my hand, ignoring searing pain as my blood resurfaces.

This may be my only chance. With the lack of food and sunlight, I'll never survive at this rate. I need to get out of here. This needs to work. I feel my chest tighten in anticipation as I conceal my hand from Alcmene when she walks into my cell. I try not to let my blood drip to the floor. As she goes to set the food down, I rush up to her, aiming my bloody hand toward her throat. Without glancing behind her, she throws me to the floor in one quick motion. Hard. I feel my breath rip away from my lungs, and I gasp for air.

"Nice try." Alcmene drops the food, and some of the oatmeal splatters off the tray from the impact on the floor. She sees me lying on my back, struggling to breathe. She notices the blood on my hand. "You're a complete idiot if you ever think I'd let you burn me with that." She starts to walk away before I speak.

"You said you need me for information, but I know that isn't true. There's no information on the Defenders that you don't already have. What do you really want from me?" I sit up, feeling a little lightheaded from my crash to the floor.

"Haven't you figured it out already?" She turns to me, grinning with an evil look in her eyes. I stand up, backing away from her. "You know your blood burns other people on contact. But that's not the only thing you can do, is it?" She stares into my eyes, knowing I'm holding something back. "I saw your eyes turn black at the battle. I saw smoke come out of your hands. You have a power."

I back into the wall. I could deny it. I could say that she was imagining everything she saw. She was angry and desperate at the battle. I could tell her that what she saw was all in her head. But I know that will never work.

Alcmene steps closer to me, her eyes never leaving mine. I can't move.

"I've seen something like this before. I can show you how to use it. How to control it. But if you ever want control, you need to join me."

I scoff. "Join *you*?" I laugh at the absurdity. "I'd rather die."

Alcmene chuckles, expecting my response. She lays a hand on my cheek. My cell door is open. I could run up the stairs and flee the castle. I could run back home and forget this power exists. But it would be impossible. Alcmene would catch me before I make it two steps, and even if she didn't, guards are everywhere, and I have no weapon. Instead of trying to escape, I freeze, giving in to her touch. I can't win. Even with my blood still smeared on my hand, I'm no match for her.

"Don't lie to yourself anymore, darling. You want to kill, I know you do. We're the same, you and I." Her voice is almost a whisper. I hear the manipulation in it.

I flashback to when my power first came out of my hands. The moment when I almost killed a Fighter. My hands start to shake, just as they did when I held my dagger to the helpless Fighter's throat.

"I told you, I'm nothing like you!" I look down at my hands, my blood capable of burning someone else. I can hurt someone with a simple touch. *I am just like her*-no. I can't be. I won't be.

"Join me," she says again, staring into my eyes, holding me in place.

"I can't!" I yell as I move away from her. I feel the pain in my eyes return, and a heaviness fills the room. Just like I felt on the day of the battle. What is happening to me?

I can just make out a wicked smile on Alcmene's face before my vision turns darker and the smoke on my hands appears. Now it feels like I'm the one being burned, but from the inside out. It feels like someone has lit a match in my stomach. Heat rises up, spreading throughout my entire body. My eyes burn so badly that I can't stop my tears from flowing out. The pitch-black smoke stings. My hands face palms up, the smoke rising a few inches like a dark cloud. I don't know how to control it or make it stop. I think of trying to attack Alcmene. Maybe now I'll have the chance to win, even through this horrible pain. But before I can do anything, something hard hits my head, and I black out.

My eyes slowly drift open. I don't know how long I was out, but everything I felt before is gone, replaced by a cloudiness in my head.

Unable to move, I look down to find myself restrained with all kinds of ropes and knots to a metal chair in my cell. Alcmene stands before me, lifting my chin to meet her eyes. Her hands are cold, and I worry she'll wrap them around my throat.

"I told you, darling. You need me." She lets my head drop. She stands in front of me with her purple-bladed dagger tight in her grip. "You said you *couldn't* join me. Not that you don't *want* to." I feel her knife graze over my skin. I can't join her. I would be betraying everything I stand for. But something in me, something deep, wants me to join. She could help me learn how to control and use my power. She is the *only* one who can. No. I can't think like that. Why am I? My mind is spinning, and a thrumming sound hums like voices arguing over my fate. What is happening to me? The cloudy feeling in my head intensifies. My eyes blur when I try to focus. My breathing is inconsistent and I worry it will never go back to normal. Is it my power making me feel this way?

Alcmene looks at my face with a knowing glare. She must know why it feels like I'm not in control of my own mind. After all, she said she knows something about the power inside of me. And now that I'm confused and vulnerable, she's using me. Manipulating me. I feel drained. Almost as exhausted as I was after we hiked for days to get here. I picture my father and Austin back at the base, waiting for me. Hoping I'm alive. But the image is obscured by a shadow. Darkness blurs my old life, as well as Alcmene's eyes staring into mine. A part of me wants to stay here. The shadow. I can hardly tell what's real and what isn't. What my power is making me believe, and what is truly reality.

Alcmene sits down in a chair across from me.

"If you join me, I will teach you everything I know about your power. I will even make you my second." She pauses. "Without me, your power will spiral out of control. You'll be a harm not only to yourself but everyone you love." She's right. If I somehow make it home and hurt everyone, I will never forgive myself.

My mind continues playing tricks on me. Stay here, in the hands of the woman who ruined my life. Leave, and suffer the consequences of my power. But would I be happier? I can't decide. Not now. It feels like every decision is the wrong one. If I join her, what would it entail? What would she make me do? Alcmene touches me. Her dagger is gone, replaced by her soft hand on my face. The warmth of her touch confuses me further. She runs a finger along the cut on my forehead, a slight smile on her face. Too much is happening all at once.

"No matter what you say, your oath keeps you here until you tell me everything I need to know."

I close my eyes, fighting whatever is happening in my thoughts. I try my best to think clearly. Alcmene moves her hand away, and somehow, it allows me to see past the darkness. Whatever this power is inside me, it's changing me. I have to fight back. If I stay, it sounds like she will let me out of this cell. She will help me train my power, and once I have enough control, I'll use it against her. This is everything I have been hoping for. If I kill her, I can finally go home and live in peace with Austin and my father. No more war. No more death. I imagine my mother painting flowers on the walls of our castle before it was destroyed. If I end this, even if it involves bloodshed, she would be proud. I open my eyes to see Alcmene's piercing stare. No oath ties me to my next words.

"I'll join you."

Part two

THE OTHER SIDE

Chapter thirty-two
ALCMENE

I have finally made some progress. Although I know she was not being completely sincere, Ember has agreed to join me. I could see her struggling with her own mind. Her dark magic was fighting against her, changing her thoughts. Soon, her mind will be plagued with darkness if she doesn't learn to fight it off. And I hope she doesn't. Darkness belongs on our side.

I get to sleep easily for once, not worrying about Ember anymore. Once the magic controls her mind, she will be among the Fighters. Permanently.

When I wake up, I groan when I remember I have to train the Fighters. My father stopped training them after a while, claiming he was above it. One of the Fighters has been training the rest, but they still aren't good enough. At least not good enough to win. Now I have to do something about it. I look at my father's sword on the wall of the throne room as I pass by, smiling. Good riddance.

On my way outside, I run into Amara. Her sword is strapped to her back, and she has a few knives at her side. Her red hair is pulled back into a messy bun, revealing her freckled face.

"Fancy seeing you here." She laughs, and we walk outside together.

Luckily, it's only misting, no crazy storm or heavy rain. A hundred Fighters are scattered around, and at my command, they line up. I have to yell to reach the entirety of them, but I have no problem with it. I tell the Fighters to pick up a sword and to begin practicing basic weapon strikes and blocks with another Fighter. After a quick demonstration, they start.

A few Fighters stand out among the rest, easily maneuvering their swords and bodies to strike and block. But as I watch, most of the Fighter's attacks are predictable. They grunt before they throw, or they're slow to the point where the other Fighter has plenty of time to block. Predictability is the fastest way to lose a battle. I sigh.

I feel a hand on my shoulder and turn around to see Amara facing me.

"Instead of people-watching, how about you and I square up?" Her voice is filled with excitement.

"Sure, but when you fall flat on your face in a second, it's your fault for suggesting it." I grin. We decide to fight without our weapons. We drop them and Amara gets into a sparring stance, as do I. "Ready?" I ask, smirking.

"Ready." I charge at her, and she blocks my first strike. Not bad. She throws a few punches, which to my surprise, I don't predict. I dodge her attacks, and send a few of my own. My fist makes contact with her stomach, knocking some of the air out of her as she stumbles backwards. I reach to hit her again, but she blocks and punches me with her free hand on the side of my jaw. It hurts more than I expected it to. I spit a small amount of blood out of my stinging mouth.

"You're not so bad after all," I tell her. Amara smiles briefly, distracting me for another second. I barely dodge another punch.

We continue to fight, and I realize we're almost evenly matched. Almost. But no one is as good as me, and eventually I land a strike that knocks her to the ground. I smile, realizing I've won, but as she falls, she takes me with her. I land on top of her.

"Are you okay?" she asks. I feel her warm breath hit my lips. We are so close. It reminds me of a similar moment from when we were kids. Amara and I used to play outside in the rain when I had time away from my father. One day, she slipped and fell, hitting her head. I ran over to her, worried sick. I thought she was badly hurt, or worse. When I touched her to see if she was still breathing, she popped up to her feet and playfully pushed me to the ground.

"Seriously?" I said as she laughed. I wiped the mud from my face. "I thought you were dead." She laughed even harder.

"I always get back up," she told me.

This moment feels the same. Except now we're older and not exactly the best of friends, but we're still together. I feel heat rise to my cheeks and I quickly get off of her. I look around, hoping none of the other Fighters saw my embarrassment. Amara stands up and brushes the dirt off her clothes.

With a slight flush on her face, she tells me, "You know, If you wanted to be on top of me, you could have just asked." She laughs. I chuckle and look away from her.

We watch the other Fighters train, and Amara and I separate to help them with their form, predictability, and techniques. When

I try to teach one of the Fighters side by side, he shakes so badly it's useless. I guess their fear of me doesn't always work out in my favor.

I look to Amara, who seems to help a woman immensely with her form. I clench my jaw as Amara runs her hands along the Fighter's arms, correcting her. I shouldn't be jealous over Amara touching some random Fighter. Amara doesn't have feelings for me like she used to. We're barely friends. Nothing more.

Soon I silence everyone and end with a statement on what we will do next lesson. With that, the Fighters head back into the castle.

"That wasn't too bad," Amara comments as we walk to the throne room.

"They'll need a ton of work before they're ready for battle. And it doesn't help that they're terrified of me," I say.

Amara laughs. "Would you rather the Fighters think they're on your level?" I glare at her. "That's what I thought." She sets her sword down. "I had fun with you, though." She lets her hair down, allowing it to fall in loose curls in front of her face. She pushes it behind her ears, and I force myself to tear my eyes away.

"I have to get going." I leave Amara and grab food for Ember before going down to the cellar. Now that she's closer to permanently being on my side, I decide bringing her food and water every day isn't too much of a burden. Once the magic digs deeper into her mind, I'll let her out of her cell. But only time will tell how long it'll be until then. I just have to wait.

Ember is standing against the bars, running her fingers in patterns along the metal. She took the braids out of her brown hair, which now runs in waves across her face. She looks exhausted. Why hasn't she been sleeping? What else is there to do in a cell?

I open the door and hand her food: a bowl of fruit and a cup of water. She takes the water from me, gulping down every drop. She eats the fruit quickly like she's worried I'll snatch it away from her.

"You haven't slept lately."

Ember's jaw tightens. "My power is doing something to me," she says.

I suppress a smile. "Tell me every detail about your power that you can think of. Start from the beginning."

She only hesitates for a moment, before telling me about the first time she felt it. At the battle when she was enraged. At the time, she didn't know I saw it all.

Every time Ember mentions the battle, she looks at me with pure hatred in her eyes. I don't blame her. Whenever I see a Defender, they somehow remind me of my father, and my anger rises. Every time I kill one of them, it reminds me that I'm one step closer to avenging Levi. I know I should regret it, but every life I take makes me feel more invigorated and powerful. No one is controlling me anymore.

"Every time I felt my power rising, I felt burning in my body and a heaviness surrounding me, like something was weighing me down but not constricting me. I felt pain in my eyes, and my vision got darker. When the smoke came the last time, it felt like my hands were on fire." It sounds almost exactly like what Levi felt. I wish I could speak to him now. I know he would be so psyched to have someone with a power like him who he could talk to.

"You said you've seen something like this before," she says.

I touch the obsidian dagger at my side. "I have. Someone I knew had a power similar to yours. He didn't have smoke coming out of his hands or blood that burns, but he had increased strength, and his eyes burned. Everything did." I don't mention that he was my brother. I don't want her to know of my past. Amara told me my anger and grief would get better over time, but as this war stretches on, it only seems to get worse. Every day it's like I'm living in the shadow of Levi. I see him everywhere I look. Every time I pick up the dagger he gave me or walk into his bedroom, I think of him bleeding to death. I think of kneeling in his blood, unable to help, unable to stop the bleeding, telling him I loved him as he took his last breath. Ember can't see my weakness.

"Where is he now?"

"Dead," I mumble. *In the stars.* I hope the pain in my eyes doesn't show. Ember doesn't ask me to elaborate, so I keep quiet. I don't want to talk about him. Don't want to think about him. "His power was activated through his anger," I tell her. Levi must have had light magic, which is easier to control than dark. A lot easier. Training Ember will be difficult. I have no idea what I'm getting myself into. "I will look into some books about your type of power and figure out how it can be activated," I tell her. I make a mental note to stop at the library later. I don't remember everything from the books my mother read. I need to find them to gain more knowledge.

"You know what kind of power I have?" she asks, her gaze strong. Shit. I haven't told her about her power having dark roots. I contemplate lying about it, but I know I will have to tell her the truth eventually. She won't be able to control and properly use her magic until she knows what it truly is.

"Yes," I sigh. "I believe that your power is a type of magic. *Dark* magic." She raises her eyebrows.

"What does that mean?" From the look in her eyes, I can tell she already knows.

"You have a darkness inside you, and your magic stems from that. I know you don't want to believe it, but you really are one of us." Ember shakes her head.

"I'm not one of you." Her words come out in a whisper so soft I can hardly hear them. She doesn't want to believe it but must know it's true.

"We already went over this when you agreed to join me. Admit it to yourself, Ember. You have an evil inside of you. Admit it!" I see the same look in Ember's eyes from yesterday. She's fighting the dark magic in her head. She closes her eyes, and I know she's desperately trying to drown everything out. I step closer to her until we're inches away. I hold her face in my hands as she opens her eyes. She tries to move away, but I don't let her. "Admit it," I say, softer this time.

"There is something dark inside me. But I don't want it to control me. It can't." She looks into my eyes, and for the first time, she almost looks afraid.

"You have to learn to control it. Not the other way around. And to start, you need to embrace your magic. It's who you are."

She moves her head away from my grasp, and I let her go.

A single tear rolls down Ember's cheek before she quickly wipes it away.

"I want to go to the library with you. I need to know more about this magic that's inside me."

I decide Ember has a low likelihood of trying to escape, so I take her.

Chapter thirty-three

ALCMENE

Before stopping at the library, I have a guard drop Ember off at the lake nearby to wash up. She's been locked in a cell for weeks, and now that she isn't actively trying to kill me, I decide letting her bathe won't hurt. When she returns, she braids her damp hair into two plaits that fall in front of her shoulders. I catch her eyeing her dagger at my side, and I almost want to give it to her. It clearly means something to her, like Leviathan's dagger to me. I want to know who gave it to her. In fact, I want to ask her a million questions. Before we leave, I give her a Fighter uniform, since her old clothes are torn and filthy. She refuses at first but eventually gives in. I think the darker outfit suits her more anyway.

We begin the walk to the library. As we travel through the castle, Fighters pass us. Some bow to me, while others glare at Ember. Everyone in the castle knows everyone else. Some of the Fighters didn't know I captured a Defender, and now they gawk at her.

We arrive at the library. It's one of the largest rooms in the castle, with hundreds of old books scattered on countless shelves. Ember seems to revel in the place. She flips through pages of books unrelated to the task, and all traces of her anger towards being stuck in my castle vanishes. Her eyes are bright and her smile is wide. There is no denying her beauty.

I never guessed Ember was much of a reader, but then again, I hardly know anything about her. Just that she has a power and wants to kill me.

Although Ember doesn't seem inclined to escape, I still keep a watchful eye on her. Trust is an unreliable thing.

I scavenge the library. As I skim through a damaged, dark green book, Ember looks over my shoulder. We both read the words and find nothing of use. As I place the book back, Ember's hand brushes my own, and I tense my jaw to get the flush of pink that rises to my cheeks under control. Maybe I'm overthinking it, but Ember seems to rush away very quickly to another area after being so close to me. I keep her in my sight as she walks to a different bookshelf. Although slightly oversized on Ember, my gray and red Fighter uniform fits her well. If I can manipulate her well enough, with the help of her spiraling power, she may wear Fighter clothes a lot longer. The thought doesn't make me angry, although it should. She may have a power, and she may be very useful in winning this war, but she is still a Defender. I shouldn't want her to stay. But for some reason, I do.

We search and search for what feels like hours, and we come up with nothing. We sit at one of the tables at the other end of the library, and Ember holds her face in her hands.

"There must be something, anything," she groans.

My mother spent much of her time in my father's room reading. All of the knowledge I have on magic is from her. These books in the library must not be the only things she read. There's nothing about what she told me here. But where else would books be? I think back to my mother's stories, and try to block out the image of my father slitting her throat. Of Levi joining her in the stars shortly after.

"Dark magic is a secret. You can't tell anyone about it," my mother told me. Back then, I had no reason to tell anyone. I didn't believe it myself. If it's a secret, then the books, the ones with the truth, must be hidden. But where would someone put books they don't want anyone to find? Where would no one look?

"You're scheming," Ember says, "I can see it." I ignore her and try to think. My mother loved those books. She would have kept them somewhere nearby. The only place no Fighter would enter, even now, is my father's room. It doesn't matter that he's dead. The room has remained untouched. He still holds some power, even after being burned. I quickly get up and hear Ember scramble to follow behind me.

When we enter his room, I so badly want to leave. I try to keep my thoughts of Levi bleeding out somewhere in the back of my mind. I haven't been in this room since I dragged his corpse out. Amara cleaned Levi's blood away in the off chance I would come back here. I'm grateful she did. Otherwise being in this room would have been a lot worse. I see Ember eyeing me, probably noticing my evident discomfort. Fortunately, she doesn't ask about it. I need to focus. If I can't find a book, Ember may never know enough to be able to control her magic. Then we may all end up dead; capturing her would have been for nothing. I throw my father's things across the room. His irrelevant books and maps, his charts and diagrams. I throw the sheets off his bed and the tapestries off his wall. Ember stands back in the doorway. I feel her eyes burning a hole in my back. The more things I throw into a pile at the center of his room, the angrier I get. Levi died in this room by my father's hand. My mother died in the bed they shared. He took everything from me. I look around, realizing I've destroyed or thrown everything he had.

"Dammit!" I yell. Where else could a book be?

I hear Ember's light footsteps as she slowly approaches me.

"There." I see her point at a scuff mark on one of the floorboards in the corner. It's so small I almost don't see it at first. It looks like the floorboard has been moved many times before. The wood is chipped slightly at the corner.

I move the floorboard, and I see two things. A necklace, delicately placed as though someone is wearing it, on top of an old book. I gasp as I recognize it.

"Whose necklace is that?" Ember asks curiously.

"My mother's." I see no point in lying about it. I don't think she ever took the jewelry off. My father must have put it in here before burning her. A part of me wants to put it back in the hole. It doesn't belong to me. But it doesn't belong in my father's room either. I place the necklace in my pocket for now. I will decide what to do with it later.

"How did she die?" I find the question invasive but more surprising than anything. I didn't think Ember would be fearless enough to ask me such a personal question. I find myself liking her boldness, so I give her an honest answer.

"My father killed her." I look at her as she stands beside me. She says nothing, not knowing how to properly respond. She simply nods, before I take out the dusty gray book. I place the floorboard back. There are no words on the cover, just chips and scratches from the book being worn. I flip through the pages until I get to one with the corner folded. I hated that habit my mother had. I would never fold the corner of a page. Ember peers over my shoulder with excitement written in her expression as she reads the same words.

"Dark magic is only found in hosts who have darkness within. It is rare and is extremely dangerous. Anyone who knows of their dark origins must hide away, as the magic is a danger to all. The magic can eat away at the host, changing their beliefs and values. A host may start with a small darkness within, only to have it sprout and grow, converting them into pure evil. The magic is unpredictable and almost impossible to control. It can kill in all different ways. It can be unstoppable."

"What if I can't control it?" she asks, her voice trembling.

"You will," I tell her, hoping I'm right. Her power sounds just as dangerous as I thought. How will I possibly be able to train her without getting myself killed?

I skim through more of the brittle pages, shocked that they don't crumble to pieces in my hands.

I read another passage to Ember, who fidgets with her hands.

"Magic is only evident in Noctifier lines. It started at the end of the nuclear war when a Noctifer obtained the power to move objects with his mind. Then more abilities at random came to light. The ability and when they came were unpredictable. The only commonalities were the feelings the hosts had and their origins. These hosts were

always Noctifiers. We haven't found any signs of Proliators or People in Between carrying magic."

I've heard the old names for Defenders and Fighters: Proliators and Noctifiers, only ever muttered by my mother when I was young. They mean "Warriors and Bringers of Night." At some point, they were simplified to the names we have now, although I'm not sure exactly when.

Ember's jaw drops as I read the passage. She must know what the old words mean, too, as her eyes start to water. I can tell she's fighting with her thoughts again. This passage only means one thing. Holders of magic are always Fighters. I knew Ember was different from the other Defenders, but I never questioned her origin.

Ember's voice is quiet and shaky. "I'm a Fighter."

Chapter thirty-four

EMBER

I sit in my cell, running my fingers along the black birthmark on my arm. I haven't even tried to keep track of the days that have passed. Only one thought runs through my mind repeatedly. *I'm a Fighter.* It doesn't feel real. My whole life has been flipped upside down before my eyes. Did my father know? My mother? Did they care? Are they even actually related to me? What does this mean for me? Should I stay in this castle, where I belong? Or should I go back to my false reality at the Defender's camp if I escape? I think of seeing my father again, who may have known this whole time, and lied to me about it. I'll have to add it to the list in my head of the things he's kept from me. But even though he lied, and even though he may not be my real father, he loves me. Even if I'm not a Defender by blood, he and Austin are my home. I can't let this distract me from my goal. I have to kill Alcmene and escape.

Alcmene's voice interrupts my thoughts as she reaches the bottom of the cellar stairs.

"You're one of *us*," she tells me. I want to scream, or cry, or punch a wall until my hand breaks. Her voice rings in my ears as she continues to speak. I don't want to accept this.

"You belong here, Ember. You were born a Fighter. The magic of our people runs through you." She's still trying to manipulate me. Weave her words into my skull when I'm most vulnerable. I know she wants me to rule by her side, to help her win the war with my magic. But how can I fight against my own family? If they are my real family. Liam is either a Fighter too, or he's not my father. But if he's not my father, who is? Who was Clara if she wasn't my mother? Or Meadow? My head spins and I feel nauseated. Maybe I'm thinking too far into it. It was just a book. It could be wrong. But D'andre's words make me think otherwise. He said I always acted like a Fighter. Now I know it's because I'm one of them.

Alcmene inches closer to me, and somehow my magic seems to grow stronger. I hate her for it. I cover my ears, trying to make her voice disappear into nothing. It doesn't go away. *I'm a Fighter.* My ears ring, over and over until I fear they're bleeding.

I throw up in the corner of the cell, and my nausea lessens, but I still feel a pulling in my chest and a pounding in my head. Thankfully, Alcmene stops talking. I don't want to be one of them. The dark magic swirls around in my mind, telling me this is exactly who I am. Who I've always been. Alcmene stares at me. The magic is corrupting my mind, my thoughts, and everything about me. But why is this all just happening now? If the book on dark magic is right, I've been living with this darkness my whole life. Why is it just changing my thoughts now, after seventeen years?

Every time Alcmene is near, I feel like I can't decipher the truth or lies that run through my mind. I know I have darkness in me.

I've known since I was a kid. I've always wanted to attack the Fighters, even when taught it was against Defender beliefs. I killed a Fighter after Meadow died, and felt no remorse after. I almost killed another one who was already bleeding out and crawling away. I'm not a good person.

I feel my magic clouding my mind. My old perspective is slowly beginning to disappear. My Defender beliefs are leaving me one by one. How do I stop it before it's too late? My magic will take over completely if I don't find a solution.

Alcmene watches me with a look that tells me she knows I'm fighting with my magic. I can't let her win. I have to kill her and go back home.

"If I've had this magic all my life, why am I only able to use it now?"

Alcmene unlocks my cell door and stands at the entrance. "Maybe it's because you didn't need your magic earlier. You said it came out the first time when I led the battle against you. You needed the magic to survive."

I shake my head. "That can't be it. There was an attack last year." I think of my sister bleeding out. I take a breath after air seems to stop traveling to my lungs. "I needed it then."

Alcmene nods.

"Why weren't you there last year?" I ask her. Surely she should have been on the front lines.

Alcmene scoffs. "My father wouldn't let me go." She grips the metal beside her. "I wanted to prove to him that I wasn't weak anymore. That I could slaughter more Defenders faster than he ever could. But he didn't want me to show him up. So he forbid it."

The thought of her killing Defenders in some sort of blood-thirsty contest with her father makes me feel ill. Alcmene changes the subject.

"I don't know why else your magic waited to show up until now."

She steps closer to me, holding out a hand to help me up. I take it, and feel my magic flutter in my chest. Suddenly, I might know why my magic didn't show up when I was younger. My magic is stronger when Alcmene is close. The first time I used my magic, Alcmene was near. It could all be because of her. I let go of her hand after she doesn't make a move to pull away.

"You're not a prisoner anymore," she tells me. "You're one of us. But that doesn't mean I won't keep an eye on you." Alcmene looks into my eyes. I try to avoid her gaze, but it's hard when she has such a pull on my magic. On me.

"I will assign you a room next to mine. My friend Leviathan's old one." Every time she lies about something, she struggles to meet my eyes. The word *friend* sounded ingenuine. I'm guessing Leviathan was something more to her. My chest starts to hurt.

"I'm not saying you're allowed to leave the castle. Even if you tried, I'd catch you. And every guard knows who you are. You wouldn't make it a foot out the door. But you can roam freely inside now. You're a Fighter, Ember." I still hear the poison in her voice. I look down at the uniform she gave me earlier. It's what the Fighters wear under their body armor. A gray shirt with a small red symbol on the left part of my chest. The same symbol is embroidered on the back but larger. I remind myself I'm only playing a part. I have to let Alcmene think I've fully accepted my role as a born Fighter. A part of that is sticking to the uniform. My magic burns in my hands. I can't let it convince me otherwise.

"It's the sacred Fighter symbol," Alcmene tells me as she notices me looking at it. My head still spins. I feel the magic moving everywhere in my body like it's traveling along with my blood.

"I accept the room," I say. Alcmene laughs like it wasn't an offer at all.

"I'm guessing this is a lot to process," she says softly, the venom leaving her voice as she guides me out of the cellar. Sometimes it seems like Alcmene has two different personalities. She's either extremely angry and manipulative or soft but full of pain on a rare occasion. She switches between the two sometimes in a matter of seconds.

Alcmene leads me to my new room. The room consists of a bed, a desk with a chair, and an empty closet. The wall is bare besides a small window near the bed. I miss my room at home, before Alcmene destroyed my castle. I miss walking around there, running my fingers along my mother's rose paintings. I miss training and Austin's cheeriness. But then my mind drifts to the smell of the filthy Fighters locked up underneath the council room, so skinny I could see their bones, so beaten and bruised I was surprised they were still breathing. That is the only reason why I'm glad the castle is a pile of rubble and ashes. At least those Fighters are out of their misery. I touch the mark on my arm, still wondering how one of the Fighter's seemed to recognize it.

Alcmene averts my gaze as we walk inside. She sits on the bed beside me, looking out the small window. The rain is a light drizzle, the thunder and lightning gone. Does she really trust that I won't try to leave? Does she trust that I won't slit her throat? I'm not sure what to do anymore. My initial plan was to get Alcmene to trust me and let me out of my cell, and find a way to kill her. But now that I'm finally out of that dark place in the cellar, I don't know what to do. I could try to kill her, but what home would I have to go back to? A home filled with lies? And what would become of my magic? Would it spiral out of control and kill the rest of the Defenders alongside me? I try to focus on the rain outside and the sound of Alcmene's light breathing. She keeps her hand close to her dagger as I speak.

"You made me answer a lot of questions," I say. She looks at me expectantly. "How about you answer one of mine?" I ask. The thought of killing Alcmene is still in the back of my mind. Sometimes the thought drifts away, my magic taking its place. But I need to fight it. I need to kill her and get out of here. Someone in the Defenders will know how to help rid me of this disease. Hopefully.

I decide to ask about Leviathan, even though I know I may not get an answer. She's lying about who he was, I know it. She cared for him more than she's letting on. And besides, I need her to trust me.

"He was my brother." She clenches her jaw but says no more. I wasn't expecting that. It's hard to imagine Alcmene with a brother. Someone she cared about. I can't comprehend how she can be so ruthless when she knows what it's like to love. I know she loved him by the way she says his name with a sorrow I recognize, as it was laced in my own voice after Meadow died.

"How did he die?" I ask, hoping that she won't lock me back into a cell for asking her invasive questions.

"My father killed him, so I killed my father," she says bluntly. My eyes widen. I know her father killed her mother, and now her brother too? I guess I know where Alcmene gets her evilness from. That must be why she killed him and took the throne. For revenge. I knew she didn't do it only for power. *Does that make her a better person than I thought?* My magic asks me. No. I can't try to humanize her. She killed so many of my people. My magic hums. We sit for a moment, hearing only the sounds of the falling rain, before I have the urge to speak again.

"I'm sorry," I say. Why am I apologizing? Just weeks ago I would have never dreamed of feeling bad for her. I tell myself it's my magic that's making me feel clouded and fuzzy. It's my magic that's making me sympathize with her. I look Alcmene in the eyes, which are slightly teary now, but she doesn't dare cry. I am a Fighter, just like her. Technically, she's not my enemy anymore. We're both on the same side. I shake my head, trying to rid the magic from my mind. I think back to when my father told me about Alcmene for the first time. I was so fascinated with her that it kept me up many nights. I've always been interested in the Fighters and their ways, but now that I know I was born one of them, everything feels different. My darkness makes me feel like I belong here, but the thought of Austin and Liam takes my thoughts back home. I shake my head again, and Alcmene glances at me skeptically. My magic is poisoning me. I can't even decide which side I belong on. What if my magic takes over, and I finally fall into Alcmene's trap? I'd become her second. I'd kill my own people. I'd be just like her. Evil incarnate. But according to the book on *dark magic*, evil is already inside me. I just never completely realized it.

I place my attention back on Alcmene, whose eyes are glued to the floor. She is full of pain but tries to mask it with anger. Leviathan is the source of her darkness. She killed her father because of him. But why did she slaughter the Defenders? Killing her father should have been enough. If Leviathan makes her the person she is, why am I like this? What made me grow up with enough darkness inside me to make me a holder of dark magic? Shouldn't *she* be the one with the magic?

"Do you still think about him? Leviathan," I ask, genuinely curious. I think of my mother and Meadow every day. D'andre and the Fighters under the council room. Grief is a constant pain.

She takes a shaky breath before looking back into my eyes. "Every second of every damn day." Her lip trembles ever so slightly. I unconsciously move closer to her. Why am I doing this? She should repulse me. I touch her hand. My magic burns. She tenses and doesn't move a muscle. I should be thinking about how I will kill her, not about her feelings. I fight my magic as I feel it swelling up in my chest. My magic wants me to be close to her and it's urging me to be near her. Why? Why is it attracted to her?

The urge to move away from her lessens as my magic burns stronger. I don't regret reaching out to her; instead, I feel heat rise to my cheeks. What is wrong with me? I remind myself again of Austin and Liam, who probably think I'm long gone. I have to go back to them. Alcmene's breathing changes. Why do I even know her breathing pattern? My magic feels like a weight on my chest, and right now, it feels the heaviest it's ever felt.

"I have to go." She quickly gets up and heads towards the door. Before she leaves, she reminds me I can't leave the castle, only this room. Even if I tried, I know I wouldn't make it a step outside before a guard would rip my throat open.

When she's gone, I fall back onto my new bed. Her brother's bed. Alcmene has an evil inside her, but she also has light, however much she tries to hide it. I can see it in her when she talks about her brother.

My mind isn't as cloudy as when I was close to Alcmene. The burning feeling subsides. Now that I can think a little clearer again, the thought of killing her returns. I have to do it before I completely lose control. I already almost have.

Chapter thirty-five

ALCMENE

After Ember comforts me, I leave the room before breaking down. Ember is a Fighter, but even so, I can't let her see my emotions. I wipe my tears as I head to my room. I stumble into Amara and almost knock her over on my way in. I don't bother muttering an empty apology. After seeing the look on my face, she follows me into my room. I sigh. Can't she just leave me alone?

"What's wrong?" she asks, her face etched in worry.

"Nothing, just leave me be." I try to walk away, but she continues to follow.

I turn around again.

"Go away!" I yell, swinging my arms toward the door. She doesn't listen. She steps up to me, grabs my hands, and holds them in front of her. I can't help but back to a minute ago when Ember held my hand in her own. Deep down, I know I didn't only leave the room because of my thoughts of Levi. I also left because of how I was feeling about Ember. Heat started to rise in my chest when she touched me. I had to get out of there before the unwanted feeling became worse. How Ember looked at me when I told her about my brother reminded me of how Amara looks at me sometimes. With an emotion behind her eyes I can't name.

I snap out of my thoughts and let Amara's hands drop out of mine.

"You know you can tell me what's on your mind. I'm here for you," she tells me.

"Leave. I won't tell you again." She nods slowly, sighing, and leaves the room. I stand over my table, my hands gripping the wood tightly. I have to let my brother go. But whenever he's brought up, all my old emotions come to light again. Hopefully, once Ember helps me win this war, and everything ends, I won't hurt at the mention of him anymore.

Wanting to get away from everything, I take a walk outside. The rain is heavier now, and the thunder returns, but I don't pay any notice. I walk over the bridge, admiring the moat filled with clear rainwater. The guards bow to me as I pass by. I try not to show my annoyance. I think of Ember, who will soon be treated as royalty when she becomes my second. That will be strange. I walk past the castle and into the woods. The forest is my favorite place to be. It's away from everyone and everything. All my burdens seem to lift away as I walk deeper into the trees. I hear the sounds of birds chirping, trying to find shelter in the storm. I throw a few knives into a tree in front of me. They easily lodge into the center of the wood, even though it's wet. I wonder if Ember is any good with throwing knives. The only weapon she had on her was her golden-handled dagger when I first captured her. I take it out of my side holster. I haven't really looked at it before. I guess I didn't care to. The dagger has two roses, red and blue, painted along the blade, with vines entwining them. It looks special, and I wonder what meaning it has to her. Maybe I'll give it back to her soon. But I still don't trust her completely. The magic is corrupting her mind, pushing her to side with me, but I know that if her mind isn't as cloudy, she could try to escape or kill me. I laugh. It would be amusing to see her try.

After a few more minutes in the forest and a few more knives lodged into trees, I head back to my castle. I dry myself off and go into Ember's room. She lies on her bed in the same position she was in when I was here earlier. She looks up at me as I enter.

"It's time to start training," I tell her. Ember gets up and follows me to the training room, which clears out as soon as I enter. We sit on the floor in the middle of the room. I try my best not to think of Levi sitting in the same spot as her, practicing his own magic for the first time. I remind myself that Ember's magic is dark, unlike Levi's. If Ember loses control, the entire castle could fall. I need to be completely focused. Maybe I could knock her out like I did before if she loses it. It stopped the magic last time.

"Levi had to get angry to summon his power, but the books said no power is the same, meaning yours can't be let out that way."

Ember nods. "Maybe I just have to think hard enough about the smoke and how to control it, and it will come out."

"That sounds ridiculous," I argue.

"Do you have a better idea?" she replies. I don't, and she knows it.

Ember closes her eyes. I scoot a few feet away from her. If the smoke touches me, who knows what it would do? Her blood burned me, so I'm guessing the smoke would do a lot worse.

Ember's face fills with concentration, and we sit silently for a few minutes. I watch as she clenches her fists and squeezes her eyes shut.

"It's not working," she grunts. "I don't know how it worked before."

I think for a moment. "What were you feeling in the moments when your power came out before?"

"I was angry," she says. Well, we know that's not the answer.

"Anything else?"

"I don't know." She looks up at me and swallows. She has the same look on her face when she's fighting her magic. She's not telling me something.

"Yes, you do."

Ember tenses her jaw, then finally says, "I was always angry. But anger comes from pain." I look into her eyes as she speaks. I'm all too aware of pain.

"Then channel that feeling and try again."

"I don't want to. Now that my magic is running through my mind constantly, I don't feel the pain as much. I don't want that to change."

Normally, I would hold a dagger to her throat and demand her to do it anyway. But I'll never convince her to stay on this side of the war if I keep demanding things from her.

I decide to try a different tactic. I move closer to her. "I know what it's like. The pain. I know how it feels when it finally leaves for a minute. It's like you can actually breathe. And I know how it feels when it returns." It hurts like hell. It ruins you, I leave out. I grab her hand, instantly regretting it when I do, as I feel something flutter in my stomach. Ember's green eyes meet mine. "But if you can't control this magic, it could be the death of you."

She nods. "Fine."

I move away from Ember, and she closes her eyes once more. I look around at the training room. Levi made me leave the room when he first practiced his power, and when I came back, everything was destroyed. I miss that day. It's like it never happened. The mirror isn't a shattered mess anymore; the damaged walls are fixed, and everything is perfectly in place. Levi would have loved to see Ember train. They could have trained together. Winning this war would have taken no effort with the two of them. We wouldn't have had to lose anyone else.

"It's still not working," Ember says. She groans in frustration. I run a hand through my hair. What if we never get her power to come out again? What use would she be to me then?

"Then I don't know what to do. You used your power before, just do it again!" I don't mean to yell, but the words come out before I can stop them. Ember doesn't react. She must be used to my anger by now.

"Can we train some other way for now? I'll figure it out eventually." Ember stands up, moving toward the knife-throwing side of the room with targets. I don't want her to practice anything else. I need her power to win the war. But I don't stop her.

"I used to wonder all the time how your training room compared to ours," she tells me as she picks up a knife from the table.

I walk over to her. "And?"

She throws the knife, hitting a perfect bullseye on the biggest target. I'm not too impressed since the target is a decent size.

"I like this one better." I don't ask why, and she doesn't elaborate. The more she likes it here, the more likely she is to stay without me forcing her.

Ember picks up more knives, hitting the bullseye on every target except the smallest one. She frowns.

"Close," I say. I would have easily hit the target. She grabs another knife to try again, and I move behind her as she lines up her shot. I feel Ember tense at my proximity. "You're angling it wrong," I say. I move the knife in her hand to line up properly with the red dot. She had it angled lower, probably because the Defender's throwing knives are slightly lighter than ours. She swallows. "Count your breaths before you release it." She throws the knife and hits the center perfectly. Maybe I would be a better trainer to the Fighters if they weren't so scared of me, but the thought of being so close to anyone besides Ember wouldn't feel right. After a few more throws without my help, Ember walks to the other side of the training room and back. Pacing, almost.

"If I can't get my magic to work, you'd have no reason to keep me here. You would kill me, wouldn't you? Rather than send me back to the Defenders." I look away from her. With any other person, I would say yes. The obvious answer would be to kill her if her power fails. She would be of no use to me. Even though she has the blood of a Fighter, she can never be fully trusted, not since she grew up on the opposite side of the war. But for some reason I can't explain, I don't want to kill her. Even if she's not as trustworthy as other Fighters, something in me wants her to stay.

"No. I wouldn't kill you." I won't elaborate. She wouldn't understand. She looks at me, somewhat shocked. But then another thought crosses her mind, I can see it in her eyes. She thinks I'm trying to trick her. Trying to manipulate her. I'm not so sure of my intentions myself. "You must work on your power during any free time you have," I tell her. She nods in response.

Suddenly I remember I have something of hers. I pull her dagger out from one of my holsters, holding the handle out to her. Her eyes widen.

"You're trusting me with my dagger?"

"Trust is a strong word. If you try anything, you know I can take you." I see a faint smile on her face; it's the first time I've ever seen her smile. It lights up her face, accentuating her bright eyes. I hand her the dagger. She looks at it like it's a long-lost treasure.

I'm about to ask why the dagger means so much to her, but she already starts to tell me before I get the chance.

"It was a family heirloom, although I've definitely gotten the most use out of it." She holds the knife, running her fingers along the painted roses. "My mother painted these. The blue rose represents the Defenders, and the red, Fighters." She touches the blood red rose. "Only now it's different, looking at it from the other side of the war." Her expression is unreadable, and I let the silence linger, wondering what she's thinking.

After a minute, I lead her back to Levi's room, as she doesn't know her way around the castle yet. As we pass by, Fighters still look at Ember suspiciously. I have to tell them soon, when I'm sure that Ember will be staying, that she will be my second. That is if she accepts it. First, she has to accept who she truly is, so it may take a while. If I announce her as my second, it may start an outrage among some Fighters, but I will be sure to silence them if they don't conform. And knowing how terrified they are of me, conforming shouldn't be much of an issue.

I've constantly been wondering one thought. If Ember ends up getting her magic under control, will the darkness have a loosened hold on her? If it does, she won't feel like she belongs on this side anymore. She'll try to escape, and I'll have no choice but to kill her.

As we enter Levi's room, I push my thoughts of him away. Ember notices this.

"Tell me more about your brother," she says. At first, I don't want to tell her anything. Talking about him yesterday was hard enough. I take a deep breath. I'm not going to tell her everything, but a little information can't hurt. We sit down on Levi's bed, as we did last night.

"Levi, as you can tell, meant a lot to me. My father was abusive." I can't believe I'm telling her this. I told myself I would never tell anyone but Amara of my past. "Levi protected me and showed me his power. We trained together until he believed he was ready to face my father in a fight to the death. He knew that killing our father would be the only way to permanently keep me safe." I push back the lump in my throat. The more I think about his death, the more I realize it was my fault. He wanted to protect me, and I let him die trying.

Ember doesn't interrupt me, not once. She looks at me with true sympathy in her eyes. I don't want her to feel bad for me. I hate the thought.

"Only he wasn't ready. I didn't see their fight, but his power must not have worked because I found him bleeding out in my father's room." My eyes start to water, and I so badly want to leave the room. But I know I can't keep running from this anymore. I need to face what happened.

Ember grabs my hand, as she did yesterday. She runs her thumb along my skin, trying to soothe me. Weeks ago, she wanted me dead. So much has changed since then. I don't want to admit what I'm feeling for her. Every time she's around, I feel a heat in my chest and a pull towards her that I can't resist. I try to shake the thoughts away, knowing she would never feel anything for me. Not after what I've done. Not after knowing I don't regret anything I did on the battlefield. Even with her magic changing her mind, I don't think her perception of me will ever completely flip.

"Why didn't his power work? Why? If it worked he would still be here, and I wouldn't be so alo-" I stop, trying to let the shakiness in my voice fall away. I don't want anyone to see me like this. Especially *her*. But why do I care more about her seeing my weakness than anyone else?

"Alone," Ember finishes my sentence. She squeezes my hand in hers, and I see a familiar look in her eyes. She's fighting with her thoughts again. I should keep my distance from her to let her figure everything out on her own. The only reason she's close to me and sympathizing with me is because her magic is corrupting her. But although I know her actions are almost certainly ingenuine, I can't bring myself to pull away.

"Even though sometimes I feel for you one minute and hate you the next, you're not alone anymore. Maybe it's the dark magic controlling me, or maybe it's just me. But either way, I'm here," Ember tells me, pulling me into her. I think I've only hugged Levi once, after our mother died. It wasn't long ago, but I can't remember how it felt. Now, as Ember holds me in her embrace, I don't think about my brother for once, just her. I feel warmth in her arms and suddenly I don't have a care in the world that I'm acting like this in front of her. When she pulls away, I feel the urge to pull her back towards me, only this time to press my lips to hers. But I stop myself, thinking the idea is ridiculous and that she's only pitying me. I see her eyes, and I think I see the black of her magic flicker across them. Why is her power activating now? But as abruptly as I see the darkness, it goes away. It just reaffirms that none of her actions are real. She's being controlled by darkness.

I should still hate Ember. She was my enemy not too long ago. But somehow, I don't. Not anymore. But that doesn't mean I completely trust her yet. After everything that happened with my father and mother, I don't know if I can ever trust anyone again.

I want to thank Ember for saying she's here for me, even though she may not have meant it. But no words come out, and I slowly leave the room, giving her one last look before I close the door between us.

Chapter thirty-six

EMBER

As soon as Alcmene leaves the room, I begin to break down. My magic was spiraling through my mind the minute she walked into the room. Why does my magic rise in my chest every time I'm close to her? The magic pulled me toward her. It made me tell her that she's not alone. At least that's what I tell myself. In a soft whisper, I start to talk aloud, trying to block out my thoughts. "I don't feel anything for Alcmene. She took everyone from me, and I have to kill her. My magic is making me feel something for her. It's not me." I state this repeatedly until I drift off to sleep.

Alcmene enters my room in the morning, waking me up so we can start training. I look at my dagger lying on the table beside her. I can kill her right here, right now. The war will end, and I can go home. Without being close to Alcmene anymore after she's dead, hopefully, my magic will go away on its own. I will never use my magic again; maybe that way it won't return. I stand up, trying to act normal. I grab my dagger for training, and she doesn't seem to think anything of it. Before she gets a chance to open the door, I slam my body against hers, pinning her against the wall. I hold my dagger to her throat.

She lets out a low laugh. "Wow. I thought you would have tried this a long time ago. What were you waiting for, darling?" She smirks, and her eyes lock onto mine. She acts confident and only slightly annoyed by my sudden attack, but I can see pain in her eyes. She opened up to me last night. Did she finally almost trust me?

Alcmene doesn't move. She doesn't try to move the dagger away either. Why doesn't she? She could take me down in a matter of a second. Take the dagger from my hands and put it to my throat. But she remains still. I feel my hand shake slightly, and I know I'm losing my chance. There's no way I can kill her now. Not when she won't fight back.

"You won't kill me," she says. "I know you. You don't have the guts."

I tense my jaw. I almost killed a helpless Fighter before, and if I almost killed someone I didn't even know, surely I can kill her. She's taken so much from me. I look into her eyes, unable to glance away. My breath hitches as I see the same softness in them that I saw last night. No. She's trying to manipulate me. I can't fall for it. I let my dagger nick her throat. I watch as a short line of blood drips down her neck. She doesn't flinch.

"Do it," she whispers. It almost looks like she actually wants me to.

My hands shake again. With a little more pressure and a swipe of my dagger, the war would end. Alcmene would fall, and no doubt the Fighters would surrender without their ruler. So why can't I do it? It would be so easy. This has been my plan all along. Kill her, and go home. I feel heat in my chest again. I know why I can't do it, but I won't admit it to myself. I let the dagger drop to the floor with a clang. I expect Alcmene to leave the room, disgusted by my sudden betrayal. But instead of leaving and slamming the door in my face, Alcmene's hands find my own.

"Listen to me." Her voice is soft again. I can't look at her. My eyes drift to the small wound on her neck. It would have been so easy. "Don't fight the magic anymore. It's who you are. Feel it. Embrace it."

I don't pull away. I feel dizzy, and my head is cloudy. Maybe she's right. I have to accept the fact that the magic isn't just a part of me I can forget about. It's who I am. It's who I've always been. My magic didn't make me want to be close to Alcmene. It didn't make me say anything I said to her. I did it willingly, and I knew that from the beginning. I've always known I've had darkness rooted deep inside of me. As much as I refuse to admit it, I am just like Alcmene and can't push away my darkness anymore.

I feel the warmth of her hands in mine, the pull of my magic toward her. I don't act upon it. A tear unwillingly makes its way out of my eye.

"Embrace it." I see no trace of poison in her words. No anger from my sudden attack.

I remember what I promised D'andre right before he died. I promised him I wouldn't fall onto the Fighter's side. I wouldn't become one of them. Embracing my magic is taking me one huge step closer to breaking my promise entirely. But right now, it doesn't feel like I have a choice. I have to embrace who I am or else it will tear me apart.

I don't say it to her, and I don't need to. I know she can tell I've given in as her hands let go of mine.

Chapter thirty-seven

ALCMENE

I leave Leviathan's old room. I wipe away the blood on my neck, and collapse onto my bed. I opened up to Ember about my brother, and that whole time, she was planning to kill me? Just like that? I think back to the way she wrapped her arms around me. It really seemed like she cared. I thought the magic completely corrupted her, but I guess I was wrong. She's been fighting the darkness, and somehow she's almost winning.

After holding her dagger to my throat, and deciding not to kill me, it seems like now she'll finally embrace who she is. But how can I trust her? Every word, every touch, may still be a lie. I close my eyes, hoping I can sleep through the day. But just as I'm drifting off, Amara shows up, shaking me.

"What?" I yell, pushing myself into a sitting-position.

"The Fighters are waiting for you to train them outside." She urges me toward the door. I groan. I just want this day to end already. As I get out of bed, Amara touches my face, brushing her thumb along my cheek. I didn't even realize there was a stray tear there. She doesn't ask me why I was crying, which is smart. She's finally learning that I won't open up to her. I gave her that luxury three years ago, and she left me.

Training the Fighters goes by slowly. Amara asks to spar with me, but I tell her no. I have too many things on my mind. I stare out at the Fighters, thinking only of Ember. I touch the small cut on my neck. How has she had such an effect on me already?

Chapter thirty-eight

EMBER

A few days later, Alcmene lets me venture outside the castle walls with her. She leads me to one of the smaller castles, although it is still enormous. I don't know what I was expecting, but when Alcmene pushes open the doors, my jaw drops.

Horses. I've never seen any in person. My father told me we had horses of our own before I was born, but then the Fighters rounded them all up and kept them for themselves. And here they are, dozens of them in stables. Brown, gray, black, and white, with long, shiny manes. They must be well taken care of. It's surprising to see Fighters having animals they care about.

A few Fighters rush down the stairs of the second floor, which I'm assuming holds supplies. They bow to Alcmene before she dismisses them with a wave. The castle is filled with the smell of hay and wildlife. It's almost calming. As I look around at the beautiful animals, Alcmene brings me to a horse in the biggest stable. It's all black, with a crimson-red saddle and a large frame. This horse is the largest of them all.

"This is Estella," Alcmene says, and almost hesitantly adds, "Her name means star." Alcmene opens the stable, and I file in next to her. She runs her hand over the horse's mane. Estella leans into her touch. Alcmene's eyes show no sign of her usual pain or hatred as she pets her horse. I find myself comfortable with her like this. Alcmene takes my hand in her own and guides me to her horse. It feels like a dream, petting an animal I've only seen in books.

I look at Alcmene. "Why did you bring me here?" Her face shades pink for a quick instant.

"Do you want to go riding?" she asks.

My eyes light up as I imagine sitting on the back of a beautiful horse, riding through the woods. "Yes." The excitement shows in my voice, and Alcmene chuckles. I'm acting like Austin on his first day of training. Oh, how I miss being a kid.

"I would let you ride one of the horses on your own, but you don't know how yet, and you know..." she trails off. She thinks I'll try to escape. I'm not sure if I would anymore. When I'm near Alcmene, my magic is much stronger. I don't think I'd try to escape with the magic swirling through my mind like it is now.

"We can both ride on Estella." Alcmene looks at me expectantly as if she's waiting for me to decline.

"How do I get up?" I ask.

Alcmene smiles. "Put your foot here." She motions to a U-shaped metal hook dangling off the horse. I do as she says. "Now, throw your other leg over his back." I reach my leg up, but I'm nowhere near reaching the top of the horse's back. I struggle as I try a few more times to throw myself up.

"Alright." Alcmene stops me when I'm about to try again. She lets out a small laugh. "Keep your foot there, and I'll lift you up." I tense at the thought of her touching me. I was the one who held her hand and hugged her when she was in pain, but she has never initiated anything. She was my enemy weeks ago. Now she's going to help me onto a horse. How my life has changed in the oddest of ways.

I let out a small sigh before she grabs the sides of my waist with her hands. I flinch at the warmth of her breath on my neck, wanting to brush away the nagging thoughts in my mind. My stomach starts to hurt. Why do I feel like this when I'm around her? Alcmene notices and loosens her grip on me, but doesn't say anything. She lifts me up, and I land on the saddle's back. She effortlessly swings up in front of me, placing her boots into the hooks.

The guards open the stable door for us, and Alcmene urges Estella forward at a slow trot out of the castle. It's weird moving without using my own legs. Alcmene begins to guide the horse to the woods. I watch Alcmene's hands lightly grip the reins and listen to hooves on the grass, and light rain pattering on the leaves. It's peaceful. I never thought I'd feel this way at the enemy's castle. I wonder what Liam would think. Austin. I try to leave them out of my mind as we enter the forest.

Estella slows as she navigates through the gaps between the trees and over the fallen branches that litter the forest floor.

"Question." Alcmene looks back at me, her brown eyes shining in the drizzling rain. "If you had horses all this time, why didn't you use them when you attacked the Defenders?"

"We don't have enough horses for all of our people. We only have a few dozen. And they would have all been killed in the battle. Then, we wouldn't have had any for farming or hunting. Besides, it was amusing, seeing the pain in the Fighters faces as they walked the long trek to your old castle," she snickers.

"I thought you liked your people," I say.

Alcmene scoffs. "I don't like them. Not at all." She doesn't say any more. Usually, I wouldn't pester her, but this I want to know.

"Why not?" I ask. I've noticed she doesn't talk to any of them as she passes. They silently bow or sometimes even kneel, but Alcmene never acknowledges them.

"I know if I become close to them, they will only use me to gain power at my side. Even when I was a kid, that was the case. Levi was the only person I ever really talked to. Now, the only one is Amara, and she wants to become my second. But somehow, even though she wants that, I know she's not using me like the others."

That sounds awful. I never thought about the price of power in that way before.

"Who is Amara?" I ask. The rain gets heavier but by now I'm used to it.

"No one, really." She looks away from me, and I know she wants to change the subject.

We continue trekking through the forest, a comfortable silence washing over us. I watch as Alcmene gently brushes her horse's hair with her hands as we ride. I've never seen her so calm. I listen to the birds chirping in the trees, and the rhythm of Alcmene's light breathing. She's not wearing her Fighter uniform, unlike usual. She's wearing all black, and I can imagine her easily blending into the darkness when night falls. She wears a vest with a long-sleeved shirt beneath it, as well slacks, with high boots that reach her knees. She has her throwing knives strapped to her sides as well as her purple dagger.

After a minute, she fills the silence.

"After the attack on your people, I wanted to get away from everything. I spent a lot of time out here in the forest with Estella." Alcmene's hair blows in the wind, concealing her scar. I still haven't asked her about it. I think I will wait a while on that question.

"I get that. It's calming, being outside of the castle with you." Alcmene smiles. I find myself wishing she would smile more often.

We continue our ride through the forest, and eventually, we stop by a pond for Estella to drink. I never take my eyes off of Alcmene. I don't think I ever would have pictured her being so caring for an animal when I saw her for the first time, ripping the throats out of Defenders. That day feels like forever ago now. We get back on Estella and continue riding until we get to a huge clearing.

"Do you want to speed it up a little?" Alcmene asks, turning to me.

"Of course I do." We both smile.

"Put your arms around me." I do, and I feel Alcmene tense up as my arms rest around her waist before she relaxes. She tightens her grip on the reins, and after a pat on Estella's side, she picks up speed.

We spend the rest of the day in the woods. I hold onto Alcmene even as we ride slowly. I forget about my magic changing me and my life with the Defenders. I spend a day only thinking about the present, even though it's with someone I never thought I'd be on the back of a horse with. The tingling sensation of my magic doesn't go away, but I revel in it for once.

Chapter thirty-nine

EMBER

Sometimes I still have nightmares about Alcmene killing the Defenders. Whenever she isn't near me, my magic is less cloudy, and I hate her more. But I don't just feel resentment towards her now. I feel other emotions, too. I don't know what to do. I'm stuck. I can't kill her, and I can't leave. Even if I did make it back to the Defender's camp, my magic might kill us all. I need to stay so I can learn how to use it. And once I learn to control it, I don't know what will come after. I feel a pull toward Alcmene and the Fighters side of the war. I'm drawn to her in a way I can't explain. My magic pulls me to her, but it's not just that. Alcmene's said many times that I belong here. But what about Liam and Austin? I can't abandon them. I can't fight them. I don't know what to do.

I have to practice using my magic, but I have no idea how to make it come out. I sit on my bed for a long time, urging the magic out of me until I begin to sweat. I haven't been able to get my magic out since I was a prisoner in Alcmene's cell weeks ago. Nothing has worked.

I look outside the window to see the storm raging on. Frustrated, I go down to the training room. By now, I know my way around the castle. There are still plenty of rooms I haven't explored, but I'm comfortable getting everywhere I need to go. The Fighters must know I am under Alcmene's protection because although they glare at me as I pass, they make no move to attack.

In the training room, I practice using throwing knives until I hit the bullseye on the smallest target. As I train, I feel the magic in my head swirling around. I feel it, so why won't it come out? I pick up a bow and arrow for target practice. We didn't have many at the Defender's castle, and I always preferred my dagger or sword, but now's a good time to try out all options.

Soon, Fighters pour into the training room. I leave after they stare at me with weapons in their hands.

I've been wondering many things since I learned I am a Fighter, specifically if Liam is a Fighter too or if he is even my father at all. And how did I end up at the Defenders castle if I was born a Fighter? I sit on my bed in my room, with my knees up to my chest. I listen to the sound of the rain and thunder for a long time before Alcmene enters.

"I have news, darling." Alcmene pulls my desk chair over to my bed and sits down in front of me. She sees my expression before she is about to continue.

"Did I interrupt something?" she asks with a skeptical look.

"I was just-" I think of the right words. "In my head."

She nods, her expression unreadable. "Some Fighters were out hunting, as usual. They didn't find anything, so they went toward the Defender territory." I have a bad feeling about where this is going. "They found a Defender near the line, and took him in. He is being held in a cell downstairs. I thought it would be a good opportunity to practice your power whenever you're ready." I tense. She wants me to hurt one of my own people. I feel the magic cloud my mind. No. They're not my people anymore. I made my choice. Right?

"I'll have to figure out how to get my magic to work first," I tell her, hoping to put this task off for as long as possible. Alcmene moves her chair closer to my bed.

"Actually, I have an idea," she says. My eyes light up. Everything I've tried has failed. "You possess dark magic. The book said that for someone to carry dark magic, they must first have darkness within them. A root that will allow the magic to grow." I nod. That's nothing new. "Close your eyes," she says. I listen. "Find the darkness inside you. It's there, but you have been hiding it for so long, it may be hidden deep. Grab onto it."

I try. I really do. I can feel the magic swirling around but can't grab it. It's like a star in the sky. You know it's there, but no matter what you do, it will always be out of reach.

"It won't work," I groan, opening my eyes.

"You haven't fully accepted the darkness as a part of you," she tells me. I've tried, but I always have doubts no matter how I see things. If I embrace my darkness and stay on this side of the war, I'm betraying everyone I used to know. But if I don't accept the darkness, I'll be living a lie. I won't be able to control the magic, and I could die for my reluctance.

I know what I have to do. I grab Alcmene's hand, and immediately, my magic feels stronger. Usually, she keeps her distance from me when I try to use my magic in case it comes out and hurts her. But when my hand touches hers, she doesn't even tense up. Is she getting more comfortable with me? Alcmene's once cold hands are now warm in my own. I feel the urge to pull away, but I don't. Yesterday we were riding on a horse together, with my arms tightly around her for hours. So why does this small touch make me feel so nervous? What's different now? I look into Alcmene's eyes. Her pupils are dilated. I take a deep breath, and shut my eyes again.

I can feel the magic. It's stronger this time but still out of reach. I need to accept it. *I will stay on this side of the war. I will learn to control my magic. I will embrace it. I will feel it.* I tell myself this over and over, while feeling Alcmene amplifying my power. Finally, I grab onto the magic.

Alcmene must be able to tell because she says, "Let it out."

Her voice fades away. I start to feel it, the pain in my eyes, the burning in my stomach. The fire in my blood. Now that I have the magic, letting it out is like an instinct. I open my eyes, and somehow, Alcmene is on the other side of the room, watching me with a small smile. Black veins cover my skin and dark smoke hovers above my hands. It's actually working. But it hurts more than anything. I think I'd rather get stabbed multiple times in the chest. It feels like my organs are on fire. I can hardly see, and I feel tears start to drip down my face as I let out a strangled cry.

"Send the magic back in," Alcmene tells me, and I can just make out a worried look on her face through my tears. I have no control. I try to send the magic back in, but it won't budge, not even a little.

"I can't." I wince, my entire body burning.

"It's your magic. You command it. Make it go back," she urges with power in her voice.

I struggle against the pain. *I can do this.* I close my eyes again and force the darkness back inside. For so long I wanted to be rid of any evil, but now, willingly, I'm letting my darkness back in. The pain lifts all at once, and I almost collapse from the impact of the magic returning. I think I'm going to fall before Alcmene rushes over and grabs my shoulders, steadying me.

"I did it." I almost don't believe it myself. Luckily, Alcmene lets go of me after her touch almost causes my magic to rise to the surface again.

She lets me rest for a few hours before I feel recharged enough to train outside. I ignore the pelting rain as we walk into the forest.

"Your blood burns. Now I want to know what the smoke can do." After about half an hour of walking, we stop at a meadow filled with flowers. It's the most beautiful part of land I've seen on the Fighter's side of the war. "Levi called this place the 'Old Meadow.' We were away from our father when we came here, just the two of us. We only got to go here a few times while Levi was still alive," Alcmene tells me. I know what it's like to lose a sibling. Places become memories that haunt you. You can never forget about the pain when it's everywhere you look.

"You want me to destroy this place?" I look at the beautiful flowers stretching far across the green land. It's a special place to Alcmene. It would feel wrong to ruin it with my magic.

I think of a time when I would have wanted to burn down everything Alcmene held dear. Now, I want to protect what's important to her.

"I don't think you'll kill everything. The meadow is too big. But it's time I let this place go. At least most of it." She doesn't meet my eyes; instead, she picks a daisy and twirls it in her fingers before letting it drop to the ground. "Take your magic out, and see what the smoke will do to the flowers."

Again, it's a struggle. I hold Alcmene's warm hand in my own, and eventually I get the magic out, but it doesn't hurt any less. I can't hold onto it for very long. I try to focus on the black smoke and what I want it to do. My vision zones in on the bright colors of the flowers, and I will my magic towards them, fighting back the excruciating pain coursing through me. The smoke expands in my hands, spreading out across the land. The pain lessens as the smoke travels away from me, but it's still awful. I start to feel lightheaded, and the world begins to spin.

"Don't pass out," She tells me, with a worried glance my way.

I keep my eyes on the smoke, and the bright yellow, white, and blue colors turn to brown one by one. All of the flowers in the area die. I watch as I turn the beauty of the forest into darkness. This is who I am now.

"Wow," I hear Alcmene mutter. She stands back from the smoke, away from me. Once everything near us is dead, I command the magic back. It takes a lot of effort, and by the time my magic is safely stored away, I'm drained. I lie in the woods for a while before Alcmene leads me back to the castle. She keeps a firm grip on my arm as we walk back, as I fear my legs will give out.

I go back to my room and lie in my bed, planning to sleep for the rest of the day. I think of the Defender in the cellar downstairs, who I may know. I feel my magic darker than ever before. I don't want to hurt him. But it's too late for that. I've accepted my magic, and now that I have, it's stronger. I feel it in my mind, clouding everything. A few weeks ago, my magic felt like a tunnel filled with fog. I thought I could see the light through the haze. But now

I can't. There is no light at the end of the tunnel, only endless darkness. I *will* hurt the Defender. I have to.

I wake up early. I look at my desk; my mother's dagger is the only thing on top. What would she think of me now? Is she even my mother? Was Meadow my sister? Or were they all Fighters, too? I look at the mark on my arm before Alcmene knocks on my door.

We go down to the cellar. It feels strange to be back in the place where I was held captive, being on the opposite side of the bars.

The Defender sits in the corner of the cell and looks up at us when we enter. Thankfully, I don't recognize him. By the look of his clothing, he appears to be from one of the outlying Defender camps who left our castle long before it was destroyed.

Alcmene whispers in my ear so the Defender can't hear. "This is your chance. Send the magic into his body, and stop his heart. If you won't, I will. I haven't had a kill in a while." Her voice sends shivers down my spine. Her whole demeanor has changed. She's back to how she was when I was in the cell. Her voice is poisonous, her eyes full of rage. She looks at the Defender, who looks down at the floor. She smiles, running her hand along her dagger's blade. With Alcmene beside me, my magic feels strong, and my mind feels cloudier than ever.

The Defender is just sitting there, helpless against the magic I will use on him. It feels wrong. I almost don't want to go through with it, but then Alcmene touches my shoulder, and my magic pushes my merciful thoughts away. Alcmene's right. I've always wanted this. I'm a Fighter and a holder of dark magic. It's who I am now.

"Do it," she whispers. I let my magic out. It takes a painful minute, and I have to hold back tears as my eyes burn. I can't show weakness in front of this man, even if he will be dead soon. He's the enemy now.

Although everything burns, I feel powerful. I feel Alcmene's hand tighten on my shoulder. It's time. I send my magic toward the Defender, who scrambles to the back of the cell, eyes wide. It's no use trying to avoid the smoke. On my command, it rushes into his throat.

Nothing seems to happen at first, and I begin to think my magic didn't have any effect on the man. But then he drops to his knees. Through his chokes and gasps, I hear him plead for me to stop. I don't. He squirms and holds his throat in his hands like he'll be able to dig the magic out. He fights and struggles, his face turning a shade of blue. He throws himself around his cell, trying with all his might to get the magic out of him, screaming so loud I worry it'll bust my eardrums. Soon, he gives up thrashing around. He looks at me, his eyes now completely black like my own. He's silently begging. I'm his last hope. I feel my magic waiver. I could let go right now, and he might still live. *No.* I can't. He falls onto his back, convulsing. He lets out one last strained choking sound before he falls limp.

Chapter forty

ALCMENE

The magic leaves the Defender and slowly makes its way back into Ember. Her legs give out, and she crashes hard to the ground. I rush over to her, worried that after using so much of her power all at once, it's killed her. Dread runs through me as I crouch beside her. I check her pulse and thank the stars she isn't dead like Levi. Only exhausted. I prop her up against the wall, and rather than call the guards, I decide to dispose of the Defender's body myself. To be honest, I'm shocked Ember actually went through with it. I thought she would have pulled her magic back before it killed him. She really is becoming one of us.

The man is lying down, facing the back of the cell, away from me. I unlock the door and approach him. A small stream of blood trickles out of his mouth, but other than that, there isn't a scratch on him. Ember's power attacked him internally. I drag his body out of the cell, up the stairs, and outside to the burning grounds. My arms ache as I drop him next to an unlit fire. Afraid Ember will wake before I get back, I call a guard to burn him. No questions are asked.

When I return to the cellar, Ember is just beginning to rouse. I watch as her eyes flutter open. "What happened?" she asks, groaning and holding a hand to her head.

"You just collapsed. I think you overexerted yourself." Ember wobbles as she tries to stand, and without asking, I grab her hands to help her up. We stand only inches apart, and I almost forget to let her go after a minute. Ember looks at the empty cell with a confused expression. "He's gone. I moved him to the burning site. Some of my guards are taking care of it now." Ember nods slowly, still staring at the cell. It feels like forever ago when I had her captive in the same place. I think keeping her down here, although I didn't really torture her besides somewhat starve her, is the only thing I've ever felt bad about. I didn't feel bad for her in the moment when her skin was pale and her mouth dry, but I do now. Now that she isn't just another prisoner.

"I'm going to go lie down," she tells me as she heads up the stairs with slow steps. I follow her into my brother's room, staying close in case she falls again.

"Are you alright?"

"Fine." She lies down on the bed, pulling the sheets over her head.

"Do you want to-"

"Go away," she mumbles, rolling over to face the wall. I know she's exhausted, but why is she acting like this?

I leave the room, already hearing her light snoring as I close the door softly behind me. I go outside and watch the rest of the Defender's body burn until there is nothing left.

I see Amara walking towards me out of the corner of my eye. I haven't talked to her since our slight argument, when I was upset about Levi and she wanted to help me, but I didn't let her. I didn't see her at training the morning after or anywhere around the castle.

"I thought you were mad at me," I say as she stands beside me.

"I'm not." She looks at the fire instead of me.

"Then why were you avoiding me?" I ask, my tone more accusatory than I mean for it to be.

"I thought some space would do you good." I take my eyes off her and join her gaze on the fire. It's burning high, with very minimal rain affecting it. I don't say anything.

I hear Amara take a long breath. "If you don't want to open up to me, that's fine. I'm only trying to help, but no matter how hard I try, you won't budge. I don't mean to pry, you know." Her voice is soft, as it usually is when she's trying to comfort me. "Look at me," she says. I don't. Who is she to give me orders? I'm the one in charge here. I continue to glare at the fire with my hands clasped together so I don't instinctively punch her.

"I know you only mean well," I mutter after a minute of silence. I don't want to spill my emotions to her, even if she wants me to. Crying about things won't make them better. She must know that. I finally turn to face her. Her emerald green eyes, sparkling like Ember's, stare back at me. She touches my shoulder with a tentative hand. I tense slightly but don't back away.

"I know what you're going through," she says as she moves her hand slowly up to the side of my neck. "You don't have to open up. I get why you don't want to. But if you ever do, I'm here. You know that by now."

I force myself to nod before I pull away from her touch.

I tread back into the castle, leaving her behind. I enter the throne room and find Ember waiting for me.

"I thought you were in a mood," I say. First Amara, now her. Ember turns to me.

"Yeah, sorry about that." Her cheeks flush pink.

"What was that about?" I ask. Suddenly, she isn't able to meet my eyes.

"I was exhausted after using my power. But that wasn't the only reason why I was acting so strangely." I move my hand to her chin, forcing her to meet my gaze. For some reason, she doesn't pull away.

"When I was killing that Defender, I was afraid of what I'd feel." She swallows.

"You were right, when you said I'm just like you. When I killed him, I felt..."

"Like yourself," I cut in.

"Yes," she replies. "And powerful." I see a hint of black fill her eyes again.

"Was it your magic that coerced you into killing him, or was it you?" I expect her to look away in shame for who she's becoming, but she never breaks eye contact.

"Both. I know I was born with darkness, and I think my magic just reinforces it."

I nod. "If you stay on our side, you will always feel what you felt today." She finally looks away. Suddenly, tears fill her eyes. I keep my hand on her face, wanting to brush them away. I don't. "What is it?" I ask.

"I don't know if I want to be this way," she mumbles, pulling away. I catch her, forcing her to look at me.

"I know this is hard, figuring out who you really are. But I've been through this, too. You told me you would embrace it. Live up to that." She nods slowly and wipes away her tears. "Trust me. I know you'll come out on the right side."

"Trust," she whispers. I let my hands fall from her face. "Not so long ago, you would have been the last person I would ever trust." She looks around the room with a spark of interest I haven't seen before. I silently hope she's considering staying here permanently.

"Maybe I can learn to trust you," she tells me.

Somehow, I know deep down I already trust her myself. I know she won't leave the castle even if I leave the door wide open. At least not now. And I trust that she will be here for me, even though she wanted me dead before. Now that she's almost killed me and stopped herself, I believe she will stay on my side. I hope.

"Maybe I do belong here." She looks down. I know what she's thinking. She's wondering if it's only the magic that's making her feel this way. I know it's not. She was born with a darkness inside her; she just had never let it out before. She's said she will embrace her dark magic, but I know it will take time for her to really accept it. I decide to ask the question I've been wanting the answer to.

"Would you fight the Defenders to end this war?" I've been dreading her answer. If I want to win, I need her by my side. But would she ever kill the people she spent her life with?

"I don't know," she replies. I let out a small sigh. I rest my hand on the side of her face again, almost instantly regretting it when I do, as I feel warmth radiate through me. I try not to think about how close she is to me or the feeling of her skin. Or how her eyes change to black again, only for an instant.

"The boy I found you with at the pond, would you be more inclined to say yes if we spared him?"

Her breath hitches, almost as if she forgot about him. "Yes. I wouldn't be able to kill him. He's like family." She thinks for a moment. "And Liam. Even though he may not actually be my father now that I know I was born a Fighter, he's still important to me. I don't want him dead either." I nod, letting my hand fall away.

"Your power could be the factor that ends this war for good. If agreeing to attack them means we have to spare two lives, I'm okay with that," I tell her. Her eyes light up. I know she wants it all to end almost as badly as I do. "I told you, I want you as my second, and I stand by that."

I see fire in Ember's eyes. "I want that too." Her voice isn't unsure like I thought it would be. It's certain and strong.

From the minute Levi died, I wanted my revenge. I knew when I saw Ember, she was the key to obtaining it. Now that she has agreed to be my second, I am closer than ever. But a warm feeling in my chest tells me it's not only that. I don't just need Ember's power to exact my revenge, I want it to be *her* power. Anyone else could have had magic in them, but I'm glad it was her. And I'm glad she will stay.

Ember eventually leaves the room for dinner, and Amara stomps in. She's mad.

"I heard what you said. You're officially making her your second." She steps closer to me until we're inches apart. I see her fighting to hold tears back in her watery eyes, masking it with anger. "Why her?" her voice cracks. "I would choose you. Always." A tear falls from her eye. I don't answer. Her anger quickly turns to sadness and then into something else entirely. Amara reaches for me, holding my hands in hers. My mind wants so many different things. I want to pull away, finally open up to her, or tell her I'm sorry for choosing Ember over her, even after everything she's done for me. But I'm unable to say or do anything, before her lips crash into mine.

Heat fills my body, and I'm drawn closer to her. This is different from the first kiss we shared. We were younger, and it was nothing more than a peck. A goodbye kiss filled with sorrow and regret. Now, Amara's hands reach for my waist, pulling me closer. The kiss is urgent and fast, but her lips are soft and gentle. Amara's red hair touches my neck, and her lips feel warm on mine. Passionate. Hungry. Part of me doesn't want to pull away, but as she pulls on my shirt, I know I have to. I don't want to admit it to myself, but I know I want someone else deep down. Amara releases her grasp on me, noticing my growing hesitation. She already knows what I'm thinking. I've wanted Amara since the day she kissed me three years ago, but now everything has changed.

"It's because of *her*, isn't it?" Her voice is sharp but filled with pain. I see hurt in her eyes, and I so badly want to embrace her. But I know I can't. I should want Amara like she wants me. She has been there for me, even when all I did was argue and push her away. She has never looked at me with hatred or fear, and she accepts me for who I am. Even if who I am is a monster. She is practically perfect for me. I should want her too. But I can't be with her, when I so badly want someone else. Someone who will never want me. I don't want to say her name. Not when what I feel will never be reciprocated. Not after what I've done. Amara quickly leaves the room, wiping tears from her eyes as she walks away. I'm left alone with the ghost of her lips on mine.

I hate myself for hurting her. I could have had everything with her. Everything I've ever wanted. We could have gone back to the way we used to be. Amara and I against the world. But not when I couldn't have devoted all of me to her. Not when my feelings lie elsewhere.

I take a deep breath, but I can't seem to calm my growing anger. I'm furious with myself. I hurt the one person alive who could love someone like me. The one person I could have had a future with. And for what? For some Defender, who although may be on my side now, will never look at me like Amara does. Not after I slaughtered her people. Not after I took her family away.

Unable to control my spinning thoughts, I walk outside, into the night. The storm rages on louder and stronger than ever, and the guards tell me it's not safe to leave the castle. But I don't care. I run into the forest, leaving Amara and everyone else behind. I hold my tears back, knowing it's useless to cry. I throw my knives into the trees, wanting to take my mind off Amara's pained expression. Wanting to forget how her hands felt on my waist. The taste of her lips. The soft sound of her breathing. I yell into the night, not caring about who will hear. The rain beats down, drenching me. The lightning strikes loudly all around, shaking the forest. I don't run back to the castle. I stay in the woods, soaked and shaking cold, until the morning comes.

Chapter forty-one

EMBER

After killing a Defender and becoming Alcmene's second, I have officially given up the person I used to be. I feel like I've betrayed everyone I have ever known. I told D'andre I wouldn't fall onto the Fighter's side, and even though I didn't know it at the time, I lied to him. I've become who used to be my enemy. Liam would be so ashamed of me. So would Austin.

I hear a knock on my door and snap out of my thoughts. I recognize the cadence as Alcmene's knocking.

"Come in," I tell her.

She slowly opens the door. "Everything alright?" she asks after seeing my expression. The only thing that will make me feel better is training. I look outside my window, and the rain isn't so heavy. Perfect for going outside.

"I want to train." Alcmene nods and follows me outside the castle. We walk in silence until we reach the Old Meadow. Alcmene places a hand on my shoulder. I try to ignore the warm electricity running through her touch as I look into her brown eyes.

"I know you must feel as though everything has changed. And I'm not sure if you realize it's for the better, but it is, Ember."

I nod, brushing her hand away. Alcmene keeps her distance from me as I let my dark magic out. The familiar thrum of energy courses through my veins. The smoke unspools and extends out to the flowers around us. I think of the Defender I killed and feel my magic react in response. It wants to kill again. Not just flowers or trees but people. Something burns inside my chest, and the magic spins circles in my head. I want the same.

As I think about the death I could cause with my magic, the smoke spirals. It travels, killing flowers at record speed and burning down trees. I'm unable to pull the magic back in. Alcmene sees my lack of control, and I begin to panic. I reach out to gather the smoke, but as much as I will it back to me, it won't budge. The darkness begins to destroy the forest. Every living plant dies around us. Alcmene runs over to me, grabbing my hands, no longer filled with smoke, as it's traveled far away.

"What's happening? You have no control!" she yells. I had control yesterday when I killed the Defender. I had control countless times before. Why is it different now? I look at Alcmene, who has anger in her eyes. She knows what destruction my magic can cause. She knows I have to control it or else chaos will ensue. "Pull it back in!" she yells. She sounds like a ruler as she barks commands. I haven't heard her talk to me like this since I was a prisoner in her cellar. Since we were enemies.

I can't concentrate with her this close to me, this angry. My magic is always stronger when Alcmene is near. I can feel it now.

The smoke that was out of reach begins to come back to me. No-not me. It travels towards Alcmene. I can't stop it. It has a mind of its own. I push her away from me, urging my darkness back inside, but it doesn't work. I try with everything I have, but the smoke reaches for Alcmene. She can't outrun it. She barely tries, before the smoke trails down her throat. She falls onto the dead grass. My magic immediately returns to me, hitting me like a wave all at once. My eyes begin to burn, but not from the magic; from the tears that well up in them. I kneel beside Alcmene. My heart stops when I realize she isn't breathing.

Without thinking, I pick her up, running as fast as I can while holding her weight. I rush past the dead forest, towards the castle. My magic runs through me, stronger than ever now that Alcmene is pressed against me. I pay no attention to it, only focusing on running the remaining distance to get her help. I hold back sobs as I run. *Please don't die. Please don't die.* I rush her to the infirmary, flying past Fighters with concerned and wary glances.

I make it to the infirmary and place her on an empty silver table. A medic runs over, and her eyes widen in shock when she sees who her patient is.

"She's not breathing," I choke out. The medic calls for help and a few more Fighters try to bring her back to life.

I panic as a medic yells to another that her heart has stopped. They press on her chest and blow air into her lungs over and over. After a minute of trying, I start to lose hope. If Alcmene dies, I will have to rule. But what's worse than that, is if she dies, I'll be alone. She was my stability on this side of the war. I know I should hate her after all she's done, but I don't. At this point, she's all I have. I would never forgive myself if she died because of me.

Tears roll down my face, and I don't care that the medics will see my weakness for her. I sit in the corner of the room, helpless to do anything for her. I look away from Alcmene's lifeless body, covering my head in my hands, letting myself cry freely. I should be happy she's dead. Only months ago, I wanted her dead more than anything.

Just before I give up on her waking and leave the room, I hear a shallow breath leave Alcmene's mouth. *She's alive.*

The magic in my chest spins in circles as I rush over to the side of the table.

"The ruler will have to stay overnight, but she will live." The medics leave, and I hear one mutter something about supplies, but I don't pay any attention to them. Alcmene's eyes flutter open. I feel my magic burn in my throat.

"I thought you weren't trying to kill me anymore." Her voice breaks.

I smile and let out a long breath. "I thought you were dead." Alcmene sits up slowly, groaning at the pain she must be feeling.

"Oh, I was for a minute." She laughs like she wasn't gone a second ago. Like nothing ever happened. I sit beside her, and she runs her thumb along my face, wiping away a tear. She smiles gently. I look into her dark brown eyes, full of life again. "I didn't think you'd care if I died, darling." She motions to the tears in my eyes, smirking.

I push her away light-heartedly.

She clutches her chest. "Careful. I haven't recovered," she jokes. I nudge her again. "Seriously though, I know you didn't want to kill me yourself when you held your dagger to my throat, but I didn't think you'd mind if I died." She looks into my eyes, and I feel vulnerable. I can't believe I lost control out there. I almost killed her. I did for a minute. My tears threaten to fall again but I push them back. Of course I would mind if she died.

I feel my magic urging me closer to her. Before now, I've been avoiding the pull to her. My magic is drawn to Alcmene, and so am I, for reasons I may never know. Instead of pushing away the feeling, this time, I give in. I push myself closer to her, and to my surprise, Alcmene doesn't pull away. I feel heat rise to my cheeks and my magic swirling in my chest. My magic rushes through me so fast I fear it'll come out to attack her again. But somehow, I contain it. Alcmene's hand touches my face. Our lips are only inches apart. Her warm breath on my face sends shivers down my spine, and I want to kiss her. More than anything. I close my eyes. Her hand moves to my neck, gently pulling me in before the door opens.

I instantly move away from her, and my magic seems to vanish all at once now that Alcmene's hands aren't on my skin. One of the medics walks into the room with bandages and water in his hands. He acts like he didn't see what almost happened between us. He hands the supplies to Alcmene, who gulps down the water and sets the bandages on the table. She never takes her eyes off mine.

"You can leave now," she says to the man. He hurries away, tripping on the doorframe as he departs. Alcmene doesn't mention our almost-kiss. If that's even what it was. She doesn't say anything at all, only takes off her gray shirt and unravels the bandages. She is only wearing a bra, and I can't keep my eyes off her toned body. I frown when I see a burn on her chest, right below her collarbone. I saw my magic trail down her throat, trying to suffocate her from the inside, but I didn't know it burned her on the outside, too. The medics must have seen it when they were resuscitating her, explaining the random bandages. Alcmene's wound is dark red and welts begin to form on her pale skin. I did this.

"I'm sorry," I say.

She shakes her head. "I'm sorry I was so angry. I thought you finally had your power mastered and then lost it. I need your power to win the war." She averts her gaze from mine.

Is that all I am to her? Just a pawn needed to avenge her brother? I should have known she doesn't care about me. I'm just a piece in her elaborate, monstrous plan. If I was the one who stopped breathing, she would have left me to die.

"And that's all I was thinking about. How much I needed you. But as much as I hate to admit it, I care, too." That catches me by surprise. My thoughts from a second ago wither away. I never thought Alcmene would care about anyone after her brother died. I never thought she'd care like I do for her.

She finishes wrapping the bandages around her body and turns around so I can secure them on her back. I feel my magic buzz as I fasten the bandage on her spine, feeling her skin under my hands. Alcmene turns to face me, and we're close again. But I know I can't let myself get wrapped up in my feelings for her. I have to focus on my magic. I have to get it back under control. And to do that, I need to be away from her. Otherwise, I risk hurting her again.

"I'm going to train. I'll see you tomorrow."

I think I see a flicker of hurt flash across Alcmene's face before it quickly vanishes. "I'll be here," she grimly replies.

I walk out of the castle into the forest. I train through the night. It's easier now that Alcmene is a safe distance away. My magic isn't spiraling in my chest and burning my lungs as much. I train until I'm comfortable and have everything under control.

Chapter forty-two

EMBER

A couple more weeks go by. It feels like I've been at the Fighter castle for ages, although it's only been a little over two months. The longer I stay here, the more used to everything I am. Alcmene has recovered from the burn I inflicted upon her, and she helps me train every day. I develop my power. Now, I am able to force my magic out of my body with minimal pain. But forcing the magic back in still takes some work, and I'm still scared of losing control again. Alcmene assures me that it won't happen, but how can she be certain?

Some of the other Fighters don't look at me with murder in their eyes anymore. Alcmene hasn't announced that I am her second yet, and for good reason. But she will soon, and I can only imagine how the Fighters will react.

Alcmene has begun to look at me differently. She still has her occasional outbursts, but we're comfortable with each other now. I can't say I don't hate her anymore, because an old part of me always will. But my other feelings for her overshadow the hate by miles. Including one feeling I still haven't admitted. It feels like too big of a betrayal to my old life to say the words aloud.

As I'm thinking, I walk in the halls, passing by Fighters. At this point, only a few glare at me. One in particular walks in front of me, forcing me to stop abruptly. I notice the anger in her green eyes. I'm suddenly very aware of the knife at my hip. Maybe I'll have to use it. The thought of killing someone again makes my chest tighten, almost in a good way.

"It's all your fault," she growls.

"What are you talking about?" I step back from her, trying to lengthen the proximity between us.

She tenses her jaw. "Alcmene and I. You're the reason-"

Alcmene comes out of nowhere and stops the Fighter's words in their tracks. She places a hand on her shoulder, who tenses as Alcmene's grip tightens.

"Amara, we can talk in private," she says through gritted teeth. I remember Alcmene mentioning Amara a few weeks ago when we were riding on Estella together in the forest. She said Amara is different and that she knows she isn't using her. Alcmene must care for her. The thought makes my magic burn as it itches to be used.

Amara pushes Alcmene away from her, and I'm shocked when Alcmene doesn't retaliate. Amara grumbles and quickly leaves the hallway. Alcmene stares daggers into her back as she flees before looking back at me.

"What was that all about?"

She sighs softly. "Nothing. Just Amara being Amara. I would steer clear of her for a while."

“Okay,” I reply wearily. What is she not telling me? Amara mentioned Alcmene when she was talking to me. She said it was all my fault. What could she possibly have been talking about? I know Amara wanted to be Alcmene's second. Does she know I stole the position?

Alcmene and I go to the forest to train, as we've been doing every day. We haven't been to the Old Meadow in some time, as most of it is destroyed, and I know Alcmene's memories there make her uneasy. But whenever we train, we still go far out into the woods to protect the land near the castle. I always see some stiffness leave Alcmene’s shoulders when we enter the forest. This is where she’s most comfortable, not in the castle where she’s bowed to or watched with fearful eyes.

I practice with my magic, feeling the darkness flow easily through my hands. Now that I've trained so much, I've learned that my magic can kill in multiple ways. At first, the smoke swirled over plants or trees, slowly killing them from the bottom up. Now, it can light plants on fire or rip them from the ground, depending on how I move the magic in my mind as I send it out. I often wonder about all the ways my magic could kill a human. When I killed a Defender weeks ago, the smoke choked him to death and drew blood from his mouth, but I’m sure there are other ways he could have died, if I knew how to command my magic better at the time. The thought of killing again makes my magic hum.

“How is training the Fighters going?” I ask after the silence begins to be too much to bear. Silence makes me think of the Defenders when we were attacked. The brief silence after the first explosion before chaos ensued. Before D'andre died.

"Slowly," Alcmene groans. "We can't attack the Defenders until our people are ready. You have your magic, which will be a huge help, but you can only take on so many people at once."

I nod. Alcmene has started to say "our people," when referring to the Fighters. Knowing she has fully accepted me as one of them is a strange feeling.

As I practice my magic, I catch Alcmene glancing at me instead of the surroundings I'm destroying. She does this often, staring at me with a soft look in her eyes, thinking I don't notice. Honestly, I do the same with her. Alcmene has been fascinating to me ever since the moment my father told me about her so long ago. Even though I'm always around her, and now I know a lot more about her and her past, she's still more fascinating than ever. And since the day I almost killed her with my magic, I've been drawn to her even more. Losing her would be a pain I'm not ready to face.

I bring the magic back to me, being sure to steer clear of sending it Alcmene's way. We sit down on the grass to take a break, covered by the thick woods above us. It's a day to be outside. For once, it's not raining.

I look at Alcmene, who sits close by my side. So close our bodies are almost touching. I try to push the heat out of my chest as I think about almost kissing her a few weeks ago.

"My father told me that no one knows your real name," I say.

Alcmene smiles faintly. "Of course, my parents did, and my brother. But no one left alive does." Just a week ago, Alcmene would have dropped her gaze from mine at the mention of her brother. But now, she's stronger. She doesn't flinch or get teary-eyed when she thinks of him. Her physical wounds have healed as well. The burn I gave her has scarred over.

"Not Amara?" I ask, hoping my jealousy isn't clear.

Alcmene gives me a look that makes me think she will taunt me for being jealous over nothing, but instead lightly laughs and says, "No. She asked me hundreds of times to tell her. I finally almost did, but then she left." Her smile fades, and she doesn't continue. What does that mean, she left? Why? For how long? Alcmene's expression reminds me of a wounded animal, and suddenly I want to know everything about her and Amara. How Alcmene was hurt by her. Why Amara was so angry because of something she claimed was my fault.

Alcmene interrupts my thoughts when she says, "You want to know what it is."

"Of course I do." I question it every day. Alcmene, meaning wrath, surely fits her, but it's not real. I want to know every real thing about her.

She smiles, looking around at the forest surrounding us, then into my eyes. "It's Crimson," she tells me, her voice soft but confident. I look into her eyes and picture how full of hate they used to be. Now they're soft and gentle, a look reserved only for me. And now I'm the only one who knows her real name. It makes me feel honored.

"That's beautiful," I say. Her cheeks turn a light shade of pink, and she looks away, trying to hide the heat that rushes to her face. I laugh and turn her face toward me, something she did many times when trying to manipulate me in the cellar. But now, every time she touches me, it's not to taunt me or manipulate me. It's a silent acknowledgement that she cares. That I reciprocate it.

Crimson's smile drops only slightly, and I think I catch her glance down at my lips. Suddenly, I feel the heat between us, stronger than ever. The moment in the infirmary comes back to me again. If the medic didn't open the door to interrupt us, would she really have kissed me? It's hard to believe that Crimson feels the same way. I'm not even sure exactly how I feel.

She swallows and moves her eyes away from mine, abruptly standing up. The thoughts I had immediately drift away. I frown as the thrum of my magic lessens, and my heart stops beating so fast. I know Crimson cares about me; she said as much, but she must not feel anything more than that. Although I'm not exactly sure what the extent of my feelings are, it hurts to know that she doesn't feel the tension between us even a little.

"We should go back," Crimson says, grabbing her throwing knives. It's strange knowing her real name after wondering what it was for so long. It fits her well. I've always associated Fighters with a blood red color, especially after my mother's roses, and it's only fitting that her name is exactly that.

"It's not raining for once," I tell her.

She looks up at the sky like she's only just noticed.

"Maybe we should do something?" I ask.

Crimson looks around. "Like what?" she asks, with a flustered look on her face.

I smile. "I don't know, maybe take a walk around?" She shrugs her shoulders before agreeing to walk through the woods. We travel a long distance, Crimson effortlessly navigating through the thick forest, while I trail behind, struggling not to trip over raised tree roots. It brings me back to when she captured me. She practically dragged me through the forest the whole way to the castle. Even in the darkness of night, she never broke her confident stride. Now,

she walks for a while and stops every so often to wait for me. I find her throwing knives in the bark of trees as I catch up to her.

Eventually, we reach a pond.

"Want to go for a swim?" I ask. Crimson looks back in the direction of the castle, obviously hesitant. "Come on." I grab her arm, pulling her closer to the water. I push her into the pond, and she gasps before she goes under. When she reemerges, she scoffs before a smile crosses her face. She swims out of the water and runs the short distance between us. I know what she's going to do. I run back into the forest, but she catches up easily. She grabs my hands, pulling me back to the pond. I try to struggle, but it's useless. I laugh as we near the water.

"Don't you dare!" I screech. She tackles me, and the freezing temperature hits me like a shock wave. I plummet underwater, silently cursing out Crimson as I swim my way back up. I make it to the water's surface, and we spend the rest of the day swimming and training.

When night hits, we race back to the castle. She wins, of course. Since there is still no rain, we lie out under the stars. Crimson looks up at the sky with a small smile.

"My favorite memory was when I was right here, under the stars, with my brother." I smile, imagining the two of them lying out here. "My father was asleep. Levi brought me out here, and we had time to relax and just be kids."

The stars twinkle in the night, and I don't worry about the war among us as I lie next to Crimson. I feel comfort in her presence, and safety. Only months ago, I felt the opposite. I saw her at the battle for the first time when she was coated in blood. I was terrified of her. I would never have dreamed of feeling safe beside her. But a lot has changed. I've changed.

"He told me that each star is a person we've lost. I never knew how much it would mean to me back then. But now it's helpful, knowing my brother is up there."

I imagine my mother and sister looking down on me. I would give anything to see them again.

"You said you killed your father and took the throne for Leviathan. Is everything you've done for him?" When I saw her for the first time at the battle at my old castle, I would have never guessed that she was anything but a bloodthirsty monster. I would have never guessed that she killed so many Defenders for anything other than power.

Crimson takes her eyes off the stars and looks at me. "I need to avenge him. I need to win the war for him. But I didn't kill all those people because of my brother. I have my own darkness in me." Just like mine. "If I wanted to only avenge my brother, killing my father would have been the end of it. But I *wanted* to kill the Defenders. I didn't want to be an abused little girl anymore. I wanted the power of life and death in my hands. Finally having it made me feel free and...alive." Crimson looks concerned, almost like she thinks I'll be scared of her need for bloodshed. Of her need to kill. But I'm not afraid.

"I understand," I tell her. My darkness urged me to do the same when I killed my first Defender. I wanted to do it. In a way, I needed to. I want to think it was the magic alone that urged me to kill him, but I know it wasn't. As I lie beside Crimson, my magic urges me closer to her. Her warmth. Her lips. I don't act upon it, but

I wonder if my magic is so strong near her because of her own darkness. Maybe it's attracted to it. But I can never know for sure.

Crimson lets out a quiet, relieved breath. We continue looking up at the twinkling stars, and the night passes.

Chapter forty-three

CRIMSON

I often find myself thinking about my day with Ember yesterday. It reminds me that peaceful days like those will all be over soon. Once the Fighters are ready, and once Ember agrees, we will attack the Defenders. Those days will be filled with endless nightmares and pain from loss. Many of the Fighters may die, but none of it matters as long as we win. I think about Ember dying. For some reason, the thought of her death hurts me more than the thought of anyone else's. There is still much to learn about her, but she's had an impact on me. Maybe it's because of how much she reminds me of Leviathan. He would have loved to meet her. But he never will, which is why this war must end. It's what he would have wanted. It's what I have to do.

I run into Amara on the way to training. She's been avoiding me since she kissed me. When Amara used to be around, I guess I kind of brushed her to the side. I didn't realize how much her caring meant to me, and now that it's gone, a part of me feels hollow. I grab her arm as she begins to walk past me. She stops in her tracks, finally looking into my eyes.

"What, Alcmene?"

"Can you stop avoiding me like this?" I want to tell her I'm sorry. I want to tell her that I wish I could be with her. But the words don't come out.

"You don't care about anything. What's the point of being here for you if you don't care anyway?" Her voice is rough, but I hear the sadness behind it. After Levi died, I never thought I'd care about anything ever again. And she's right. I didn't care when I took the lives of countless Defenders. I didn't care when I destroyed their castle. I didn't care when I tore Ember away from her family. But things have changed since then. I don't care how many lives I need to take to avenge my brother, but I do care about Amara and Ember. If they died, I know it would hurt me. But pain is something I'm used to. If they die in battle, it would only add to my never-ending hurt.

"I do care," I tell her.

Amara rolls her eyes. "Don't lie to me." She moves her arm out of my grasp and continues her walk down the hall. I think about chasing after her, but decide against it. I turn around and walk outside. It's time to train the Fighters, hopefully for one of the last times.

As I watch the Fighters train, I feel the absence of Amara by my side. I will have to get used to it. She may never forgive me.

I let my mind drift to Ember. I'm guessing she's training in the woods, killing flowers and trees, sending her darkness into every living thing. She's come so far. She's ready to fight. The only problem is whether or not she wants to. Ember told me she would fight a while ago if we spare her father and Austin. But how will anyone survive once the fires start and the Fighters start swinging their swords? How can I promise her they will live? This is why I have been continuously training the Fighters. I know Ember could probably kill everyone in the battle single-handedly, but I'm not sure if I trust her to do so. She grew up with them, and that kind of bond doesn't just go away.

Once training ends, I walk into the castle. Ember isn't in her room. I travel into the forest, enjoying the calm feeling that washes over me as I enter the tree line. The songs from the birds. The light rain. I continue to our usual training spot, finding her sitting against a tall tree. Everything around her is brown and dead, except the tree behind her.

"Hey." I sit beside her.

Black smoke flows above her hands. Her eyes are black as well. It's almost captivating seeing her engulfed in darkness. It's beautiful.

When Ember sees me, she forces her magic back inside her body. "How did the training go?" she asks.

"I think they're almost ready. In a few more days, I will make a plan. Soon, the war will be over." Ember looks out at the dead plants around us. I see her hesitation. I reach to grab her hand. "They are not your people anymore," I insist. She nods slowly. "One last fight and the war ends for good."

"What about Austin and my father? They need to live." I hear despair in her voice.

I squeeze her hand lightly. She doesn't pull away.

"We have to come up with some kind of plan that will keep them alive," I tell her, although I don't want to. I want to kill all the

Defenders. I want none of them breathing at the end of it. But Ember would never accept that, and I need her to win this war. I have to settle for a compromise.

She nods again, more confident this time. “If we can do that, then yes. I will end this war with you.” She looks into my eyes and squeezes my hand back.

“Your magic is the most crucial element in winning. You have to be ready.”

“I am.” I really hope she’s right. She took down that Defender weeks ago easily, but it was only one. Soon, she will face hundreds. Now that she’s been training hard every day, she may have the ability to do so. But I need to be sure.

“There are smaller Defender camps two days out. If you can take down a camp of about a hundred, I will be confident in your ability to kill more when the time comes.”

Ember lets the smoke out of her hands, holding it in front of her. She shoots it into an already-dead plant, lighting it on fire. She smiles.

“I will. Just tell me where to go.”

Ember collects a sword from the training room, and I load up on throwing knives. I told her to focus on using only her magic to kill the Defenders at the small camp, but her sword is a back-up.

Before we depart, I take Ember to the castle holding the horses. I assign her a horse that no one has claimed yet. The horse is dark gray, with a long black mane and gray eyes. Over the past few weeks

I've taught her how to ride. It took a lot longer than I thought it would, but after many frustrating hours, she was able to ride Estella through the forest with minimal guidance.

Ember tries to get onto her horse, struggling for a second before clumsily throwing herself onto the saddle. As we ride out of the castle together, off into the woods, a few Fighters watch us skeptically. I glare back at them, and they turn away.

"How are you able to leave the castle for multiple days? There will be no ruler or second," she asks.

"The Fighters know that if I get back and find out they did something stupid, they won't be around for much longer. They will stay in line, no matter how long I'm gone," I assure her.

Ember and I travel through the woods, heading toward the nearest Defender camp. She is more fidgety than usual, and I worry about her moral standing in all of this. I really hope she will go through with it. These Defenders won't be anyone she knows. They're not from her old castle. It's a perfect stepping stone for her.

It is a long ride to the Defender's camp, and I decide to fill the silence between us as she rides next to me.

"You never really told me much about your family." I keep my horse in line with Ember's, making sure she is stable. She is wearing one of my outfits. I need to get her some of her own, as mine are slightly big on her, but I like seeing her in my clothes. Light rain drizzles down on us, but it's nothing we aren't used to by now. Ember's wet hair, darker from the rain, isn't in braids for once. It falls in waves down to the middle of her spine, perfectly framing her face. "I know your father and Austin are all you have now, but did you have any other family?"

"My mother and sister died in the battle last year." I look at the trees. So she knows what it's like to lose people who mean everything. "My sister was ambushed, and my mother died in my father's arms." She doesn't elaborate any further, but a gloomy look crosses her face. She's probably wondering if they'd hate her for joining me. For what she's done. I know I would wonder, if I was her. I often think Levi wouldn't like who I've become. I don't think he'd support the fact that I want to burn the whole world down for him. That it's turning me into a monster. Maybe Ember and I have more in common than I thought.

"This war has to end," I mutter. For Levi. For Ember. And for me.

"Yes, it really does."

We let our horses stop to drink when we reach a small river. Nightfall is almost upon us.

"I want to travel for a few more hours, covering as much ground as possible. Then we can rest," I tell Ember. I help her onto her horse. It still shocks me that she isn't repulsed by my touch. When we first met, she would have tried to cut my hands off if I grabbed her waist like this. But now, every small touch is natural and comfortable. I don't think twice about it, and neither does she.

When we finally stop to camp for the night, I make a pit for a fire. Ember begins to gather wood and joins me after making a decent pile. It's hard to see her with only the moonlight shining through the thick leaves. But her eyes are bright in the dark.

"Remember when I took you from the Defenders, and showed you how to make a fire without a match on our hike to the castle?" I ask.

"Yes. However, I wasn't listening very much. I was preoccupied with the thought of Austin and my father." I nod. She was planning to kill me back then. Sometimes, I still wonder if this is all some elaborate plan of Ember's. Joining me, getting me to care for her and trust her, just for her to stab me in the back when I least expect it. It would be devastating, to say the least. It would be a whole new kind of pain. But I don't think I'd be shocked, more hurt than anything. Trusting or caring for people has never ended well for me, and I'm not sure it ever will. So, I can't say I have complete faith that Ember is actually on my side. I just hope she is.

"What about now? Do you still think of them often?" I continue talking to wash away my thoughts of betrayal.

"Not as often as I used to, considering how much I've changed. But sometimes. I still want them to live. They deserve to live. Especially Austin. He's too young and too kind for this cruel world."

"I understand. If Levi was on the opposite side of the war right now, I would want him alive, too." I grab two sticks, placing them in front of me.

"Remind me how to do this again," Ember says. I laugh and remember how useless it was the first time I tried teaching her how to make a fire. This time, she watches me intently, with a look I always crave to see in her eyes, although I can't quite name it.

Chapter forty-four

EMBER

Crimson and I wake up early. We want to cover the rest of the trip before nightfall, meaning we will have to keep a brisk pace. Crimson puts the fire out, spreading the ashes and covering any evidence that we were here. Then we mount our horses and head toward the camp. I decide to ask why Amara was angry at me the other day as we start the trek.

"I'm sorry she acted that way towards you. She was just..." she looks into my eyes, "jealous."

Before I can ask what Amara would be jealous about, she continues.

"Nyla, Amara's mother, was the ruler of the Fighters long ago. She stepped down, but Amara never told me why. She didn't know herself. Now her mother lives in the smaller castle, away from soldiers and people who would try to kill her for giving up the throne. Amara wanted to be my second, to follow in her mother's footsteps and eventually become the ruler. But she figured out I was planning on giving the position to you. That is why she was angry." I never knew rulers were able to step down willingly. I never thought anyone would want to. Why would Nyla want to give up so much power?

"Is that what the second, smaller castle is for? I know one of them is for horses, but is the other for people like Nyla?" I ask as I guide my horse around a fallen tree.

"Nyla is the exception. People that live in the small castle aren't soldiers or can't be. They're elderly, injured, or families with infants. My father also had people live there if they gave him something he wanted, and in return he didn't make them fight in the war." I can only imagine what Crimson's father would have wanted from his people.

We continue our trek through the forest, and I feel my magic run through me, especially when Crimson brings her horse slightly closer to mine. Before I know it, the camp is in the distance. I take a deep breath, preparing myself for all the people I will kill.

The camp has at least one hundred wooden huts. No tents from what I can see, so I'm guessing many of the Defenders were probably born out here. From our vantage point in the trees, I can make out the smoke of two campfires, and people everywhere. This is it. Everything I have been trained for has led to this moment. This will determine if I am ready to attack the larger camp later, the one that holds people I know.

"Ready?" I feel Crimson's hand on my shoulder and my magic hums. I turn to face her, and my magic screams at me to move closer. I pull away from her, only slightly. I need to focus my magic on the battle ahead, not its draw to Crimson.

"Ready." We tie our horses to the trees a safe distance from the camp before moving up.

"Make me proud." Crimson's voice in my ear sends shivers down my spine. I hear her take her sword out of her sheath, and we move out of the forest.

Instantly, multiple Defenders spot us. My eyes turn black, the pain nothing but a nuisance at this point. I let the smoke unravel in my hands and feel my magic burn like fire through me. I feel Crimson's eyes on me. Without a word, I send my magic into the closest Defender and down his throat. He was pulling the weeds out of the ground near his hut, but as the magic seeps into him, he stops what he's doing and begins to claw at his neck. I let my magic run its course. I watch as he falls to the ground, gasping for air with tears streaming down his cheeks. After a few seconds, he stops fighting and goes limp. Dead. My magic moves back to me, and I let it hover above my black-veined hands. The same feeling from when I first killed a Defender returns. I feel powerful, and as I watch the Defenders begin to run, I want to feel more of it.

Crimson charges with a sword above her head. She shouts something, but I don't hear it as I focus on sending my magic into multiple huts, burning them to nothing within a minute. At this point, everyone is alerted. I cut both my hands with the blade of my mother's dagger, and I rush forward. I send my magic into more Defenders. Some choke to death, some light on fire. I catch up to a few who make a run for it. I use the blood on my hands to burn through their necks, watching as their skin rips apart and their blood turns the green grass to a shade of dark red. After every kill, I feel my magic burn for more. Crimson takes out many Defenders, swiping them down with her sword and decapitating a few with pure strength. But for all the lives she takes, I take double.

I send my magic into ten huts at a time, burning them immediately. Defender's start to choke on the smoke as they flee the area. Some make it to the forest but don't get far. I topple down trees, crushing the runners. I set fire to the forest, making a circle around the camp. Now no one else can make it into the woods alive. A Defender runs at me, screaming some kind of incoherent profanity while swinging his sword my way. He doesn't get close to me before I send my magic into a cut in his hand. He drops his sword and falls to his knees as his veins turn black. The darkness spreads, and his screaming silences as it reaches his face. His skin melts off and his bones dissolve, leaving him as a pile of ash.

Crimson is at the other side of the camp by now, taking down anyone who tries to hide or run. The flames consume everything, but the smoke doesn't bother me. I see Crimson using her throwing knives. Her favorite. She smiles as she lodges her knives into Defender's necks, taking them down in one hit. There aren't that many people left now. A few more men try to attack me, but they die before they can get up close. I let one get near me, and burn his face apart in a second once he thinks he has a fighting chance. A couple of Defenders are on their knees, heads to the ground, praying for me to spare them. I don't. I kill the last of them, watching as my magic kills them slowly, poisoning them, burning them, before I pull it back to me. Crimson retrieves her knives from the dead and sheathes her sword before returning to my side. I turn to face her. She is covered in blood, none of which is her own.

"I didn't think you had the guts." She laughs as she looks around at the bodies surrounding us. The blood-stained grass.

I force my eyes back to normal, and the pain disappears. Crimson lays a bloody hand on the side of my face, threatening to bring my magic back to the surface. I feel a warmth spread through me, which feels different from the fire I felt seconds ago but somehow more intense. I feel my heart pounding so fast and loud that I wonder if she can hear it.

"Every time I'm near you, my magic feels stronger. Why?" I ask. After killing all these people, I never once felt any kind of strong emotion other than power. But now, I feel incredibly nervous. My stomach feels like it's doing flips.

She grins. "You have dark magic. Maybe it's attracted to my darkness, too." That's what I've been thinking. I'll never know for sure, but I think I'm okay with that. I look into Crimson's eyes, full of a darkness I have grown to accept. I feel more powerful than I ever have before. But the best part is how freeing it feels. The small smile on Crimson's face, for once, stays. I feel the fire slowly inch closer to us, but I pay it no mind. Instead, I focus on how close Crimson is to me and the feeling of her hand on my face. As I look into her brown eyes, I finally realize she feels the same way I do. I've been pushing my feelings away, knowing my feelings for her may be the biggest betrayal to my old life out of them all. Especially when I thought she never wanted me back. But I forget about that now as her other hand reaches for my waist, filling me with warmth.

I used to hate silence. It always reminded me of the feeling right before the end. But the second of silence between us, right before the distance closes and our lips touch, is the best feeling of them all. My magic whirls and spins, and the burning in my eyes return as they change to black, but I don't care. I pull Crimson closer by the back of her neck as my other hand tangles in her hair. The blood from the open wounds on my hands drip down her spine as her tongue slips into my mouth. It's overwhelming, but not in a bad way. Kissing Crimson is electric and warm and terrifying. I want to keep doing it.

As her lips find mine again and again, I know that my desire for her will grow to be as addictive and consuming as my magic. Intoxicating and unnerving, unlike anything I've ever felt before. I won't be able to stop myself from falling even harder than I already have.

I expected our kiss to be rough and fast. We hated each other not too long ago. But Crimson's lips are gentle, and her hands are soft and sure, as if she hasn't just murdered so many people with them. I forget about everything else, only thinking of her. We are standing in a circle of fire and burned corpses, and to be honest, kissing her in the midst of it all is everything I've ever wanted.

Chapter forty-five
CRIMSON

I don't break away until I have to, until the fire is so close that it grabs at my boots. After our kiss, I see that Ember's eyes have turned black. Secretly, I hope the magic pulling her toward me wasn't the only reason why she kissed me. I hope that deep down, beneath her darkness, it's what she really wanted.

We put out the fire at the entrance to the forest, leaving just enough room to both enter the tree line. After I rip a piece of my shirt off to patch up Ember's hands, we walk back to the horses and mount them, leaving the camp filled with bodies and blood behind to burn through the night.

As we begin our trek back, I ask Ember, "How do you feel?"

She looks at me with a grin plastered on her lips. "Perfect."

I smile in return. When I first met Ember, I never would have believed I would end up being so connected to her. I've opened up to her more than anyone, and kissing her made me feel even more vulnerable with her. Vulnerability is something I never thought I would be capable of. Not after Amara left me, and Levi joined the stars.

"Sounds like you're ready to take down the big camp." From what I saw today, she'd be ready to take on anything. I was shocked by how many people she killed without hesitation. She has come a long way. I just hope her need to spare her father and Austin don't ruin our chance at winning this war.

"I am," she says.

We travel through the dark and only stop to rest the next night. Ember makes a fire just how I taught her, and I walk through the forest with my throwing knife in hand, looking for a kill. Eventually, hopping in the soft grass is a rabbit. I throw my knife, hitting it right in the eye. The rabbit falls limp. I take it back to Ember, and we clean it, then cook it over the fire. I sit beside her in the dirt, my legs lightly brushing against hers.

"So much has changed since you first captured me," she says.

"I would never have imagined this." I gesture to the two of us, and she chuckles.

"When you first dragged me into a cell, me neither." We laugh.

"There was always something there. From the moment I saw you, I could tell."

Ember smiles. "I know what you mean. As much as I hated you back then, I was drawn to you before I even met you."

I look into the fire, and I brush away the thoughts of burning Levi's body. Ember notices my expression.

"Leviathan haunts you, doesn't he?" She grabs my hand in hers.

"He does," I answer. She doesn't ask me anything more. I don't think Levi's death will ever leave me. His pooling blood. His final words. The last of him, burning away in a pit of flames and smoke.

But maybe it will get easier. Just not anytime soon. I change the subject, suddenly becoming overwhelmed with the image of his eyes as they glossed over. I try to focus on the warmth of Ember's hand as I speak. "Now that you're on this side of the war, do you ever think about the people I killed in the battle?"

Ember looks at the fire. "I do. Like I said, a part of me will always hate you. But now, I know a part of me will always hate myself, too."

I squeeze her hand softly. "What do you mean?" Her face glows from the fire's light, and I can make out her shining green eyes, which remind me of Amara's. I feel horrible for choosing Ember over her, especially after feeling like Ember would never understand me or accept me like she does. But I was wrong. Ember really has become one of us, and she accepts me just as Amara does. But it doesn't make hurting her any less painful. I know she may never forgive me. If Ember never had a power and I never dragged her here, I'm sure Amara and I would have ended up together. I would have made her my second and ended the war with her by my side. Kissed her under the light of the stars. Bonded over our shared grief. But Ember has a power for a reason, and I believe I was destined to end up here, with her, one way or another.

"I know that I've always had darkness inside me." Ember releases black smoke from her hand, hovering it above her palm. "But I let it out, and I didn't have to." She looks at me, still holding her other hand in mine. "I'm not saying I regret it, because I don't. This darkness, this magic, it's who I am. But I know I'm not on the good side of this war, either." I nod. The smoke goes back into her hands. "I accept my darkness. And I accept the fact that I am a Fighter." She takes her hand out of mine to brush it along my jaw. "The old part of me would never forgive what you did, and it would never forgive who I've become. But that's not me anymore." She pauses. "I forgive you now."

I smile and pull her towards me. We share a brief, gentle kiss that leaves my lips tingling, before we go to sleep.

I wake up next to Ember. The fire is still burning, but I feel more heat from Ember's body next to mine than the heat of the flames. I brush her hair out of her sleeping face, and I get up. I put out the fire, scattering the ashes, before waking her. We leave, traveling the rest of the way back to the castle.

When we walk through the doors, I'm immediately greeted by Amara. Her red hair isn't tied up like usual, instead in a loose mess of curls, impersonating an angry lion.

"Where the hell have you been?" she fumes.

I motion for Ember to head to her room, and she goes. "I went with Ember to a Defender base. I needed to know that she was ready to attack the main camp, and she is," I tell her.

"So what, you just leave without saying anything?"

"Sounds like someone I know." I start walking to my room, taking off my soaked jacket.

"Is that what this is all about?" Amara grabs my shoulder, stopping me. "You're choosing Ember over me because I left you three years ago?" I grunt in annoyance as she holds me in place.

"No, it's not about that." I look into Amara's eyes and feel shame for how I've chosen her last, when she would have chosen me first.

"You know I felt something for you. I always did. But it's different with Ember. I don't know how to explain it." Amara's grip loosens as her eyes begin to water. "I'm sorry," I whisper.

She nods before she turns and walks away. That's all she ever does. Leave.

After shedding my drenched clothes and pulling on dry ones, I go into the throne room, smiling as I pass by my father's blood stain on the floor. I walk over to the table and lay out a sheet of paper. Now that Ember is ready, there is no time to waste. I have to plan an attack on the Defenders main base that will end the war for good. It may not be wise to attack them head-on, as we did last time. But the Fighters are better suited for combat after my teachings, and I have Ember now. Why plan at all, when she can walk back in there and easily kill them?

A thought pops into my head. The Defenders would never guess that Ember would turn to my side. She can walk back into the camp, acting like she's escaped somehow, and then take them down from the inside. As she causes a distraction, the rest of the Fighters can be on the outskirts in the woods, ready to attack on her command. Just as I begin to write this down, Ember walks in.

"I was just thinking of a plan." She walks up to me, looking at the empty paper on the table. She has changed out of her wet clothes and into a Fighter uniform. She smiles at me and redoes the braids in her hair.

"Doesn't look like you have much," Ember chuckles.

"I was just about to write my idea down." She looks up at me expectantly. "The Defenders still think of you as one of theirs. You can walk in without question and attack them from the inside while we take down the perimeter. It would be quick and easy. I just have to place my Fighters accordingly."

She nods, thinking. "What about my father and Austin?" she asks. Dammit.

"Maybe you can get them out before everything starts happening?" I question.

"Maybe." Her voice is full of doubt.

I outline the plan, sketching the camp as I vaguely remember it. Ember helps me fill in the missing pieces, holding her hand over mine as she fills in lines with my pencil. She draws the tents, including her old one.

"Did you like living with the Defenders?" I ask.

"They were all I knew. I never thought I could be happier than I was because I never knew the world outside of their castle. But I was fine with my life there, at least up until I discovered The Council's secret."

"What secret?" I ask.

Ember takes a deep breath and puts the pencil down. Her green eyes meet mine. I think back to our kiss the other day, her eyes black from her magic.

"I always thought the Defenders were pacifists. I thought they wouldn't hurt Fighters unless they absolutely had to. But I found out they were torturing them under the council room. Starving them, beating them. It was a shock to me."

I'm not angry, because I do the same things to their people, and I don't feel bad about it. But it is shocking, as Ember said, to realize the Defenders are not as full of light as they make themselves out to be. No one is truly "good" in this world. Everyone crosses a line at some point.

"My father was a big part of it. He lied to me." Her voice is rough.

"You want to save him and Austin, but everyone they know will be dead. They won't want to join us. What will we do with them?"

Ember looks outside at the pouring rain. It's the beginning of another storm.

"I don't know," she says honestly. I know what I want. I want to kill them. I want them *all* dead. But it would hurt her, and I can't do that to her. We have to figure something else out. Ember looks back at me, tracing her thumb along the scar on my face. "You never told me how you got this." Her voice is soft. I grab Ember's hand and try to alleviate the shudder in my voice.

"My father. It was the first time he did worse than hit me. It was ten years ago." I don't tell her how bad it hurt or how much I cried that night. I don't tell her how scared I was. Maybe one day I'll tell her everything. How exactly I went from an innocent young girl to who I am today. How my father was the biggest part in it. But right now, Ember doesn't ask for more, so I don't elaborate any further.

She squeezes my hand. "I'm sorry about your father, Crimson," she whispers.

I smile when she calls me by my real name. It's been so long since someone has. Too long.

We look back to the paper and the plan we still have to draw out. After a minute, I tell her what I've been wanting to say.

"I want to announce you as my second in front the Fighters. They may be outraged, but I will silence them. You are one of us, and they will have to accept that."

Ember picks up the pencil and draws Fighters surrounding the camp's perimeter, with her in the middle.

"What are we waiting for?"

I smile and take her hand.

Chapter forty-six

EMBER

I stand beside Crimson as she sits on her throne. When the Fighters file in, she stands. Amara, standing beside who I'm assuming is her mother, is in front of the crowd. I see the similarities between them. Amara's mother, Nyla, stares at me for a long time, making me somewhat uneasy. She must know Amara hates me. But her expression isn't angry, it's completely unreadable. Like looking into the face of a ghost. I put my eyes on Crimson. She gives me a comforting glance before seriousness clouds her face as the Fighters start to look at her. Once they all arrive, she begins to speak.

"I have an announcement to make." Her voice is cold like it was when she interrogated me in the cellar months ago. I don't think I'll ever forget the tone of her voice or how she looked at me when I was her prisoner. I'm glad I'm out of there now. All of the Fighters fall dead silent as she continues."I have chosen a second in command. As you all know, my second will become the new ruler when I die. My second holds the same power as me, so I expect her to be treated as such. If I leave for any reason, she will take my place on the throne." The Fighters cast wary glances my way. "I have chosen Ember, who you may know as a previous Defender." Fighters glare at me, daggers in their eyes. Some begin to chatter amongst themselves. "Silence." She doesn't yell, but her voice raises slightly. "Ember is not a Defender anymore." I straighten beside Crimson. "She is one of us. And she is the key to ending the war." More Fighters talk, and some start to yell. "I said, enough!" She shouts this time, and I hear venom dripping from her voice. Everyone stops talking. "You will listen to her, you will obey her, or you will be betraying me. And you all know what happens if you betray me."

A Fighter in the corner of the room yells again, and within a second, Crimson sends a throwing knife his way, stopping his breath and sending him to the floor. Blood spurts out of the Fighter's jugular, coating the side of the room and the other Fighters in blood. No one is talking anymore. Everyone stands perfectly still, staring at Crimson with terror in their eyes. She was prepared for this.

"Anyone else?" Crimson growls. No one says a word. "Good. Then it is decided. We will attack the Defenders and win this war by the end of next week when you will all be ready. Ember will help lead us through battle as my second." With that, the Fighters leave the room, some tripping over each other to escape the body. Crimson calls for a guard to clean it up after she retrieves her throwing knife, wiping the blood off the blade with her hands.

Amara and her mother linger in the doorway.

"What is it?" Crimson looks over to Amara. I expect Amara to start shouting at me again, like she did days ago, or to tell Crimson she's making a mistake. But it's Nyla who walks up to us. Up to me. Without a word, she pulls my sleeve up, revealing the black birthmark on my arm. Recognition flashes in her eyes as she runs a finger across my mark, the same look the Fighter under the Council room wore. I want to pull away from her. She's a stranger. But for some reason, I can't. She looks into my eyes, and I can see how similar we look this close up.

Her voice is powerful, like the voice of a former ruler, but riddled with disbelief.

"You're my daughter."

END OF BOOK ONE

Acknowledgements

First and foremost, I want to thank my mom, who not only helped me write and edit *When Embers Fall*, but supported me every step of the way. She believed in my story years ago when it was merely an idea, and when I began writing, she was always honest and helpful about the changes that needed to be made. Without her, this book wouldn't exist.

I am thankful for my Aunt Heidi, who guided me on the journey of releasing my debut novel. She answered all my questions and assisted me whenever I needed it. The minute I announced that I wanted to write this book, she was onboard and contributing her ideas. I am grateful for everything she has done and continues to do for me.

I want to thank my teachers throughout high school who supported me when I started writing, specifically Mrs. Revoir, who I was always so excited to share my progress with.

I am grateful for my editors who made my rough draft into a publishable novel. Their ideas and experience allowed this book to flourish in ways I didn't believe were possible.

Thank you to DanaeIllustrations, who brought my characters to life with her amazing work. Stumbling across an incredible artist at a pride festival was only fitting for my sapphic book.

I am so grateful to my fellow LGBT authors, who allowed me to have a path when writing this book, and made sharing queer stories possible. Thank you to everyone who continues writing inclusive stories to add to the growing genre. I am so lucky to be a part of the wonderful community.

And last, but never the least, I want to give a huge thank you to my readers, especially my queer readers. I am beyond thankful to everyone who picked up my novel and fell in love with the characters as much as I did writing them. I am so excited for all of you to rejoin the world of Alcmene and Ember in the sequel, *When Embers Rise.* I promise that all of your questions will be answered in book two.

I will never forget everyone who has helped my dream become a reality. For so long I never thought this book would become published, and it is because of everyone mentioned above that it has. So one last time, thank you.

Made in the USA
Middletown, DE
26 August 2024